THE DRIFTER

Book 10

AMERICA FALLS

Scott Medbury

ISBN: 9798848852776

Also by Scott Medbury

You can listen to my audiobooks free here: **https://www.youtube.com/c/scottmedburyauthor**

The America Falls Series:

Hell Week
On the Run
Cold Comfort
Rude Shock
Luke's Trek
Civil War
Lone Wolf
Texas Fight
Messenger
The Drifter

The Rabid States Series:

Unleashed
Alpha Pack
Fox Hole

Standalone novels:

INGA

www.scottmedbury.com

Table of Contents

Part One: The Last Old Man

Part Two: Bakerstown

Part Three: The Bad Penny

Part Four: Lynch Mob

Part Five: Eye of the Storm

Part Six: Wolves at the Gate

PART ONE: THE LAST OLD MAN

CHAPTER 1

Blood orange smears dashed the evening sky; the sun melting behind a ridge of chestnut oaks and pine trees found native to the state of Pennsylvania—where the worn boots of the drifter traveled.

Ten long years since the fall of America. It felt like a century to Joshua Ragland. His travels across the ruined remains of his home, the United States, showed it to be a shadow of its former glory.

For most who survived, memories of the old life had faded. Not for Ragland. He had been twenty-four when America fell, when nearly all who survived the virus had been seventeen at the most. Now at thirty-four, the world before the virus was like a home he could never go back to. A town across a gorge without a bridge to reach it.

Reaching down into his pack, Ragland pulled out a metal flask with an inbuilt filter he'd ripped from another bottle long before it fell apart. He took a long gulp, wiped his beard, and surveyed the hills. This will do, he thought. This will make for a good camping spot.

He'd left it a little later than usual, rushing to erect his small tent in the twilight before darkness engulfed him. Around him, in the woods, he could hear the scurrying of possums and cottontails in the leaves. In the distance, the cry of a bobcat echoed, bouncing off the ridge faces and into the inky sky.

A tall man, Ragland always had to negotiate and tuck himself into the tent. At over six-foot-three, it often meant smacking his head on low-hanging branches, too. His collection of bruises and welts were plenty.

Happy with the campfire crackling away, which would keep until the early hours, Ragland had just one more chore before bedding down for the night.

Traps.

He set them most nights and with a bit of luck, he would have a fresh breakfast waiting for him when he woke up.

Ragland was comfortable living off the land. In the world after The Fall—as he called it—law and order existed only in pockets. On the eastern seaboard at least. Gangs of wild kids roamed the lands now. He'd not required the relay of rumor to know of feral gangs and cannibal hordes. Ragland had seen it all.

And they didn't just stick to one place. With his own grey eyes, he'd witnessed them scurry and loot in the big cities, desecrate towns, and burn down small villages and settlements. That was most. Some, however, sought the wilds. The spaces between our fallen civilization.

One rumor he had heard was of their superstitions. They believed that ghosts claimed dominion of the old places, and said it justified their riotous acts. To him, it was the same old bullshit, but he could never shake the idea of a haunted dimension alongside their own, a dimension filled with the hundreds of millions of souls lost in the space of a few weeks, ten years before.

Standing poised over one of his tripwires, stuck in a reverie, Ragland reached instinctively to his chest, feeling for the necklace. On it, a birthstone. Onyx. The color of deep darkness.

It had belonged to someone special to him. Someone who died long ago when the virus came and wiped out over half the population.

His little sister.

Melanie.

Ragland's scarred and calloused hand gripped the stone on its leather thong and tried to picture her face again. Like a teardrop, with their dad's signature blue eyes. His whole family had blue eyes. Not him; he'd drawn the short straw.

The snap of a twig put him on high alert. Dropping his hand, he reached for the hunting knife at his right ankle and drew it, peering into the darkness. After a few minutes of listening intently, he considered himself safe, sheathed the blade, and ensured his tripwire was in order.

Back at the tent, Ragland fell straight to sleep, dropping off within minutes. It was the one benefit of living the apocalypse. Back before the virus, he had always suffered from sporadic insomnia. But now, with the world outside as good as ended, and society in America in tatters and set back a century or more, he had never slept better.

When he woke from his tangled nest, Ragland pulled himself straight out from his sleeping bag, grabbed his knife, and walked blurry eyed into the trees in search of breakfast.

He'd not walked far—perhaps a hundred feet when he found the squirrel snared in his trap. Bending down, one of his knees poking out of his worn jeans, he prized it free and took it back to camp. He usually caught a rabbit, but squirrel would be enough for him to get started.

With plenty of experience, Ragland got the dead fire going again after clearing away the ash. Once he'd skinned and gutted the squirrel, he skewered it on a sharpened stick and held it over the fire

The animal was lean and cooked well enough to eat in ten minutes. The meat was tasty, not as good as rabbit but close, and he savored the fatty juices, licking his fingers after he had picked the carcass clean.

Leaving no time to watch the sunrise, he packed up his gear, breaking down the tent and stacking it neatly into his backpack. As customary, he cleared the site he'd had the fire, throwing away the rocks and brushing the ground with a leafy branch until there was no trace he had been there.

He never liked to stay in one place for longer than was necessary. It invited comfort, laziness and predictability. All of which could come back to bite him if the moment struck advantageous to a group of raiders or cannibals. No sense sleeping in if it meant waking up with his feet cut off, spit-roasting over his own fire.

Tossing away the what-if notion, Ragland threw his well-worn backpack over his shoulders, ran a hand through his long brown hair and tied it back from his face with a bandana, as he surveyed the way ahead.

He decided he'd go north.

His last loop around the northern part of Pennsylvania, south of Canada's Lake Erie, proved to be a gold mine for abandoned towns and villages, some still stocked with canned food that would probably last another century. All well and good, but hunting was still his preferred option for food where possible.

Sweeping across the eastern states, he'd hunted everything from small fish to elk. The upside to a vastly depleted human population meant the animals thrived and were plentiful in most areas, even returning to their former master's urban domains, now just concrete and steel shells. Vestiges and relics of a world long gone.

Of course, the abundance of game and the toppling of the former apex predator—man—brought its own problems. There had been a population explosion of predators, and barely a day passed where he didn't have to avoid an animal with the capacity to kill him. Wolves, cougars, mountain lions, bears... he had seen them all.

Predators weren't the only ones flourishing though. A year ago, a group of traders had told Ragland of a rumor that bison had returned to the sweeping hills of Wyoming. He had yet to set his eyes on this miracle. Lucrative though it might be, the traders risked a lot by heading west into the occupied territories. He hadn't yet taken the chance but thought he'd like to before he died, one last, long trek all the way west to the beaches of California.

That said, he had witnessed many other miracles in his lonely travels. Of course, he stopped at the occasional town or village to re-supply, but only his time out in the wilds revealed the new world's most incredible beauties. Tranquil lakes glistening under a golden sun, untouched by man for years. Farmland gone wild, as far as the eye can see. A rich explosion of life.

He'd seen so much.

With the sun now rising cleanly from behind the pines, its pale light illuminated his lean, bearded face, and he smiled. He'd always hoped to have a backyard with his first house. Now, he had over six million square miles to play with.

The apocalypse wasn't without its silver linings.

CHAPTER 2

Ragland's descent from his campsite was less treacherous than he had anticipated, the ground not so slippery, with plenty of grip on his old boots granting him purchase.

The plan for the day would be to navigate the small stream to the north, climb the next ridge and get his bearings on any nearby settlements, so as to avoid them. Almost fully stocked, he had no reason to entertain the presence of people.

Around him, as he navigated the way down, he could hear a chorus of birds above him, dancing and fluttering between the branches. The further he descended, the more he could make out the distant trickle of water.

Beneath his boots, small twigs snapped, and the first leaves of fall wedged themselves into the grooves. Despite the time of year, Ragland had earned himself a decent sweat by the time he reached the bottom. Taking a breath, he drained the rest of his filtered water and followed the sound of the stream.

'*Out on the streets*,' he suddenly started singing

to himself, spying the glint of midday sun off the water between the trees. '*That's where we'll meet.*'

A song he once heard his dad sing. A song he hadn't heard played in a long, long time.

Ragland would give anything to hear recorded music again and a device he had looked for on his travels—one which was top of the list—was a record player. One he could finally use to listen to music the way his dad's generation had. He'd heard of some still lying around but he was yet to come across one that didn't require power from a grid that no longer ran. A battery operated one was what he needed.

During his many supermarket raids in the early days, batteries were a dime a dozen. He found old MP3 players, Walkmans, and even a cassette tape player that all worked on batteries. During the first few years, he'd listened to a lot of music. But it didn't last.

Over time, as others sought to ransack those last vestiges of technology, the batteries dwindled and became extinct. Now, only some major towns and cities had any left, but they were still hard to come by.

Ragland felt like each year that passed took them further back in time. It didn't feel like the twenty-first century anymore, not even the twentieth.

And traveling had proven that notion.

Crouching and still singing, Ragland dipped his water flask into the stream, the filtering device at the top already at work.

His badly out of tune song played to a small family of Elk drinking on the northern shore.

He paused then. Watched. Took in the gleam of their fine, chestnut coats. Their shiny bauble eyes beneath long eyelashes. A scurry to the east had a few of them raise and crane their heads.

The buck noticed Ragland and gazed at him warily. For some reason, he found himself raising a hand in greeting.

The buck blinked.

'Come here often?'

The buck dipped his head back to the water.

'Not much for chit chat, I see?'

Smiling, he rummaged through his bag and pulled out a bag of nuts and berries he'd been collecting. A skill he'd taken the time to perfect —not keen on finding an abandoned bus to shit himself to death in.

Thirst quenched, and belly full, Ragland saw off the bucks as they traveled west down the stream, leaving his way open to cross the shallow middle to the other side. The gradual incline of the valley opposite meant he could keep his pace without tiring himself for hunting.

Back between the pines, he bent low to look out for signs of life, keen to start hunting early before the sun set in six or so hours. He'd quickly learned in his first year in the wild that time slipped away when you got busy hunting.

It didn't take long for him to find the prints of a medium-sized bird. A wild turkey if experience served him well. Gripping his bow carefully—it was always strapped vertically to his backpack—he took out an arrow and held it against the limb of the bow, not yet wanting to notch. That would come later.

And turkey was his favorite.

With males weighing in at over twenty pounds if they were big and healthy, just their heart boiled in salt water would provide him enough for a good snack, the rest of the carcass easily feeding him for the next two days before it spoiled.

Unlike the hellish episode he'd had recently with groundhogs, Ragland found he had much better luck with turkeys. Their wing and claw marks on the ground, and the little dust bowls they left on the forest floor were all telltale signs.

Today, he was feeling a bit cocky. Today he would feast.

His mouth was already watering when he caught what sounded like, at the very least, a small flock of wild turkey. Ragland clambered across a particularly rocky outcrop, kneeling to spy his prize. And there they were.

Foraging just twenty feet ahead, they remained ignorant to his presence. Using this window, Ragland notched an arrow onto his bowstring, pulling it back, feeling the resistance, keeping it in line with his chin and nose. A straight, accurate line for precision shooting.

He'd seen other hunters prefer the more unorthodox method of pulling it to their cheek, but he felt it never guaranteed accuracy like his way. And he'd never gone hungry.

Taking measure of the distance, the stillness of the air, and the cool temperature, he exhaled slowly, feeling his chest depress, and then loosed his arrow.

Feather and shaft cut through the air like a knife, finding its way home in the lower neck of one of the turkeys. The others scattered instantly, dashing between the trees in different directions, their wings scraping the forest floor.

Feeling uncharacteristically smug, he continued to admire his shot, and it almost cost him his dinner.

A bobcat's whiskers, then its head appeared from the shadows between a few closely knitted trees, prowling toward the dead turkey. Ragland paused, stock still, not having heard it coming. In all his time in the wild, he'd heard the cry and scream of a bobcat maybe a half-dozen times. They were incredibly agile and silent hunters.

Sensing Ragland was poised to move, the bobcat moved quickly to claim the turkey, grabbing the scrawny neck between its jaws.

'Fucker!

Ragland bolted forward, scaring the bobcat away, but as he did so, a sharp, hot pain seared in his ankle, and he came crashing down.

'Christ!' he screamed.

The lynx rufus—the scientific name Ragland knew from reading books on his journeys—had vanished, along with his dinner *and* his precious arrow, leaving him sprawled on the muddy ground, clutching his ankle.

A lesson for you, you cocky bastard, he admonished himself.

He'd let his long years of successful hunting and ego best him for just a split second, and it'd come back to bite him on the ass.

Wincing and pulling himself up slowly, he tested the weight on his twisted ankle and felt it to be much more manageable than he'd anticipated. In fact, he had the feeling he would walk it off in a few hours. The same could not be said for his pride, which was significantly battered.

Ragland continued towards the top of the ridge, checking absent-mindedly for any other tracks to pursue. After an hour of fruitless tracking, he found a fresh set of claw marks. But his attention had been drawn to something else.

A voice.

Dropping down to his haunches, Ragland immediately froze, scanning the woods around him for the source of the voice.

Male.

No, two voices. No! Three…

He tilted his head, and held his breath as he

listened to pinpoint their location. They were downwind, further east along the hill. Maybe a little higher up. Torn between curiosity and caution, Ragland decided to gain height and vantage.

With bow and arrows stashed away, and running in a low crouch, he closed the distance to the voices and made his way further up the incline to a large outcropping. When he was settled, he saw them below, some fifty feet away. Three rough looking young men, in all black.

One of them turned toward the lip of the precipice that hid Ragland, and he could see the smears of crimson on his cheeks.

Blood.

'Cannibals,' he mouthed, ducking lower, so only his eyes peeked through the undergrowth, his right hand touching the knife in his boot to make sure it was there.

They were talking amongst themselves. Hurriedly. Debating about how to split up. Then, catching Ragland off guard, one of the cannibals screamed, pointing further down the hill toward another figure.

'Meat!' he screeched.

The words fell cold against his skin, making the hairs on his neck stand on end. The war cry was something he'd heard plenty of times before. Cannibals did not see people for who they were, only *what* they were.

Meat.

The figure in the distance froze for a second, then took off but stumbled as they ran, falling, and they were quickly set upon by the cannibals. Ragland stayed hidden, an audience to their hunt. Their movements were quick, decisive, and merciless. He saw their quarry was a female and as he watched, the laughing cannibals took her arms and legs and carried her back towards the small camp they'd made below Ragland's hiding spot.

The prisoner screamed. As they drew closer, Ragland could see she was young, perhaps only in her late teens. She was putting up a pretty good fight, reaching across to bite one of the cannibals on the arm.

He dropped her, and she took a chance to leap up and kick another square in the balls.

A howl from him went up, piercing the canopy above.

Ouch.

Ragland thought she might just fight her way free and make a run for it, but the third cannibal, the biggest of them, stepped forward and unleashed a roundhouse punch that took her on the temple.

Like a ragdoll, she fell in a heap on the leafy floor.

'No!' Ragland gasped involuntarily.

Though not a yell, his voice carried, stirring the ears of the cannibal who had been bitten. His dark, murderous eyes scanned the ridge where he hid. After a few seconds, with Ragland holding his breath and blood pounding in his ears, the cannibal decided it was nothing and moved to help tie up their meal.

As they turned the teenager over, Ragland caught sight of her face and froze. It was Melanie…

No. She's dead, Josh. Dead. You're seeing things again.

But the resemblance was unmistakable. The same long black hair. The same Roman nose. The same brow.

She looked just like his sister, Melanie.

Taking stock of the situation, wanting to take advantage of their vulnerability, Ragland pulled his knife from its ankle sheath and was seconds from pouncing when a fourth man approached from the west, slow and deliberate in his movements. He spoke in a deep voice.

'We take her to the pack,' he spoke, surveying the girl who lay motionless, her arms and legs bound. '*He* will want to see.'

The other three nodded, the large one picking her up and throwing her over his shoulder. He was easily as tall as Ragland but broader across the back. It would take a lot to put someone like that in the dirt, but a well-placed arrow would be all he'd need.

As the cannibals moved off, heading northeast away from him and up the ridge, Ragland decided against his better judgement that he would need to get involved.

He was going to kill every one of them.

CHAPTER 3

Ragland's stomach growled like a wolf as the crescent moon peeped over the swaying treetops. A sweet breeze reached his nose but soon soured with the greasy sweat of his prey. The cannibals were close.

For the last few hours, he'd kept slow and at least a quarter mile away. The last thing he wanted was to alert them. At this distance, he could easily track and keep them in sight. If the day had taught him one thing, it was to stay true to his own habits.

Be slow. Be cautious. Be deliberate.

He had no idea where their camp could be, or how permanent it was. His familiarity with the area wasn't the best. But as they crested the ridge by dusk, he could see a few winks of light below in a clearing. No doubt their camp.

How many would be there, he thought? Would he be met with a whole pack of them? If so, how would he free the girl? As good a hunter as he was, he wouldn't be able to take on more than half a dozen of them and even then, stealth and surprise would have to work in his favor.

Ragland let the distance between he and the cannibals grow as they moved down the slope, descending to the camp. He was keen to avoid dislodging stray rocks or making any noise that might give away his presence.

His patience paid dividends when they reached the camp just a half-hour later, his existence still undetected. Sticking to the shadows just outside the camp, Ragland began to survey and recon the area to get a good headcount. The cannibals—four to the party—had mentioned another, so he knew already there would be a minimum of five to deal with.

Circling slowly, avoiding any dry twigs underfoot, he soon learned that the hunting party was only the four, plus one. Their leader. Dressed only in black pants, he was a gruesome sight, his lean, muscled torso covered in dried blood and other markings. To top off his outfit, he wore a gruesome necklace of ears and fingers.

Once he was satisfied it was only a party of five, Ragland pinpointed the girl's location. She was tied against a tree at the center of the camp, head lolling on her chest where she sat, legs bent to the left.

How are you going to do this, Josh?

He closed his eyes and listened to their muttering. Their footsteps. The crackle of logs on the campfire. He could smell the musky smoke, the pine charring in the heat. It whistled in the night. A sound Ragland had grown to love like a friend.

As he circled them, a plan formulated in his head.

He noticed the ringleader was hanging around the girl, pointing and prodding as she recoiled from his touch. She was gagged with no chance to scream for help. The other four were split into two pairs.

Closer to the girl and their boss, the two smaller men huddled together, nudging, and pushing each other between laughs. These two were clearly Zoms.

Cannibalism had become rife in the years after the attack and the retreat of the invading army. A lot could be said of their Chinese conquerors, but at least they fed the children they enslaved. No one knew where or how it started but over the years, the consumption of human meat had taken its toll on the very young. Those whose brains hadn't fully developed before they chose or were forced into the gruesome eating habits.

Whilst eating human flesh was repulsive, it was no more dangerous than other meat if cooked properly. Unfortunately, the starving children and teens who had started the horrible practice hadn't been fussy about cooking meat properly or supplementing their diet with vegetables. It left them with poor brain and physical development, with some even incapable of speech.

The ones already in their teens had fared better, those in their twenties now, but many still suffered from their appalling diet.

The result was that the cannibals had developed a two-tiered society. Zoms, the developmentally challenged, and Norms the older less affected ones who ruled over them.

Ragland could make out between the giggles that these two were deciding what parts of the girl they would eat first. He felt the embers of rage begin to glow deep inside him.

He continued around the camp in a southerly direction. On the western side of the big campfire were the other two. They were Norms.

The largest man leaned against a big tree about twenty-five feet away facing south and relieving himself in the dark, while his shorter friend sat on a fallen tree ten feet closer, sharpening a knife on a whetstone. His back was to the bushes where Ragland lurked. Hidden from the other three by the roaring fire and surrounding dark, he saw his chance.

Thick fingers gripped his knife as he crept up on his first victim. Reaching out, he clasped a hand over the cannibal's mouth and sliced his throat open with a quick movement. He held the struggling man as he bled out, spraying the foliage and ground black in the darkness. The struggle didn't last long and with his eyes on the larger cannibal, he eased his victim down to the ground.

He took a split second to visualize his next move. This man was the biggest of them, and he needed to make sure he got it right first time. His life and that of the girl depended on it.

Sprinting forward to apply as much force as possible, Ragland launched his left foot into the back of the man's left knee, buckling him just as he was zipping up. Before the man could cry out, Ragland had already gripped him by the hair and reefed his head backward, before hammering his blade deep into the man's right eye. He fell without a whimper.

Two down. Three to go.

Wiping his hands clean, he circled back and reevaluated his chances. The Zoms were so hectic and noisy that an attack silencing them would almost certainly alert the leader. He would put a knife in the girl's belly, and it would all have been for nothing.

No.

He'd have to cut the head off the snake first.

He moved forward, pressing a finger to his lips, so the girl wouldn't give him away. It was too little or too late. Her eyes widened at the sight of him, and the cannibal leader spun around before Ragland could close the gap.

The cannibal's yell of alarm tore the silence and echoed from the trees. Bats fluttered out from the canopy, and rodents scurried with fright. With his bloodied knife in hand, Ragland was momentarily frozen as his mind sought a solution to this new problem.

A half-second passed before he spun the knife, pinched the tip of the blade, and raised it to his ear before launching it and breaking into a run to follow its course. The steel blade found its home, buried hilt deep in the cannibal's muscled chest, and he dropped to his knees looking down at the worn handle as if trying to figure out what it was.

'MEAT!' one of the Zoms screeched behind him.

Ragland decided the leader posed no further threat and spun around, drawing his bow. Adrenaline was thrumming through his system and his rapid heartbeat drowned out the noise of his surroundings.

Nocking an arrow, he took aim at the Zoms who were running helter-skelter towards him, drool flying from their mouths.

His arrow whipped through the dark and suddenly came still in one of their eye sockets. The Zom wobbled, as if confused, before his legs stopped working and he fell face first into the dirt.

His friend didn't notice and continued his charge.

Ragland drew another arrow but fumbled the shot and watched as it whizzed by the bastard's pointy head. It was too late to nock another, and the cannibal hopped then skipped and then launched himself from a rock and crashed into Ragland, sending them both sprawling to the dirt beside the campfire.

'MEAT!' he shrieked again.

Ragland saw the crazy in his eyes and he had no doubt the teenager was mad with whatever rotten disease you earned for eating the meat of your own species. His attacker's charnel breath took his breath away and as he struggled; he turned his face away to avoid the drool dripping from the sharpened teeth.

The son of a bitch was strong for his size.

The crazed Zom pressed a forearm down on Ragland's windpipe and secured his legs so he couldn't wriggle away. Ragland punched his face and rock-hard head, but all it did was irritate the cannibal and hurt his knuckles.

With the air slowly choked from him, he started to see static crawl in the edges of his vision. He was passing out. In a last-ditched effort to survive, his hand scrabbled at the edges of the campfire, until it found a smoldering stick. The pain from the heat was immense, but he ignored it and drove the glowing point as hard as he could into the cannibal's ribcage.

The other man squealed in agony, falling from Ragland as if he were molten to the touch, and writhed on the ground trying to pull the stick out.

Staring down at the angry red welts on his palm, Ragland ground his teeth in both pain and anger. He didn't waste time tending to the wound, but quickly turned to the leader, who was still kneeling looking dumbly at the knife in his chest. Ragland gripped the handle of his hunting knife, put a foot to the man's chest and ripped it free, kicking him onto his back before turning to face the Zom.

The surviving cannibal was in no state to fight; he lay on the ground in the fetal position crying pitifully. Ragland felt no pity. He knelt and drove the blade deep between the C2 and C3 vertebrae of the cannibal's neck, driving it until it protruded from his gargling mouth like a silver tongue.

He glanced back at the leader. The man was on his back staring sightlessly at the sky. With the job done, a huge sigh escaped him. He had almost forgotten the girl in the heat of battle and his heartbeat was only just beginning to slow as he staggered over, covered in dirt and blood, with his knife at the ready to cut the girl's ropes.

'It's okay, I'm not going to hurt you,' he said, watching her flinch as he knelt beside her. The blade sawed through the bonds with ease.

He reached up for her gag and paused.

'Don't scream, okay? I'm here to help. They're gone now. Dealt with.'

Ragland pulled the bunched cloth from her mouth. While she didn't scream out loud, she did scream with her big, round eyes and stayed rooted to the spot in absolute terror. He wagered that it may have been the first time she'd seen such violence.

That surprised him, living in a world like this.

Once she was free, Ragland helped the girl up, but she lurched away from his hands and climbed to her feet before stepping a safe distance away and casting an eye over the bodies and blood.

She promptly bent over and vomited, the hot rush splattering in the dirt like lava on sand.

'Easy there,' Ragland said. 'We need to get you out of here. Where's your settlement or village?'

The girl's shoulders heaved again. Then stopped. Wiping her mouth, she rose slowly, suddenly shaking from the cold. Ragland spied one of the cannibals' jackets nearby and threw it to her.

'Here.'

She caught it wordlessly, draping it over her shoulders.

Ragland had to close his mouth. In the poor light, this girl really did look like Melanie; the same fine features and complexion framed by long black hair. He rubbed his eyes to make sure the campfire wasn't playing tricks on him.

'Where do you live?' He asked again.

No answer. She stood silent. Helpless.

A howl nearby pricked their ears. The smell of blood would have cougars and wolves eager for a midnight snack, here in no time. Not wanting to waste any more time, preferring to take their chances in the darkness, Ragland grabbed her by the arm and tugged her away from camp, heading down into the trees.

'We need to go. Now.'

She resisted at first, then stumbled on reluctantly, keeping pace with him as they descended into the shadows, the flickering light of the cannibals' camp vanishing in the thickets and tree branches behind them.

In the distance, echoing across the wooded hills, the howl of a wolf spurred them on.

CHAPTER 4

'Keep up!' Ragland rasped, glancing back to see the girl trudging behind.

He'd assumed the sun had risen. Assumed, only because he couldn't see it through the thick fog that clung to the valley they'd walked into. The trees grew thin on the valley floor, opening into a vast grassland before the next ridge.

She jogged, matching Ragland's speed, and glanced at him, fearful still. Cautious. Wondering where he was going.

With not a single word spoken since he'd rescued her from the cannibals, Ragland had no information about where she had come from, where her settlement was, or even her goddamn name.

'You don't speak much, do you?' he grumbled, cleaning one of his arrowheads with a cloth.

Nothing.

'If you don't speak by noon, and I know you *can* speak. I know it. Then we're gonna have to part ways, you and I.'

She frowned at him, measuring his words but

said nothing.

'Well then,' he smirked. 'That settles that. I think we best get us breakfast.'

His arrows were quickly bloodied, finding not one but two cottontails whipping through the field. Back as a kid, he'd loved animals. Couldn't bear the thought of harming a single hair on their heads. Not even a mouse. Now, ten years deep into the new world, he didn't so much as blink. It was just life. Eat or die.

He cut them and pulled the furs off the carcasses like a glove with a soft *thrup* sound, revealing the purple-red meat beneath.

The girl didn't blink, which told Ragland she may be new to human violence but was no stranger to hunting or butchering.

With the ground damp, it took him a little longer than usual to find enough dry kindling for a fire. As sure as it always was, the fire was soon popping; two rabbits spitting across the flames, fat dropping onto the logs and hissing.

The girl sat on a rock, knees close together, arms wrapped tight around them. She stared at the rabbit, not blinking, and once again, Ragland was reminded just how much she looked like Melanie.

Her stomach growled as loud as any hungry bear's.

'Eat,' he said, pointing his knife at the rabbit.

No movement.

'It ain't a request, kid. I need your strength for the hike tomorrow. Nothing but hills and ridges north of here.'

She glanced at him, shuffling her weight a little, but decided against it.

Wow, he thought. *Those fuckers really did a number on her.*

Sympathizing, he took the second rabbit off the fire, stuck one end of the stick into the ground between two campfire rocks, and cut off a wedge of cooked meat like a kebab, handing it over to her.

Her hand flashed out and grabbed the food. Ragland had barely blinked, and she'd consumed the entire piece.

'There we go. You're gonna have to sort the res —'

But she had gotten the hint, tearing at the rabbit with her bare fingers and wolfing the meat down like she hadn't eaten in days. And maybe she hadn't.

Ragland watched her ravenous movements with a pang. The resemblance didn't help things, and he found it difficult to compartmentalize what he was seeing - to separate himself and his emotions. For all his travels, he'd witnessed a lot of suffering and pain. New mothers not able to feed their babies. Young kids orphaned by the virus, fighting for scraps outside trash heaps.

Yet, for all of it, this sight hit the deepest.

Sighing, almost choking on the smoke that

suddenly turned in his direction, he went back to his own meal, methodically peeling the meat away from cartilage and bone.

A habit Ragland knew had been essential to his survival this long had been traps. And not just the kind that secured his breakfast. No. These ones were the others who followed, hoping for a quick finish.

Ragland always deprived them of that.

Just before noon, he knelt to check the tracks he and the silent girl had made on their walk north. The grass before had left deep, sodden impressions, with numerous twigs in the woods snapped and ripped from nearby shrubs. Perfect.

Choosing a particularly overgrown section of the climb, Ragland reached into his bag and pulled out a shotgun slug. Something he only used in emergencies. The girl watched as he worked the trap; her curiosity piqued for the first time since he'd rescued her.

Setting a thin piece of fishing wire from one tree to the next, he hooked it to a small trap on the bark shrouded in leaves and attached the shotgun shell to it.

Standing up with a groan, feeling his left knee pop, he motioned to it as he walked back up to her.

'Just in case we're followed. Won't kill 'em, but we'll hear them from miles off.'

A blink.

Ragland supposed that was as good as it was going to get with her, jokingly wondering if he'd arrived after they'd cut her tongue out. It was silence from the trauma. Had to be. He'd seen it a few times before when he'd helped a few folks out here and there. The terror of what they'd endured would render them frozen. A defense mechanism and a way for the brain to protect itself.

Maybe it was the same for her? But he'd never seen it last for more than a few hours and it was now almost a full day since he'd found her. He let his mind ponder what might have happened to her if he hadn't been on the scene.

Thankful he'd put down the trap sooner rather than later, he shivered; not from the cold, and lugged his weight up the ridge to the top, the girl in tow, making no complaints. He had to give her that, she never complained.

The rest of the day fell away to the night quicker than he'd anticipated, with the pair falling into a rhythm that felt hypnotic and regulated their breathing to keep them going. But with moisture in the air, he felt damp from the exertion—sweat seeping into his clothes.

Reaching the top of another ridge, he spied a slightly flatter area of terrain toward the northeast, toward a route he'd take to hike to New York and eventually Maine.

'We'll stop here for the night,' Ragland called

to her as she hid behind a set of trees to relieve herself.

Setting his backpack and things down in a spot blanketed by pine needles, he stretched and rolled his shoulders to relieve the stiffness. Next, he cleared a spot in the earth, then moved off to find wood for the fire that would be supplemented by a fistful of spare twigs he'd collected at their morning camp.

The silent girl loped off to help.

'Not too far,' he said.

She nodded, and with another pair of hands, he had a pile ready and a new fire going within minutes. Thoroughly pleased with the efficiency, he found himself grinning as he fed some of the twigs into the fire to stoke it.

'You know, I can't recall the last time I had a camp companion. God. It must have been at least three years ago. Maybe more…' He stopped; suddenly aware he'd spoken more words in twenty-four hours to his mute audience than he had in months.

Noticing the pause, the girl looked up from warming her hands to regard him with big inquisitive eyes.

'Not gonna say a word, are ya?'

She stared.

'We doin' this? Because I did say, I'd cut you loose if you didn't tell me at least your name. In fact,' he grumbled, checking the setting sun through the clouds. 'I'd say I've given you a good few hours' leeway, right?'

Nothing. She went back to warming her hands.

'I want you gone by morning,' he said.

And he meant it. Without knowing who she was or where she came from, regardless of who she looked like, it could bite him right on the ass. She could be part of a group that would make the cannibals look like a knitting circle, people who might slit his throat in the night as easy as they would a turkey.

Thinking about turkey, he ducked into the pack and pulled out the cut remains of their rabbit from the morning. It would be good to eat now, but any left would have to be thrown away, with no way to keep it from spoiling.

His dark eyes buried themselves in the crackling fire. He fell into another one of his reveries, so lost to the world that he almost missed what she said.

'Kit.'

Ragland almost choked on his rabbit, thumping himself in the chest to wrestle himself back from death.

'Jesus fuck! She speaks! What's that? Kit? That your name?'

'Yes.'

He'd imagined a softer voice coming from that delicate face. But instead, it was something far raspier, not exactly like a bartender who smoked ten a day, but certainly husky.

'Great,' he said. 'Guess you get to stay at the Ragland Motel for another night. Watch out for the bed bugs, they're everywhere.'

She smirked, which only fueled his freshly minted good mood.

'Want the rest of mine?'

'Sure,' she repeated, reaching out to take the leftover rabbit, munching away happily.

'I'm gonna have to teach you to hunt the way you eat. Goddamn!'

'I hunt.'

'What?'

Kit swallowed the last of the food, wiping her mouth with the back of her jacket sleeve. 'I can hunt.'

'Like, small game? Or bigger?'

She nodded.

'Both? That's good. That's good,' he said, twisting the tip of his blade into a log next to him. 'Is that how they got you? Out hunting too far from your settlement?'

Kit looked to pull back in on herself. Building back the walls he'd finally managed to break down.

He'd hit a nerve.

'It's okay. You don't have to say a thing.'

'It's fine,' she sighed, shoulders rolling forward as she poked a long stick into the fire, causing a dusty of sparks to leap up from the ash. 'It was my own fault. They warned me before.'

'They? Your group?'

Kit nodded, then pointed to his chest.

'What's that?'

Ragland looked down, plucking up his sister's onyx necklace. 'It's... something I keep to remember someone close to me. I lost her; my sister, at the start of The Fall, when everything happened. I've been alone ever since.'

Speaking the words seemed to hit him harder than the nightmares had in years. It took a great deal of control to compose himself, thankful the night had drawn in quickly, leaving the light of the fire little chance to illuminate his expression.

'I'm sorry,' Kit said. 'How old was she?'

'Seventeen.'

'That's rough.'

'Yeah,' he said. 'But what about you? We need to get you home. Are you ready to tell me so we can call time on this rescue operation, or am I going to get that silent treatment again?'

'No,' she said, looking back at the fire. 'I'm sorry about that. I just didn't trust you.'

'Trust me? I saved your goddamn life.'

Kit threw the stick into the fire.

'Well, for me it was five men with weapons taking me, and then another took their place.'

'Wow,' he said. Incredulous. 'I fed you and kept you safe. I don't see any bonds on your wrists or ankles.'

'I didn't ask for you to save me.'

Ragland threw his head back and barked with laughter.

'So, what, you were just biding your time before you took them all on yourself?'

Kit remained silent, picking up a fresh stick to stoke the fire. Afraid he'd lose her again, Ragland reined in his ego, shook his head, and gestured toward her, but before he could make the speech, she was already speaking.

'I've decided I trust you.'

Ragland was pleasantly surprised.

'Why's that? Ragland Motel serves the best cottontail roast in Pennsylvania?'

'No, jerk,' she smirked. 'That necklace. A lady in our town has something similar. Different type, but she keeps it to remember someone too. She's the nicest one there. At least, in my opinion. But whatever. So, yeah, I guess I trust you, old man.'

'Old man?' Ragland scoffed, slightly offended.

'Yeah, go figure. All the old ones died out except you. What are you, like fifty?'

He got up from his perch, knowing he'd be about ready for bed after a quick check on his traps. As he rolled out his sleeping mat, he looked over his shoulder at her silhouette against the dwindling campfire.

'I'm thirty-four, you cheeky shit.'

'Damn.'

'And you?'

'Seventeen.'

That figured. Not only like Melanie, but the same age too.

Busying himself with checking the traps shortly after the tent was ready, he staggered back, yawning, suddenly aware of how tired he was from having to worry about another human being. It had sapped him of his energy.

'Nice to meet you, Kit,' he said before rolling over to sleep. 'Let's get some shut eye.'

CHAPTER 5

Once the dam was breached, Ragland couldn't stem the flow of words. From the moment the sun rose the next day, Kit wouldn't stop talking. She would recall the last time she hunted. Her favorite food to eat. The meals she disliked most. On and on it went.

But nothing about where she was from or her people. That nugget of knowledge, clearly, she kept locked away.

Ragland had a name. Kit. And that was a good start. Perhaps if he could gain more of her trust, he'd finally obtain the name and location of her settlement so he could deliver her and be on his way. As nice as it was to have company, Ragland was a loner and somewhat of an introvert. Large crowds, or even the occasional companion, were a big no in his rulebook.

Things were never simple with people. They bred trouble. Small talk turned to conversation. Conversation became gossip. Gossip became lies, which then turned into arguments. Arguments became fights, and then before you knew it, all hell broke loose.

No. Best that he kept well away from people and their problems.

'So, like I said,' Kit rattled on, storming through the last of Ragland's ration of nuts. 'I go out hunting all the time. It's no biggie. All the guys do. Most of the girls don't, though, but I don't give a shit. We all need to eat, so no point just, like, sitting around making blankets or whatever, right?'

Ragland was trying his best not to listen. The sun was high in the sky, and she'd been talking for hours, and now it was to the point that he was silently wishing he'd never heard her screams in the first place.

This is what you get for getting involved, Josh.

'Right?'

'Tell you what,' Ragland huffed, putting down his pack. 'Take my bow, go get lunch.'

He pulled the worn limb from his shoulder and handed the bow and a few arrows to Kit, who suddenly didn't look too enthusiastic.

'What?'

'Go get us lunch,' he said.

'Like, right now? You want me to go find game?'

Ragland nodded, trying not to lose his patience.

'Sure.'

'Okay, er... you trust me with this? I mean, you don't even know me, and you're just giving me your gear that you need and—' He stared at her with raised eyebrows and folded his arms. 'Okay, okay, geez, I'm going!'

She put the bow over her shoulder and holding the arrows in a tight grip jogged off into the trees, missing some tracks Ragland had hoped she'd spot.

Great going, he thought. *We'll be lucky to eat by sundown.*

With his pack rearranged to accommodate new supplies of foraged food, he made to put his feet up and take a quick nap when he heard footsteps approaching from the west.

Jumping up and reaching for his hunting knife, Ragland ducked low and scanned the undergrowth. Then, with a turkey in each hand, an arrow in her mouth, and the bow slung over her shoulders, Kit practically swaggered into their campsite and dropped them at his feet.

'What d'ya reckon to a pair of gobblers, old man?'

She spat the arrow into her free hand and handed it and the bow back to him.

'Thanks,' he said, hiding how impressed he was.

'No trouble?'

'Nope. Easy like Wednesday morning.'

'You mean easy like *Sunday* morning...'

'It's not Sunday,' she laughed, oblivious to the song reference. 'It's Wednesday.'

Ragland closed his eyes and pressed his thumbs into them.

'That's not what I... never mind. Grab those turkeys. We're heading north before we break again for camp and dinner. And stop calling me old man, will you?'

'Sure thing, Gramps.'

He ignored it. His spirits lifted by the fact her bravado about hunting wasn't bullshit after all. She was quick with her words, but so far, none of it had been a lie.

As much as he could tell, anyway.

Their hike carried them over a set of low, rolling hills covered in more woods. When they came across old roads, they crossed with caution. The tarmac in this part of the country was long weathered by mother nature, cracked, and crumbled by wild grass and encroaching tree roots. It would be reckless to navigate the old ways in their present condition, particularly when one could also run across more *human* problems too.

He'd learned a while ago, when their deterioration truly started to take hold, that it was best to go horseback by daylight or cross-country by foot. Never in a wagon, and never at night.

He heard the gentle trickle of water running over rocks to his right, so they detoured and stopped briefly to refill his flask. Ragland was getting through at least twice the water now, with his sidekick.

Mid-afternoon came in cooler than he anticipated; winter was just around the corner. He debated taking out an extra layer from his pack but decided against it, removing his water flask instead. It was then, pausing for a break, that he'd realized he'd finally tuned Kit's incessant voice out.

He found out because she'd thumped him on the arm.

'Hey, Gramps, you home? You hear a thing I said back there?'

'Not really.'

Kit shook her head, folding her arms.

'Asshole.'

Ragland tossed the bottle aside and raised his hands above his head. 'That's it, I can't do it. I tried. Really, I did. Just tell me where your goddamn town is, right now, or so help me god...'

Kit froze, pursing her lips together. Melanie used to do that, too, and it only pissed him off more.

'Goddamn it!' He picked up his bottle, tucked it back into his pack, and grabbed the turkeys off the girl, who still stood rigid, refusing to speak. 'Have a nice life and good luck getting back!'

It'd be a lie to say he didn't feel a little betrayed to not have more trust from someone he'd saved from being beaten, raped, and eaten by cannibals. Then again, he understood her side too. He really did, he just lived better on his own.

He had only taken a few dozen steps south when she called out.

'Bakerstown.'

Ragland stopped. Debating whether it was still worth the trouble. He felt the onyx necklace against his chest. It sat at a slight angle and was digging in where the bow's limb met it, almost like a divine sign from beyond the veil. His sister telling him what an ass he was being. And maybe she was right.

He turned, walked back up the hill, and gave her the turkeys back.

'How far?'

'Not far,' she said, glancing at her surroundings. 'We were walking in the right direction anyway. Another half-day northeast, and we should reach Rubin's Hunting Lodge.'

'Hang on, I thought you said you were from Bakerstown?

'I am. The Lodge is a half-mile outside the town. It's a checkpoint for anyone who travels south to hunt.'

'Is that why you kept your mouth shut? Because I just so happened to be heading the way you wanted?'

A slow nod.

Ragland swore and decided it best to get a good pace on. With any luck, this time tomorrow, he'd be free of her and back to his nomad life in the mountains.

Alone and happy.

CHAPTER 6

Ragland's knees welcomed the gradual slope down into the wooded valley. They'd been hiking for hours and were now just a few miles away from Rubin's Hunting Lodge according to Kit. His joints were a far cry from their glory days, the creaks and aches signifying his nutrient deficient diet and accumulated injuries during his ten years of trekking through rough landscape.

How long could he keep it up, he thought, until he'd need a Gandalf staff?

He let a laugh best him, which drew Kit's attention.

'Holy shit, was that genuine?'

'Sure, why not?'

Kit shrugged.

'Just sayin', you don't laugh so much, Gramps.'

Ragland knew she was right, but he failed to see how it made a difference to surviving. The less noise, the better. Another reason it'd been difficult to tolerate her rambling.

'You should laugh more. It's, like, good for you.

When life is taking a shit on things, you got two choices, right? You can either cry, or you can laugh.'

'That one of yours?'

'No,' she said pensively. 'Someone... Something someone told me a long time ago.'

'They sound wise.'

'They were.'

Ragland didn't miss the past tense and wondered then about her past. Perhaps—just like his—it was stained with trauma and loss?

'So, that's your mantra?'

Kit shook her head; frown turning into a grin.

'Nah. My mantra is talk trash, get mashed. And I live by it, old man, so don't try any of that knife kung-fu on me, or you'll be eating dirt.'

'That so?'

'Uh, yeah.'

They both exchanged a quick look to see who would break first, and both laughed.

Above them, the sky was clear. A pale, metallic blue, turning to a navy beyond the next ridge as the day marched on. Ragland squinted at the sun, almost missing a circle of birds just a quarter mile from where they stood.

He threw out an arm to stop Kit, almost winding her.

'Hey, what the fu—' She stopped, seeing the birds Ragland was pointing to. 'So what? It's probably a dead animal.'

'No,' he said. 'Something seems off.'

Kit rolled her eyes.

'Oh, sure. What could it be, Gramps? A body? Maybe even a trap? After what you did to those cannibals though, it can't be them unless they came back to life...'

Ragland raised a finger to his lips.

'We go check it out. Might be nothing but might also be nothing good. If so, then we detour west. Stay low and quiet.'

She decided to obey, not wanting to neglect the unease that had crept into her bones. A prickling that ran along her arms and up her back. Something did feel wrong.

When the pair broke through a throng of tightly set young pines, Ragland motioned Kit to copy him and squat down low. With the sun setting, she couldn't see a thing in the half-light, but he pointed a finger ahead.

'There, just by the fallen tree,' he whispered.

Kit's eyes scanned the area and finally saw it. A dead buck.

'I see it.'

Ragland notched an arrow into his bow and waited. And waited some more. Kit grew restless, shuffling her weight from left to right.

'What now?' she said.

'It's a trap. We leave. Now.'

A rogue cloud swamped the sun which was now low on the horizon. Darkness fell over them, and the howl of a wolf pierced the temporary twilight.

Kit and Ragland looked at each other and he saw her eyes were filled with terror. Not needing to be told, she turned and followed Ragland at a quick pace back west up the valley side, moving so fast she nearly stumbled.

'Oh, God. Oh, God. Oh, God,' she repeated, breathing heavily and trying her best to keep up with Ragland, who had lengthened his stride.

'We need to keep going,' he called back. 'Their pack will be in the area.'

'Won't they be occupied by the buck?

'No, he'd already been gutted.'

Kit clutched at a stitch, navigating an outcropping on their right.

'So, they've eaten? Great. Can we slow down?'

'No,' he repeated. 'It was a trap. Someone left it there. They'd taken what they wanted. The wolves will be in the area now, and we need to leave.'

'Who? How do you kn—'

'I don't know who, but I saw their footprints.'

Kit cursed. She hadn't seen the tracks. Ragland didn't blame her - he'd been hunting and tracking a lot longer than she had.

Sweating from exertion, a few more howls to their left alerted Ragland, and so he changed course, making a more northern direction this time. At the top of the valley side, the trees thinned out into an open area of grassland. He could see it ahead and knew that while it would leave them vulnerable, it would also give them sight of anything—or anyone—following them.

He hoped the latter would be unnecessary but had a feeling that was wishful thinking.

Kit and Ragland broke out from the trees, panting now, and raced across the open ground to its center. They turned on the spot and surveyed the tree line where they had emerged, chests heaving from the effort.

'What now?' she breathed, bending over to suck in some air.

'We wait a moment. Here,' he handed her his bow, taking out the hunting knife on his ankle. 'Don't hesitate, and don't notch the second arrow.'

Kit frowned, strapping his quiver to her own belt.

'Huh? Why?'

'It will take too long to draw again. Take them in your hand and stab them. They'll be on us before you can get a second shot off.'

'Oh, great. Shit. That's reassuring, Gramps. You save my ass from the cannibals just to serve us both to the wolves?'

He gritted his teeth.

'Not if I can help it.'

The air grew still. Blood pounded in his ears, and after a few minutes of painful waiting, a single wolf emerged from the trees to their right. Then, on their left, two more. The animals' heads were bowed low, eyes fixed on them.

A larger wolf followed; nose raised as it sniffed the air. The alpha. Then four more.

Seven. They were well and truly outnumbered.

Ragland felt his stomach drop. This would be more than they could survive. He could no longer hear nor taste the salt in his mouth. The world around him was muffled by the adrenaline coursing through his body. He twisted on his heels, grabbing Kit by the arm.

'RUN!'

The jerk of her arm caused her to drop the bow, and she was in no position to retrieve it, having to pump her legs as hard as she could just to keep up with Ragland. Chased by the wolves, she could hear their ragged breathing gaining on them, imagining their sharp teeth ready to sink into vulnerable flesh.

Ahead, Kit could make out a wooden structure. It was an old railroad bridge that looked like it had been decommissioned decades ago. She tried to find the breath to tell Ragland, but he had already seen it.

'Go! The bridge!'

No shit, Sherlock, she thought.

Now with a destination, they poured on a new burst of speed, but the wolves were eating up the distance quicker than they were closing the gap to the railroad bridge. Ragland knew it would be a close thing.

Kit heard wolves yapping barely yards behind her and she screamed, almost tripping, before running onto the old wooden sleepers.

Now sprinting over the dilapidated structure, her eyes widened at a new danger. The wooden beams were creaking under their weight. She could see ahead of Ragland that it crossed all the way over the narrow, yet deep gully, but also saw that many of the supports under the bridge, along with a good number of the sleepers on top, had given way years ago. The steel rails were long gone.

The drop was enough to kill them both if it gave way.

Ragland, who was a few yards ahead of Kit, skidded to a halt and turned with his hunting knife in hand. He moved to the side as Kit flew past him, then stepped back into the path of the huge wolf on her tail and lunged, sweeping the weapon in an upward arc as it leapt at him. The force of his blow embedded the blade to the hilt, but the momentum of the animal sent the wolf sailing over his head.

The rickety bridge shook as the shrieking animal landed, then skidded over the edge, taking his hunting knife with it.

'Nooo!'

The rest of the wolves slowed their charge and cantered cautiously onto the bridge, now wary of Ragland's threat.

Kit continued her wobbly run across the bridge, arms out like a circus acrobat.

Good, he thought. *At least saving you from the*

cannibals won't have been in vain.

Deciding the wolves wouldn't delay for too much longer, Ragland took his chances on the bridge and ran after Kit.

The wolves gave chase. Ragland yelled for her to keep going. His lungs were on fire. Heart pounding in his chest, as the wolves gained, snapping and snarling as they got closer. He caught up with Kit.

'Keep going!" he urged her before he felt sharp teeth clamp down on his calf.

The pain was searing. Ragland tripped and knocked Kit over in the process. The combined weight of the wolves, him, and Kit hitting the old timber sent up dust, and a creaking wooden groan punctuated by three ominous cracking sounds.

He kicked out at the wolf, still biting and pulling the denim of his jeans, intent on getting to the flesh beneath. It didn't flinch, and its packmates were moving in warily to get their share of the pending kill when the bridge began to tilt to the right.

'Run, Kit!' Ragland screamed his throat raw. '*RUN*!'

It was too late. As Kit rose to make an escape, the structure beneath them gave out with an explosive *CRAAACK!*

'No!'

Ragland dropped, desperately grabbing Kit's ankle and with his other hand a fractured support beam on the rotten substructure of the bridge. As gravity bit and Kit stopped falling, the sudden weight of her almost wrenched his arm free of his shoulder socket.

His cry was louder than the wolves' yelps and squeals as he watched them, along with sleepers and splintered debris from the bridge, plummet into the gully where they were dashed against the rocks and scrub below.

Ragland struggled to contain his panic and regulate his breathing. He looked up and saw the baleful yellow eyes of the pack leader eyeing him from the edge of the broken track, sniffing the air as though weighing up the risk of leaping down onto the narrow beam his erstwhile meal now clung to.

Dismissing the wolf as an immediate threat, Ragland peered down at Kit, who had her eyes closed and a splash of blood on her scalp.

'Shit!' he said. 'Hey Kit. Hey! You awake? Argh!'

His shoulders burned with the strain of holding their combined weight, and he felt his little finger slip and lose purchase on the beam. Just three fingers and a thumb now held him in place, dangling over the huge drop.

With a wolf above, certain death below, and Kit hanging unconscious from his rapidly slipping grip, Ragland knew without a doubt that the long streak of luck he'd enjoyed since America fell, had finally run out...

PART TWO: BAKERSTOWN

CHAPTER 7

Ragland liked to pride himself in finding solutions to problems. All those years tracking, hunting, and surviving the new world had taught him how to handle most things that came up.

Now, hanging eighty feet over a gorge, with the unconscious girl in one hand, and the splintered beam in the other, he was finally stumped.

Another finger slipped.

Three left.

It wouldn't be long now.

For a horrible but fleeting moment, he considered letting Kit fall to her death so he could try and save himself, but with epic timing she spared him that moral dilemma by blinking back to consciousness and beginning to thrash wildly when she found herself hanging upside down over the deep gorge.

'Stop! Don't move!'

Kit cried, her breathing coming in quick bursts as she hyperventilated.

The girl waking up spurred him back into survival mode and he looked around for something... anything to get them out of their predicament. He found it, three feet away. The one remaining support beam that connected both sides of the bridge, one that had run parallel to the broken beam he hung from. It was their only chance.

'Hey, Kit. Listen to me. Listen,' he pleaded. 'You see that beam there? That thick piece of wood that spans the gap?'

She dared open her eyes and tried to find what Ragland was talking about from her upside-down perspective.

'Yeah, I see it. Oh my God. Oh my God.'

'Good,' he said through gritted teeth. 'I'm going to need you to work with me here, Okay? I'm going to swing you toward it, and I want you to grab it.'

Kit started to hyperventilate again, and he couldn't blame her. His third finger was cutting into the wood and blood from it was trickling down to his wrist.

'I know! I know but look. If we don't do this, we both die. You got this! Here we go.'

The wolf above became agitated, perhaps sensing this last-ditch effort at escape, and paced along the edge of the fractured bridge above him, dipping its head and sniffing at the very beam he was going to try and swing Kit too.

Ragland clenched his jaw and started slowly

building momentum. At first it felt fruitless, with the wind creating a challenge, but after a few twists, he was creating enough pivot from his shoulder to develop an arc.

Kit clawed the air as she gradually swung closer to the beam, her hair dangling beneath her, damp with blood and sweat.

'I can't get it!' she moaned, her fingers swiping a good six inches from the beam.

'You can!'

He gave her another swing and felt his third finger slip right to the edge, the tendons in his wrist popped in protest and he let out an involuntary cry; this seemed to spook the wolf, which dashed out of sight.

This time, Kit's fingertip brushed the edge of the structure before she swung away.

'I- I almost got it!' she shouted. 'One more!'

Ragland didn't know if he had another. Closing his eyes and biting down hard, he let out a howl and with all his might threw her, releasing his grip and in the same move, reaching up and grabbing his own beam with the newly free hand.

Dangling with his eyes closed in dread, he waited for the scream as she fell. Instead, he heard a thud and the sound of Kit scrambling onto the unbroken beam.

Looking across and suddenly feeling a hell of a lot lighter, Ragland saw her pull herself up and begin crawling along the beam until she reached safety at the edge of the remaining substructure. From there she had a quick climb to the surface of the bridge.

Thank god.

'You good?' he shouted.

'I think so...'

She bent over, sucking in deep breaths. She looked shaken and he couldn't blame her.

Even though he was free of her weight, he still struggled to pull himself up; his muscles were fatigued and trembled violently. He took a deep breath when he had half crawled onto it then carefully got to his feet. Once upright he dared a glance in the direction of the wolf. It had retreated to the end of the bridge and stood with its sole surviving packmate, but as soon as it saw his head and shoulders peak above the bridge surface, it barked and ran towards him.

Staying calm he leapt across to the other beam. Kit screamed as he teetered with his arms waving wildly before finding his balance and turning towards her.

'Hurry! It's coming!'

No shit Sherlock, he thought, as he began speed walking along the beam with his arms out like a tightrope walker.

He heard claws scrabbling behind him as the predator came to a skidding halt. He didn't think it would attempt to jump down onto the narrow beam but regardless, he awkwardly ran the last two yards when he thought he was within range of Kit's outstretched hands.

He came in too fast and leapt onto the surface, barreling into her, causing them both to fall to the weathered sleepers. Once he knew he hadn't killed her, he rolled onto his back and began to laugh. It started as a giggle, then turned into a deep belly laugh. Kit joined in too. When the laughter finally subsided, he nursed his left hand and stared up at the sky, which had rapidly fallen into night.

Never had the stars looked so beautiful.

'Shit,' he panted.

'Let's get off this thing, like, right now,' Kit said, her face still pale.

'Yeah, good call.'

He rolled over onto his side and wearily climbed to his feet. The two wolves still watched. He was tempted to flip them the bird, but turned and hastened after Kit, not wanting to tempt fate or linger any longer in case they plucked up the courage to attempt to jump down onto the beam and follow.

It was certainly possible. It was wide enough, and he knew it was only the jump of five feet from the surface to the intact beam that was stopping them. They were undoubtedly nimble enough to traverse it.

Once safely off the bridge, they both jogged a short distance and fell to the earth. Kit was back up again within seconds to throw up into a bush to the left, hucking up all the turkey she'd eaten earlier.

Wiping her mouth with the back of her plaid shirt, she staggered back and fell to her knees next to Ragland, trying in vain to wipe the blood from her forehead.

'That was too close.'

'You did good,' he breathed, feeling for his gear. 'Real good… Ah shit.'

He walked back to the edge of the gorge, but darkness had swallowed it and Ragland couldn't make out the bottom, let alone see if his bow or knife were down there with the dead wolves.

'Goddamn it.'

'Sorry,' he heard Kit say behind him, sniffing. 'I didn't mean to drop the bow.'

He shook his head, trying not to feel personally wronged, because ever since he rescued her, things had been a hot damn mess.

'No,' he said, helping her up from the dirt. 'Not your fault. We have what we need. Our lives. Besides, I still have the pack, I can replace the bow and knife eventually. For now, we just have to make it to Bakerstown. Know the way?'

Kit looked back at the bridge, then surveyed the trees. For a second, he was worried she was lost, and that after everything they'd survived, it was all for nothing.

'This way,' she said, finally.

'Sure?'

Kit nodded. 'I'm sure. We'll reach the Hunting Lodge first. It's always got someone there for lookout. Probably Peter or Alex.'

'And what are these folks of yours like?'

'They're good people, old man. I wouldn't have stayed there if they weren't. So, like, let's just get going. This place is giving me the creeps.'

Ragland looked around. He felt it too, like someone was watching. Not wanting to chance their luck any further, they made off into the woods. Luckily it was a full moonlit night, but they still had to tread carefully to avoid stumbling in the dark.

CHAPTER 8

'Shhh,' said Kit, stopping and cocking her head, after an hour and a half of difficult trekking.

Ragland paused behind her and then heard what she was listening for. The babbling of a stream.

'This way!' she said and moved off again without checking to see if he was following.

The cold night bit at their exposed skin. Both hungry, Kit more so for throwing up everything in her stomach, and exhausted from the ordeal, they staggered down a rocky path between the trees, following the noise of the stream to their right.

It sounded closer with every step they took.

'We're here,' she whispered finally, her feet practically dragging themselves through the dirt.

Ragland was about to ask where exactly, but before he could open his mouth, the flickering of torchlight winked at him through the branches.

The woodland path opened onto a narrow walkway over the rocky stream that cascaded down from the higher ground to their west.

Water always calmed Ragland. The soothing slosh and trickle as it rolled its way over rock and pebble. But not tonight. Instead, despite fatigue, he was on high alert, eyeing the balcony of the big log cabin on the other side of the water. A large man in a cutter's cowboy hat and holding a long rifle at the ready stood at the railing watching them cross.

Kit jogged in front of Ragland, waving her hand.

'Hey, Peter, it's me. Kit.'

If he was smart, Ragland thought, *he'd have his gun pointed on me within a heartbeat.*

And he was.

No sooner had Kit crossed the short lawn to the decking than Peter swung his rifle up to his shoulder and brought it to bear on Ragland, his feet spread and a cold look on his face.

'That's about far enough.'

'Peter,' Kit protested, grabbing her savior's arm. 'His name's Ragland. He saved my life. Twice! We owe him. Food and a bed for the night at least.'

'I'll decide what we do. Where the hell have you been, girl? We was worried sick. Thought you'd gone and got yourself lost. Me and Alex were fixing to go lookin' for ya tomorrow.'

'Peter, please.'

Ragland remained stock still on the lodge end of the bridge, his hands up and waiting patiently.

'Toss that bag over here,' the man ordered, not paying Kit any attention.

'Listen. Peter, is it? I'm no bother. I can just leave right now, and we don't—'

'I said, toss the bag! You deaf or just dumb, old man?'

It was all he could do not to groan. This scrawny hero, Peter, looked at least a decade younger than him, with his jeans held up by a too big belt whose excess length flapped down beside the gun holster on his hip.

'You sure I can't persuade you?'

'Throw it here!'

Peter clicked back the hammer. Ragland didn't like the look of his trigger discipline—or lack of. He took off his backpack reluctantly and threw it towards the deck.

Peter nudged Kit, who stepped down off the veranda and picked up the bag. She looked at Ragland, mouthed *sorry*, and took it back to Peter, setting it on a wooden table near him.

'Pull up your shirt and give us a turn, princess.'

He's not messing around, thought Ragland.

This Peter, no matter how young, knew the rules of survival, at least when it came to strangers. Feeling only mildly humiliated, he lifted up his shirt to show no concealed weapons and turned slowly.

'I'm unarmed,' Ragland shouted, when he had done his three-sixty turn. 'Just give me my gear and I'll be gone.'

'No can do.'

'Why's that?'

'Don't trust you. This could be some sorta trap, or something. You don't get to come any closer, so on yer bike and don't come back.'

Ragland turned to Kit.

'Is this the welcome party you mentioned?'

'Peter,' she said. 'For god's sake. Stop this macho shit, right now. No one cares. You've stripped him of everything. Can you at least let him in?'

The young cowboy seemed to think on it. It was clear he wanted to show he was in charge, but a flash of doubt crossed his features in the torchlight. That doubt made him look more like a kid with a button nose trying to play adult, than a hardened sentry.

'Look,' Ragland said, his already sore arms aching from being held up too long. 'I don't know you, and you don't know me. But I figure, if word got around in this town of yours that you stripped the guy who saved one of your own, before sending him helpless into the woods, it won't earn you any brownie points. You don't have to roll out the red carpet, kid. Just let me take my stuff and I'll be on my way. I never wanted to get mixed up in this anyway.'

Kit glowered. He could see the words hurt her, but he'd had enough. This was exactly why he kept to himself and got involved with others as infrequently as possible.

'What's going on here?'

The woman's voice came from inside the lodge and a figure emerged. She was shorter than both Kit and Peter and her voice was soft but held a tone of authority. Not unlike a mother who'd just found her kids causing trouble.

As she stepped into the torchlight, Ragland saw she was a petite woman, much closer in age to him, maybe 27 or so, with sleep-tousled blond hair. She was wearing a denim shirt under a thick puffer jacket and jeans.

'Well?'

Ragland's eyes met with hers. In that instant, he knew she was the real boss around here. Someone who meant business and didn't need to point a gun to take control.

'He wandered in here with Kit. Don't know who he is and what with Kit missin' and all... come on, Marly.'

The woman named Marly walked over to Kit, putting her arm around her shoulders.

'Good to see you back, kid. Want to tell me the story?'

'This old man saved me. Twice. If it wasn't for him, I'd be lunch and dinner for a pack of cannibals a few days walk from here. Seriously, like, I owe him my life. But Peter, here, is fu—'

Marly held up a hand, smiled, and stepped down off the veranda and walked across to Ragland.

'What's your name?'

'Ragland, ma'am. Joshua Ragland.'

'True, is it? You saved her from them?'

Surprised to see her waltz on up to him without a blink of hesitation, he looked down at her and nodded. The height difference was almost comical, and she had to crane her neck up, hand on her hips, to get a good look at him.

'Yes, that's pretty much how it went down.'

She regarded him a second longer, then nodded.

'I can tell when a man's lying. Peter!' she shouted over her shoulder. 'Put that rifle down, you big lump, and go send word to Claire.'

Peter hung his head, embarrassed, and skulked off back into the lodge.

'So we good then?'

'Sure. Sorry about him. Peter. He gets awful protective about what we have here. Doesn't take kindly to strangers.'

'It's no bother. Mind if I get my stuff?'

She gave him a quick once over then nodded.

Ragland side-stepped Marly and grabbed his backpack from the table on the veranda. Kit was still there, and she looked on the brink of collapsing.

It was after throwing his backpack on, that he considered the issue of losing his bow and hunting knife. He'd had both for a very long time and had grown attached to them. He was lucky to still have his pendant.

Holding the onyx stone in his hand, he knew,

in his heart, that venturing back out into the wild without a weapon and the means to hunt would be suicide. He needed to stay, regroup and replenish his energy before figuring out his next moves.

Marly joined them, smiling at Kit and rubbing her arm.

'When Alex gets here, we'll get you right on over to Claire. Okay?'

Kit nodded.

Given how uncharacteristically quiet she was, Ragland thought she must be on the edge of exhaustion.

'Who's Claire?' he asked, adjusting the straps on his bag.

'Our town medic.'

Ragland's eyes widened.

'Those aren't too common these days.'

'We're lucky to have her. Here, let's get inside and start a fire. Alex will be a while yet.'

Still on edge, and checking shadows, Ragland followed Kit and Marly into the lodge. The interior was, as expected, dark wood, dusty taxidermy, flags and badges over the walls, and a big old gun over the stone fireplace.

A long couch ran for a good fifteen feet next to a shaggy rug that had seen better days. Kit slumped onto the lounge, taking up a moth-eaten blanket and tucking her legs in. Poor kid, he thought.

Opposite the living area, an island bench that looked like it had been surgically removed from another building entirely and grafted into the lodge, designated the kitchen.

He wandered over to the kitchen island, wiping his muddied hand over it; newer it might be, but it was thick with dust.

'Hey, sasquatch, wanna help me with the fire?' Marly called to him, bending down to poke the charred remains in the hearth, making room for fresh wood.

'Sure,' he said. 'What you got?'

'Tinder's over in the basket there,' she pointed. 'And some more logs out on the porch. You get those?'

Ragland smiled. She sure had a way with managing people. She'd known him all of five minutes, and already had him running around doing errands.

His boots echoed across the floorboards on his way to the front door. Next to it, in the half-open drawer of the side table, he could see the rotten covers of old fiction titles and a few magazines. On top, there were a few melted candles and a tin dish filled with coins and screws that no one would have a use for ever again.

Out on the porch, the cool air ruffled his hair. North facing, the lodge's front caught most of the weather, feeling substantially colder than the back where they'd entered. To his right was a porch swing covered in leaves with an old book face down on the seat. To his left, the logs Marly had requested.

Grabbing an armful, he returned to Marly, who had cleared a good space, adding plenty of smaller kindling. Ragland knelt, knees clicking, and arranged the logs across each other to maximize oxygen.

'Got a match or lighter?'

'No matches, sorry. We ran out years ago. Same with lighters. You don't have any yourself, do you?' Marly asked, looking vaguely hopeful.

'No, sorry. Flint then?'

Marly picked up a rock and a small piece of flint from the top of the mantelpiece and handed it to him. Ragland took it and noticed the scratches and burns across the rock where it'd been used hundreds of times.

He'd used matches and lighters, in the early years. Then, when they ran out, he'd taken to using flutes of wood and kindling to generate a fire. An old trick he'd picked up from books, but one that played havoc on his hands.

It was only after a year that he decided to start collecting flint when he could. It proved to be a game-changer. The shame of it taking him a good year to move to flint still stung on occasion, the callouses on his palms a permanent reminder.

'Thank you,' he said, striking the flint just twice on the rock, sparks leaping off and catching in the kindling immediately.

Orange heat flared and glowed hot. Ragland bent close and blew gently on the kindling, creating a thick plume of grey smoke to fill the space between the logs. He stopped, took a breath and blew again.

The fire took, flames belching into life, curling their hot fingers around the wood. Ragland sat back on his haunches and glanced over at Marly.

'Should do.'

She nodded with a smile.

'Not bad, old man.'

'Hey, I get enough of that from the kid,' he said, pointing a thumb at Kit, who was already fast asleep.

'For good reason,' she said, frowning now as the same light lit up Ragland's face. 'You're the oldest person we've seen in a very long time. We thought the virus had killed them off. How old were you when it happened?'

'Twenty-four.'

'Wow, life must be hard out there on your own. You look like you're pushing forty with that beard. No offense.'

Ragland felt exposed. He couldn't remember ever meeting someone so capable of seeing right through him. She was right. The years in the wild had been hard on him. He felt like each year aged him by three.

'I'm gonna go grab some air on the veranda until your guy comes down.'

Marly grinned.

'Your old bones weary, huh?'

He was of course tired and sore from the ordeal over the gorge and the long trek to the lodge but didn't want to give away just how vulnerable he was.

'No, just have some thinking to do is all…'

Ragland left her to it, glancing over his shoulder to see her watching him and knowing she didn't buy it. He knew he desperately needed the chance to recover after what had happened. Kit was just mature enough to know when she was beat and needed rest. He could be a stubborn mule at the best of times.

Out on the front porch Ragland went to the swinging bench and picked up the hardcover book, marveling at its pristine condition.

Stamped in gold leaf on the black bound cover was: *Dubliners, by James Joyce.*

Before he could flick through the pages, a man's voice boomed from the trees in front of the porch.

'Best not be losing my place there, sir.'

CHAPTER 9

Ragland looked up and saw a tall black man, in a dark winter jacket and blue jeans. He had on him a small backpack and a rifle slung across his right shoulder. As he walked closer, he noted stubble on the newcomer's chin and bright, intelligent eyes beneath a Red Sox cap.

'No problem,' he called back, placing the book down slowly and standing up.

Alex stepped up onto the porch, giving Ragland a quick once over, wearing an expression far more relaxed than his friend Peter had.

'You must be the old guy Peter mentioned?'

Alex looked no older than nineteen, maybe twenty. Which meant, like Kit, he'd spent half of his life in the post-virus apocalypse. Something about the young man's demeanor put Ragland at ease. A relaxing aura he couldn't put his finger on.

He gestured to the book.

'And you must be the town scholar?'

Alex laughed.

'Peter didn't say you were funny. But, then again, Peter wouldn't know funny if it bit his ass.' He rubbed his stubble, nodding to the door. 'They inside?'

Ragland nodded. 'Kit's resting up.'

The two men stepped back into the lodge. Marly sat on the edge of the couch with Kit, using a damp cloth to wipe the blood and dirt from her face. Alex took care to be quiet, as he put his gear down.

'Hey, just got in. What happened?'

Marly glanced at Ragland, then placed a hand on Alex's shoulder as he sat opposite, next to Kit's feet. Ragland remained standing by the fireplace, warming his back.

'Don't know the full story yet, and I'm not sure what Peter told you, but this man saved Kit from some bad trouble and brought her back to us.'

Alex looked back at Ragland, a smile brightening up his face. He nodded, then took off his hat.

'Thank you.'

Ragland nodded.

Kit stirred at the sound of voices, peeling her eyes open to see Alex. She sat herself up quickly and wrapped her arms around him. Alex did the same, burying his face in her neck, before kissing her on the forehead.

Marly got up to leave them to it, shoving her hands into her pockets. She walked over to Ragland.

'Alex will swap over from Peter for the night watch. We'll walk back with Kit to Bakerstown. I'll get you a bed for the night and feed you breakfast tomorrow. After that, what you do is entirely up to you. But I must emphasize that what you did was a good thing. The town will be thankful for it, and you'll be welcomed. There's enough food to go around, and another pair of hands would go far. So, if you ever—'

'I appreciate the offer,' Ragland interrupted, averting his gaze from Alex and Kit whispering and kissing each other. 'But that's just not me. I'm happy to have helped, but food and shelter will be a fine payment. Really.'

Marly's eyes studied him again. Searching. She stopped, dropping her gaze and placing her hands on her hips.

'Very well, Mr. Ragland, let's get us all back to Bakerstown. Alex, you all set up and good?'

Alex was in the middle of softly admonishing Kit. Ragland heard snippets about leaving without warning or backup. He was inclined to agree with the boy, who appeared to have a good head on his shoulders.

'Yeah, all good here,' said Alex, before standing up, walking over to Ragland and holding out a hand. 'I mean it. Thank you. Let me know, and I'll repay you in whatever way I can.'

'Don't even mention it, kid. A life is gift enough.'

'I'm serious. Name your price.'

'And so am I. No payment needed.'

'Kit,' Marly said, grabbing her own small backpack. 'You think you can manage the hike back into town?'

She nodded. 'Yeah. Just a little tired. I'll be alright.'

Groggily she climbed off the couch, throwing aside the blanket and grabbed a jacket from the clothes peg by the front door.

'Hey, one more thing,' Alex said to Ragland before he left with Marly and Kit. 'Sorry about Peter. He told me he had you at gunpoint. He's always been like that. Protective. Go easy on him. The other folks will be happy to see you.'

Ragland frowned.

'How many people know I'm here?'

'Ah, it's not like that. Peter doesn't gossip.'

'Sure.'

'Thanks again, old man. Say, what's your name? I only got your surname.'

'Joshua. You can call me Josh.'

Alex smiled, slapping him on the arm. The contact surprised Ragland. The sort of jovial interaction between men that he hadn't experienced in a long time. 'Alright then, Josh. Good meeting you.'

The slow walk through the trees, onto a small asphalt road, and up to the wooden gates of what he assumed was Bakerstown, had been more pleasant than he'd anticipated. Cool air, quietness and the soft chatter between Marly and Kit soothing to his aching head and muscles.

The scent of pine hung in the cold air, mingling with the earthy aroma of soil. He snapped off leaves to pick at as he walked, soon appreciating the more level surface of the road that led up to the town entrance.

As they approached, Ragland could see the night sky glowed with light from the town. It was clearly bigger than he'd thought, assuming all that light was coming from torches.

Ahead, erected to what looked like roughly twenty feet high, stood a timber wall. Obviously built to keep strangers out, it was not dissimilar to the barriers and fences around many other towns that he had seen on his travels, although this one was perhaps the most impressive he had seen. It was constructed from big, rough-hewn logs, laid horizontally and strapped together with iron bands.

The gates were reinforced with iron plates and looked heavy enough to withstand a battering ram for a good hour or two. At the top of the gates, torches silhouetted two figures with guns pointed down toward their party.

Marly walked out in front, waving.

'It's Marly. One of ya'll go fetch Claire. We've got a couple of injured people to look at.'

'Open up!' boomed one of the voices.

The rumbling creak of the gates sounded in the night as they rolled and scraped over the road, two figures, pushing them open.

'Looks a lot of effort,' Ragland remarked.

'We had a winch mechanism before,' Marly replied. 'Long story short, shit happened, and we had to rebuild quickly. It'll do for now.'

'Fair enough.'

'Well get you through to see Claire, make sure you're alright.'

'If it's all the same, I think I'll just catch some Z's.'

She shrugged, already several paces ahead of him.

'Suit yourself. Don't expect a marked grave if you die in your sleep.'

Ragland smiled.

Passing through the gates, he looked at the folk standing guard. All eyes on him, the stranger to Bakerstown. They all looked young. Much younger than he'd been when he'd gone from his last year of law school to living in the after days. And yet their faces spoke of hard experience. The grim reality that one didn't get to choose—it just came knocking at the door and had to be dealt with.

Ragland felt a small sadness then, just as he had when he'd seen it before, in other kids across the country. Childhoods ripped away from them when the virus took their parents. Their friends. Their ordinary lives.

He didn't see the sadness reflected in those faces. Just grit and their will to survive.

They might be young, but they weren't to be underestimated.

'Thank you, Rufus,' Marly shouted up onto the wooden walkway that had been built like scaffolding behind the perimeter fence.

A skinny white kid with curly hair nodded. Next to him, an Asian kid pointed to Ragland.

'Who's that?'

'None of your business, Charlie. Keep the watch. You did ask for it, remember?'

Ragland saw the kid's shoulders slump but had already moved on.

In front of him was the town, similar to any other from the age before America fell but changed by necessity. The road they walked acted as the main avenue, bisecting the town. A big sign proclaimed *MAIN ST.*

On the left and right, several smaller streets led off from it. Ragland noted that many of the original buildings were still intact—some even refurbished.

He concluded from the rough bricks and new mortar, that they had a stonemason in their ranks. Not bad considering that the oldest person he'd seen would only have been seventeen at the most during the Fall. Even in the dim light, he could tell that some of the wooden structures also looked just a few years old. And there were a lot of them too.

As the trio walked down through the town, deserted due to the time of night, Ragland could see that Kit's hometown was sprawling, full of growth and sustainability.

It occurred to him that Marly's offer to stay as a much-needed pair of hands, was just kindness. They didn't need him at all. If anything, he'd probably just get in the way.

Bakerstown was thriving.

Opposite what looked like a converted bookshop, Ragland saw a tall brunette emerge from one of the repurposed shops. Judging by the large red cross above the window, this was the town medic, Claire.

'Hey,' she said to Marly, smiling at Kit and taking a furtive glance at Ragland. 'Everything okay? Peter and Alex told me.'

'Just a few scratches and bruises, but we should be sure. If you take Kit, I'll get our guest here to his quarters for the night.'

'Sure you don't need looking at?' the doctor offered, looking Ragland over.

He held up a hand.

'I'm fine, will be good as new after a few hours shuteye.'

'Whatever you say, stranger.' She turned to Kit, rubbing her shoulders. 'Hey there, you okay? Let's get you cleaned up.'

The doctor led Kit back across the street and into her office, which looked to be lit by a few lanterns.

Ragland often wished he'd trained to be an electrician or another useful trade. There was no call for lawyers in Post America, but to be able to work on a plant and revive an electricity grid, even a small one, would have been something exceptional.

Instead, they were in the dark ages. With such a miniscule number of adult survivors after the Fall, lanterns and torches and the occasional small generator would be the best they'd ever have.

At least until an industrial rebirth.

'You there?' Marly called, clicking her fingers. 'Don't fall asleep on me now. That there was Claire. She's an angel. She looks after this town more than anyone. Including me.'

'Claire? Right. Yeah, sorry. I guess I'm tired.'

'No bother, let's get you over to the shack. We have a small house at the end here, where we put up travelers or people passing through. We call it the Creaky Motel.'

'Creaky?'

'It wobbles like a bitch. One of Charlie's first projects. Rahul helped. You'll meet them all tomorrow. They're some of the handymen in town who keep things going.'

'Right.'

The two walked down the rest of the avenue in silence, Ragland turning his head left and right to soak it all in. They passed more stores and buildings converted into living space. Some were demolished on the outskirts of town, fenced up and used to grow crops. To the left, a church and then to the right, what looked to be the original town's school, looked after and according to Marly, still used for its original purpose.

The juxtaposition of original buildings and new wooden structures reminded Ragland they were living and breathing a real American apocalypse. Thrown back into the Wild West, with wooden swing doors, horses as main transport, and canned beans the new delicacy.

'Do you ever miss it?' Ragland said, deciding to break the quiet. 'The old world? Before the virus hit?'

'Sure I do. You know how long it's been since I've seen a meme?'

They both laughed, shaking their heads at the lost technology that used to seem so important.

She tapped his arm.

'Not sure I miss all that. But I miss how easy it was. My biggest gripe back then was mom waking me up too early on a Saturday...' He saw a sadness cross her features and he reminded himself she really was just a kid too, early twenties at the most. 'Now it's how to help the town survive another winter without losing another soul.'

'I'm sure you've seen it on your travels. The struggles and harshness of life now. Seems funny that most people back then were more concerned about whether you were a Democrat or a Republican, or the price of gas, or Bitcoin or Elon's next tweet. I think the virus was more like a time machine, than anything else. Took us back a century, but who knows, maybe that's what we needed?'

Ragland liked the analogy. It did feel like getting hurled back in time by an invisible hand and waking up living in an old western movie.

'Elon Musk! I haven't heard that name in years. You know, I heard a rumor about a year after from someone, that he lifted off for Mars in one of his rockets a week before the attack. It was all on the hush hush of course. Just him, his family and a select group of scientists.'

'Naw! Bullshit!'

'You know, it probably is bullshit, but a tiny piece of me hopes it's true. That he got to live out his dream.'

They both looked up to the stars and were silent for a minute, contemplating the possibility it was true.

'What about you?' she asked. 'You miss it?'

His hand touching the onyx stone on his chest didn't go unnoticed by Marly.

'A few things. Sure. Certainly took electricity for granted, didn't we?'

'Sure as hell did. Though, I heard a rumor last year of folks a state over trying to rebuild a plant and learn how to run it.'

'Really?'

'Hell yeah. It's not over for us yet, Mr. Ragland.'

They had finally arrived at a rundown-looking shack, with a front door and no windows.

Scrawled in white paint above the door was *Creaky Motel.* A big, old Coca-Cola sign, made from tin and spotted with rust, was nailed to the wall. Ragland wasn't sure it was there purely for decoration.

'Thank you,' he said, opening the door to peek in.

It was bare, with only a fireplace, a bed, and a chest of drawers on the opposite side. A small fire was crackling away in the fireplace.

'You're welcome. Had Peter come by and set it up for us.'

'How'd you know I'd stay?'

Marly smiled, giving him a wink.

'You'll get to know my ways. Sleep tight now. Come by the square at sun-up. I'll introduce you to the town and organize you some breakfast.'

'Sure thing,' he said, nodding. 'And call me Josh.'

She returned the nod and pulled the door closed. The weary drifter stowed what little he had left, then collapsed onto the bed, asleep almost as soon as his head hit the pillow.

CHAPTER 10

Three loud gunshots ripped Ragland from a deep sleep. He bolted upright, the room dark, feeling for the hunting knife he'd lost the day before. He was still getting his bearings when the bangs came again. No, not gunshots. It was some damn fool rapping on the tin Coca-Cola sign next to the door.

He climbed off the battered mattress, rubbing his back, and realized just how cold it was with the fire out.

Grumbling, he staggered over and pulled the door open.

Kit, patched up and in fresh clothes, stood with her arms folded.

'You been sleeping this whole time?'

Ragland squinted up at the cloudy sky.

'What time is it?'

'Time you got dressed, old man. Here,' she bent and picked up a bag she'd left on the steps and flung it into his arms. 'Fresh clothes. Towel. Home-made soap. There's a shower behind this shack.'

'A shower?'

Kit smirked.

'Well, more like a bucket. I'm sure it'll be an upgrade from bathing in rivers though. It'll be cold. We don't heat water for bathing until it gets to winter, just to conserve our resources.'

Ragland nodded. 'Makes sense. Listen, about yesterday. You doing okay? It was a hell of a getaway.'

'Yeah,' she said, fidgeting with her jacket sleeve. 'Claire checked me over. Nothing major. So, like, I guess I'm invincible, or whatever. Anyway, I just swung by to wake your ass up and give you the clothes. Marly's expecting you in the square, so I'd hurry up if I were you. She hates tardiness.'

'Roger that.'

She was right. The water was cold. He took an old dishcloth from the bag and used it with the soap to wash off the worst of it. Not knowing how full the tank was, he hurried himself up. It took vigorous scrubbing to shift the dirt and blood from his travels—especially his matted hair. He'd turned half-wild.

Feeling rejuvenated from his baptism, he rummaged through the clothes and pulled out a pair of black jeans, a white t-shirt, socks, and some underwear. Pulling them on, the jeans were a little loose, but otherwise, everything fit.

Ragland smiled to himself, as he pulled the socks on. That Marly knew how to measure by the eye, that's for sure.

With no mirror to check, he swiped his fingers through his long hair and beard, hoping for the best. He grabbed his old jacket, which was still dirty, and took it with him on his walk to find the town square.

Bakerstown looked very different in the daylight. The streets were filled with people coming and going, most busy with tasks or errands, by the looks of it. Men, women, and children delivering everything: long pieces of timber for the houses; wagons filled with water tanks; horses strapped with tools for the workers, and others loaded with fresh produce.

Spying the wicker baskets, Ragland had a hunch they'd be heading to a town square to share out the crop. He'd seen similar behaviors in other smaller towns and villages before. It seemed at the end of the world communities gravitated towards socialism in the real sense of the word.

Backpack over one shoulder, Ragland followed the two kids up the side street, getting constant side-glances and looks from the locals. A few stopped their DIY projects, or paused their chatter, eyes searching and studying.

Don't worry, he thought. *I won't be here for long.*

The kids rounded left onto another road, where horses and wagons were running back and forth with goods and equipment. It felt eerily like stepping back to a time well before the virus. Civilization here in Bakerstown was thriving in a symphony of trade and primitive industry.

Navigating the horses, earning a few more stares, Ragland continued his tail of the two kids, as they turned onto another side street. It opened up onto Main Street. This section saw the road widening for what had once been on-street parking opposite the town hall. Now the entire area had been repurposed as a market, with rudimentary stands and tables laid out in a semi-circle.

Ragland could smell the food from a mile away, lifting his head to catch every last scent.

He closed his eyes and listed everything: earthy potatoes, apples, peaches, cabbage, beans, tomatoes, and even cherries.

'Can I help you?'

Ragland peeled open his eyes and looked down to his right. A kid no older than eight, with scruffy brown hair and big eyes, gawked at him with a single eyebrow raised.

The drifter smiled.

'Hey, kid.'

'I'm no kid, jerk face. You're not from here, are you?'

'You got that right.'

He turned to survey the market. No one had noticed a stranger talking to one of their own just yet, everyone was too engrossed with handing out the food. It looked to Ragland like they'd formed a rudimentary system of bartering.

'Know who Marly is, kid?'

'My name's Jackson, not kid. Don't call me that. Call me Jackson. Everyone knows Marly, jerk face.'

Ragland held up his hands in mock offense.

'Hey now, I'm just asking where she is.'

'She's right here,' a familiar voice spoke from Ragland's left.

He turned to see Marly standing hands on hips and glaring at Jackson.

'Now what have I told you, Jackson, about calling people jerk face. It's not nice, is it? What would your mom and pa, say? Huh?'

The kid looked abashed, looked sideways at Ragland and started chewing something in his mouth.

'Sorry.'

'Been called worse. Don't worry about it, ki- Jackson.'

Marly flapped a hand. 'Get. Erica will be wondering where you're at.'

Without another word, the kid bolted, sprinting up the street. Marly turned to Ragland, smiling. She tucked some loose hair behind her ear, giving him the once over.

'I see you found the shower. Anyway, I promised you a tour. Have you eaten yet?'

'No, ma'am,' he found himself saying, which made her laugh.

'We can nip that in the bud right away, old man. I'm not your ma'am. Call me Marly. The kids call me Mayor Marly for fun. Whatever gives you your kicks, I guess.'

'Marly it is.'

'Let's get you fed then. Simon will have some oats ready for ya.'

Marly was straight into the action, saying goodbye to a few of the folks at the market, and waving at others as she turned back toward the avenue. For a short person, she sure had a stride on her. Ragland had to focus to keep up.

'That right there's the florist. Casey and Fred run that.'

'A florist?'

She laughed.

'I'm guessing you're wondering why we'd need one, right? Low on the priorities? Well, Bakerstown doesn't just exist for function. Not anymore. We saw the value in the little extras. Keeps morale up and offers more purpose to our lives than turning over human waste for fertilizer and digging up crops.'

He wasn't convinced. The land around them was their garden. A florist shop felt tacked on and unnecessary, but what did he know about running a town.

'Sure.'

'Don't you get all grumpy on me again, old man. I'm sure some honey oats will flip that frown of yours.'

'Honey?' he found himself asking.

'Oh yeah, we do alright, us Bakerstown folk.'

Their tour to wherever Simon was located, led conveniently through most of the settlement. It allowed Marly to stretch her legs and introduce Ragland to what felt like half the population.

Not far from the florist was an old civil building. They were in time to see a tall, shaven haired woman with tattoos and glasses carrying a load of books through the main entrance.

'That's Jenny,' Marly said. 'She's the town librarian and chronologist. She makes sure we keep record of everything. That we don't lose our little bits of history. As you know, with the virus wiping out the adult population—well except for you apparently—there was no one to keep the power on, let alone servers or computers running. So, we're back to paper. Jenny keeps us from going all the way back to the dark ages.'

Next up, outside the refurbished school, a chunky-looking man, also wearing glasses, was theatrically gesticulating in front of a group of young kids sitting cross-legged on the lawn outside the building.

'That's one of our teachers. Clint. His parents, before the virus, were teachers. He's a quiet one. Stoic, you would say. Bit like you. But when he's around kids, he lights up. Has near boundless amounts of energy, too. He and Erica, who I mentioned earlier, are the two in Bakerstown who help educate the next generation.'

'The next generation?'

'Sure. Claire has helped deliver quite a few little sprites since the fall.'

'Oh.'

'We lost a few too, but...'

Marly's pause was a stab of melancholy in their otherwise enjoyable introduction to the Bakerstown people. He was still dwelling on it by the time they reached Simon's Café and Bar.

'Here we are,' she said, waving at the sign.

'Wow.'

A lot of work had been done to the building in front of Ragland. Peering closer at it, he could see from some of the base brickwork that it had once been two buildings, a separate bar and the smaller café next to it, but now supports had been placed and the middle wall knocked through with a serving window. From the kitchen there was a direct view into the bar and vice versa.

Ragland crossed his arms, nodding his head slowly in admiration.

'Nice handiwork there.'

'Sure is. Charlie helped Rahul with the project when he was just fifteen years old. Hell of a kid. You saw him when you came in last night. You haven't met Rahul yet. He's the local blacksmith, as if this place isn't quite wild west enough for you.'

'All that's missing is a saloon and hitching

posts,' he laughed.

'Anyway,' she clapped. 'I have to go. Hey, Si. Got a new one here. Give him a bowl or two of your best honey oats, okay? Don't want our reputation slipping!'

Simon, a red-haired man almost as tall as Ragland, with a long ginger beard and thick arms, waved Ragland in.

'Sure thing Marly.'

Marly winked, already speed walking back the way she came.

Ragland, shifting the backpack on his shoulder, ducked into the café side of the building, breathing in the fresh smell of hot oats and the sweet tang of honey in the air. It smelt so good. Stomach growling, he ambled over toward the counter, where Simon gave him a polite smile.

'So, you're new to Bakerstown, eh? What's your name?'

His Canadian accent was strong, soft, with a musical tone to it. Despite his size, Ragland felt Simon was someone who wouldn't cause him any trouble.

'I'm not staying long. Listen, I need new gear. I lost my knife and bow out there and need to trade to get something new. Tell me where I can go, and I'll get out of your hair as quick as I can?'

'The hell you will, hoser,' Simon barked from behind his great beard.

'What did you call me?'

'Listen. Marly tells me I gotta feed you. So, I do as I'm told and you sit yourself down and relax and eat, then we can talk.'

Ragland shook his head with a grimace.

'Is everyone so stubborn in this goddamned place?'

'Welcome to Bakerstown, old man. Finest hot oats and the stubbornest people you ever did meet. Here.'

Simon slopped a ladle full of porridge into a bowl, then topped it off with a generous spoonful of honey. It was the first fresh batch of the stuff Ragland had seen in years. Plenty of settlements didn't bother with the luxury, preferring to keep away from bees. He didn't blame them.

Ragland sat at the counter and took the bowl and spoon.

'Thank you.'

The bearded Canadian threw a towel over his shoulder and leaned over the counter, peering at him. Ragland wasn't fond of being watched and felt himself bristle.

'What?'

'I want a verdict.'

His patience was wearing thin, but he humored the guy because he just wanted to eat and get moving. He took a decent spoonful and put it into his mouth.

Then it hit him.

'Jesus,' he whispered, refilling his spoon and taking another mouthful.

Simon crossed his arms.

'You're welcome. Have I at least earned your name now?'

His eyes half-lidded in pleasure, Ragland swallowed his third spoonful of oats and nodded.

'Joshua Ragland.'

'Surnames too, huh? Well, pleased to meet you, Joshua Ragland. I'm Simon Tremblay.'

CHAPTER 11

By the afternoon, Ragland had met with more of the people in town and had returned to Simon's for lunch. Simon had been happy to serve him the spicy bean casserole now that they were on a "first name basis".

One of the other townspeople who had impressed him was the town butcher, who supplied their very limited stock of fresh meat. His name was Jack, a Scottish lad who had come over with his family before the virus hit. He had been stranded in the States ever since and Marly had given him a home, she told him on their continued tour, because he had no one else left.

'His father was a butcher and Jack had been helping out in the store since he was ten. He's been a godsend. We keep our dependency low. Hunt enough to offer it to the town a few times a week.'

'Seems a good kid,' Ragland muttered. 'Hunting and butchering is a key skill.'

'Sure is. I hear you're a dab hand yourself, old man.'

Ragland smirked.

'Kit?'

'Yup. Spoke with her after I left you with Simon. She's doing well and back to helping Erica with the kids at school.'

'Great.'

He could still feel the stares of the locals. Little itches at the back of his head, then when he turned, the low murmur of suspicion. It was the one thing he hated most when passing through settlements. He would always be a stranger to them. A wanderer. A drifter.

Being alone was in his blood. He liked to help where he could, but Ragland always made sure to draw back into his own world when enough was done. Already, he'd allowed himself too many comforts. Honey oats. Beans. A shower. It was time to go.

'Listen. I've stayed too long as it is. I need to replace my gear. Do you have somewhere I co—'

Marly nodded. 'Why don't we pay Rahul a visit?'

On the edge of the town, beside an open plot of unused land, a large double-door garage belched heat. Inside, Ragland could make out workshop benches, an anvil, a furnace rigged to the roof to remove the smoke, and endless rows of shelving filled with tools and equipment. Like a thin veneer, charcoal dust and filth coated the floor and walls.

By the anvil, a big man in an apron and large protective gloves pulled back his tinted face shield, revealing eyes that were such a deep brown they were almost black, and a bushy black mustache.

The man drilled him with an intense stare that he returned in kind. Neither man dropped their gaze and Rahul finally jabbed the hammer toward him.

'Who's the asshole, Mayor?'

'This is Ragland, the asshole who saved Kit from a pack of cannibals two days' walk from here,' she said, marching up to him and crossing her arms. 'How're the nails coming along?'

Rahul finally let his eyes stray from Ragland.

'Good. Managed to smelt some struts off an old pylon out east, which will give us another few hundred or so.'

Marly nodded.

'Good. Listen. Our friend here is looking to part ways, as much as it pains me,' she emphasized the last two words, glancing at Ragland. 'But he lost his gear getting Kit back to us.'

'And it's my problem, how?'

'Jesus, Rahul.'

'I make stuff for the town, Mayor. I don't pawn my shit off to out-of-towners. That ain't how it works.'

'Well,' she said, pointing a finger at the blacksmith's chest. 'We owe him. And we always pay our due. So, what will it be? You gonna brood or are you gonna fetch this fine hero a hunting knife, so he doesn't starve by sundown?'

Rahul's eyes narrowed. He worked his jaw, a lot like Peter had when he leveled the rifle at him back at the lodge. Finally, he huffed and stalked off and through an adjacent door.

The pair heard banging and clanging—Marly giving Ragland a wink—before the smith returned, holding what looked to be a seven or eight-inch blade in one hand and a leather sheath in the other.

'Here,' Rahul grumbled, sliding the knife home and shoving it toward Ragland.

'Wasn't so hard, was it?' Marly said, shaking her head.

'A word?' Rahul snapped.

The pair stepped away from Ragland. They got into it, their hands gesticulating and their voices rising enough for him to catch a few words about limited resources and helping strangers.

Marly returned, with a glint in her eyes.

'Shall we go?'

'All good then?'

'Yeah,' she said.

Ragland watched the sour Rahul pull his visor down and go back to work, re-heating the rod he'd been working on when they arrived.

'Listen. You mind if I say goodbye to the kid?'

'Kit?'

'Yeah. Wouldn't be right if I... just left.'

Marly smiled, inclining her head.
'No. It wouldn't. Come on now.'

CHAPTER 12

Kit stepped away from the group of young kids after placing a crayon and piece of paper next to them. Her expression clearly painted her disappointment in the news.

'When are you leaving?'

'Now. I've just re-stocked. Marly helped me out with a knife and some food for the road.'

'What about your bow? Isn't that, like, key for hunting or whatever?'

'I'll manage with traps for now. Have done it before.'

The classroom Ragland and Marly had interrupted proved too loud for conversations to continue, so the three stepped outside into the cool, crisp air that was signaling a turn toward winter.

'Why not stay until spring, when it gets warmer?' she said, rubbing her upper arms. 'The weather will only get worse. Can't imagine how friggin' cold it gets out there, you know? And you're no young buck neither, right?'

'I'll be just fine.'

Looking uncomfortable, perhaps sensing that trauma had created a certain bond between the two, Marly cleared her throat.

'I'll leave you two to say your goodbyes. Mr. Ragland, I'll be at the gate.'

He nodded.

After she'd walked a good distance away, Kit fired up, detailing all the idiotic consequences of his decisions and why it made more sense to stay, even if it was for the short term.

'You're being such an ass, you know that? No. A jerk face, as Jackson would say. A friggin' jerk face.'

'Listen. You wouldn't understand. Besides, I've gotten you home safe, like I promised. There's nothing more I can do for you or this town.'

'Maybe there's something we can do for you?'

Ragland wasn't getting through to her and didn't like how her attitude echoed that of his sister when they argued. It made biting back that much harder.

'Damn it, kid, I'm going. I came to say goodbye out of courtesy.'

He turned to leave, but Kit stopped him in his tracks with her next words.

'Would she want you to be out there in the world alone?'

'What did you say?'

'Your sister,' Kit said. 'I think she'd want you to make a home, you know?'

He spun and crossed the space between them

in a flash.

'You don't know a goddamn thing about her! Just because I saved your life, doesn't mean you get to talk to me like that. I don't owe you a damn thing.'

Kit's eyes welled up.

'Asshole!'

Their shouting had alerted one of the teachers inside. A woman poked her head out the door.

'Everything okay, Kit?'

'Yeah,' she said, wiping her eyes and stepping away from Ragland. 'All good here, Erica. Just, er… saying goodbye. You know?' She looked back to Ragland, a look of betrayal and hurt on her face. 'Have a nice life.'

And then she was gone, leaving Ragland alone in the street, with more eyes on him.

Now itching to leave, guilt for his harsh words a mighty motivator, Ragland speed-walked the quarter mile to the gate, where he saw Marly with a few faces he didn't recognize, and one he did.

Alex, Kit's boyfriend.

Marly's arm went up when she spotted Ragland approaching, and the guards began to push the gate open.

'You sure about this?' she asked one last time. 'You know you're welcome to stay, so long as you pull your weight. Offer's still on the table, old man.'

Ragland sighed, which Marly decoded within a

heartbeat.

'Guessin' she didn't take it too well, huh?'

'No,' he replied, searching the tree line outside the perimeter. 'She did not.'

Alex overheard.

'Everything okay?'

Marly rested a hand on his shoulder.

'Everything's fine. You get to sleep. You've earned it after that watch.'

The young kid eyed Ragland.

'What did you say to her?'

'Nothing.'

'Don't lie to me. Kit doesn't upset easy, and I'm not stupid.'

Ragland shifted the backpack on his shoulders, threading his left arm through and clicking in the straps. He made sure the knife on his hip was secured properly; he had already checked the blade and couldn't help admiring the work Rahul had done on the weapon. It would serve him well.

He couldn't find the words to answer Alex. Instead, Marly found them for him.

'Go see her then, Alex. She's just upset that Mr. Ragland has to leave. A visit from her boyfriend will cheer her up.'

'Yeah, I think I will,' Alex said, then looked back at Ragland and held out his hand. 'I know my manners. Thank you again for bringing Kit back to us. Whatever you two said is between you, but if you upset her... well then, maybe don't come back.'

Ragland nodded, his first impression that he was a loyal, good-hearted kid reinforced.

'Sure thing kid,' he said, before turning to Marly. 'Thanks for everything Mayor Marly.'

'Anytime.'

Ragland glanced back to see them watching him as the guards pulled the gates closed. When they snapped shut, he filled his lungs with the cool, pine scented air. It'd only been twelve hours at most, but he'd missed it all the same.

In just a day, Ragland managed a modest five-mile hike south from Bakerstown before making camp. In the morning, he intended to head east to the coast, before heading south for winter.

He got to test the efficacy of his newly acquired hunting knife. Clean, and sharp, it made quick work of a raccoon he'd been lucky enough to trap.

I suppose it wasn't all for nothing, he mused, as he worked.

But still, he wished he hadn't lost his bow. It'd take him some time to replace it, he'd need to either make a replacement, or travel into a ghost town or city to try and find one.

For now, he'd stick to traps and the knife.

The campfire had been quicker to light too, the sharp blade sparking the tinder in one go.

The fire snapped and popped as Ragland held a piece of his small game over the flames, staring into the fire.

Would she want you to be out there in the world alone?

Kit's words swirled in his mind, bringing back regrets and memories.

The smell of charred meat jerked him back to the present. Ragland swore, pulling the meat up and inspecting the damage. Half of it was blackened beyond saving, so he took the knife and sliced it in half, chewing on the rest.

Above, shifting and winking around and through the plume of wood smoke, the stars of the cold night drew his attention. Ragland leaned back on his elbows and squinted at them, his eyes adjusting to the dark around him.

I think she'd want you to make a home, you know?

He threw the last bit of gristle into the trees, angry at the tormenting thoughts. The kid didn't know shit. She'd known him for a day or two. Not long enough to unpack a decade of grief and regret.

Ragland was away in his head, the camp still not fully set up, when he heard the scuffle of feet behind him. He had no time to react before a boney arm wrapped around his neck.

Cursing, Ragland clutched the arm, leaned forward, then threw his head back as hard as he could. It was like hitting rock, but he was rewarded with the muffled crunch of a nose breaking and a shriek that almost burst his eardrums. As warm blood gushed onto the back of his head, the arm loosened and he scrambled away.

He rose to his feet and turned to confront his attacker. It was a cannibal. Clearly a Zom, half-dressed almost more creature than man, with blackened teeth, long fingernails, and bloodstained lips.

Slowly, it rose from where it had fallen. Ragland's mouth dropped. It didn't seem possible. The bastard was huge. At least six foot six. As he scrambled frantically for his new hunting knife, the creature leapt at him, knocking him to the ground and began trying to claw his face and throat.

Suffocating under the immense weight and retched stench that filled his nose, Ragland desperately felt the ground around him until his fingers happened upon the handle of the knife. He gripped it just as the cannibal bit down hard on his ear.

Ragland screamed and warm blood oozed down the side of his face—he could feel it slicking his neck. Wasting no time, he thrust the knife up into the Zom's throat. He gave the blade a quick jerk to the right and a waterfall of blood gushed from the seam, drenching him.

The cannibal, eyes wide in shock, twitched, gurgled, then flopped backwards, clutching frantically at the mortal wound.

Panting, Ragland sat up, watching it die, then heard the distant cry of more of them in the night. A branch snapped behind him and he turned holding his knife out in front of him, only to find a familiar face illuminated eerily by the glow of the campfire.

'Let's get you the hell outta here, old man,' said Alex, from Bakerstown.

PART THREE: THE BAD PENNY

CHAPTER 13

'Open the gates!' Alex roared up to Charlie, who vanished behind the fence, then reappeared moments later, pushing open the entrance to Bakerstown.

It would be the second time in three days that Ragland would enter the settlement in the dead of night, covered in blood.

Better be careful or I'll start to make a name for myself, he thought.

Alex and Ragland marched through, helping Charlie shut the gates immediately, the crack of wood snapping to with a satisfying echo through the square.

Charlie, the young guard Ragland remembered from before, stared at him with wide eyes. He must have looked like a horror show.

'It's not ours,' Alex spoke for them, his chest rising and falling rapidly. 'Well not mine at least.'

The pair had jogged nearly the entire distance back to Bakerstown, and hadn't encountered anymore cannibals.

Ragland wiped the blood from his neck, it

coated his hand like a slick red grease.

'We might have a problem.'

'Yeah, you think?' Alex replied.

Charlie turned his head between the two large men, pointing to Ragland's bandaged ear.

'What happened out there?'

'Never you mind, kid,' Ragland growled.

'I'm no kid!'

'The hell you aren't.'

Alex shook his head.

'Charlie. We need you back on watch. We need to go speak to Marly.'

'But wh—'

'Charlie...'

Alex's hard look seemed to encourage Charlie's reconsideration of protest. Huffing, he mumbled something under his breath and climbed back up onto the walkway, glancing down briefly at the two.

'Come on,' Alex said, tapping Ragland on the arm. 'We need to go see her, now.'

Just like before, barely a voice stirred in the night. It had been too long since Ragland kept a timepiece on his person, but he figured the hour was late enough that visiting Marly meant waking her up.

'Listen, kid. We can catch her up in the morning.'

'No,' Alex said, his stride almost a match for Ragland's, as they marched through town, taking a few turns toward an area that looked to be more residential. 'We can't.'

'What does that mean?'

'It means we have a bigger problem on our hands than you think we do, old man. It means we gotta tell Marly ASAP.'

Ragland grabbed Alex by the arm and whirled him to a stop. The pair stood shrouded almost entirely in darkness beside a large stone building that must have once been a series of department stores.

'What do you mean, a bigger problem?'

Alex shifted. 'The cannibals.'

'They've always been a problem.'

'Not like this.'

Ragland ran his fingers through his hair. 'Only forever.'

'I know what a fuckin' cannibal is, old man, don't preach to me like I don't.'

'Oh? That right?'

'They have leaders. Order. Even a government. They send out feral packs like scouts. Rangers. Looking for the most vulnerable settlements and people. People like us. Meat. Then the others move in force. More organized. More deadly.'

Ragland bit the inside of his cheek to avoid his face telling too much. Truth is, he had been away from people a long time. There were gaps in his knowledge..

'You're not kidding, are you?'

'No. I'm not. This is the closest I've seen them, which is why we need to get to Marly.'

On the edge of Bakerstown, an old three-story house stood first in a neat row of others that looked identical, although more ramshackle. The garage, lot size, and the windowed loft on the home informed Ragland it had likely belonged to someone quite well off.

'Wow.'

'Yeah,' Alex said, wasting no time to indulge and stomping right up the main path to the front door.

Inside, in the top window, a light flickered to life. Shadows of candlelight danced across the ceiling. Ragland heard a staircase creaking underfoot a second or two before Marly threw the door open, her irritated gaze falling on Alex.

'Where in hell have you been..?'

Her face softened immediately upon seeing Ragland, covered in blood and with a bandaged ear.

'Well now, what's this mess?'

'Cannibals,' Alex said, gesticulating urgently and stepping in front of Ragland. 'More of them and closer than usual. I think we've got a problem.'

'Hang on,' Ragland said. 'There was only the one...'

'Only the one that we saw. You heard them too.'

'Marly,' Ragland said. 'I'm sorry for the intrusion. Alex here has himself all worked up—'

Alex raised his voice and a few more lights

flickered on in the houses opposite.

'I'm not exaggerating! We have a problem, Marly. A big problem. We need to talk.'

'Can this wait until tomorrow?' she said, rubbing her eyes.

'No, it really can't.'

Ragland stood silent, not quite believing the discussion unfolding before his eyes. It had only taken him two days to stumble back into people drama. Two damn days.

Marly patted down her bed hair and looked up and down the street.

'You best come on in then before we wake the whole town up with this racket. Come on now.'

The mayor led them into the open hallway, Ragland closing the door behind them. Marly picked up the candle she'd placed on the stand by the door before she'd opened it.

'This way,' she said. Alex and Ragland followed wordlessly, the soles of their boots drumming on the wooden floorboards.

She guided them down the hallway and left into a small room. The walls were lined with bookshelves, leaving space at the end for a window. In the middle sat a long table with coasters haphazardly placed on it.

Marly pulled out two seats, then walked around to the other side and sat down opposite. A hand motioned for them to do the same.

Ragland caught the smell of printed paper as he navigated the table, placing his backpack down beside his feet before sitting in the chair next to Alex.

Marly placed the candle on the table, casting an eerie glow over her features.

'From the beginning. Tell me what happened. Alex, you go. We'll get to you last, old man.'

CHAPTER 14

Alex began to explain how he had left to follow Ragland later on the day he had departed. A lot of the story came as a surprise to the drifter, and he was annoyed at being tracked without his knowledge and worse, that the kid had seemed to track him with ease. Still, he gritted his teeth and listened.

The tale continued until it reached a point Ragland hadn't foreseen. Alex had been distracted by smoke in the southeast and had briefly veered from Ragland's trail to investigate. Half a day in that direction he had come across a big encampment.

Turning back, he'd decided to catch up with Ragland and let him know he had been tracking him and warn him about the danger to the south. He arrived just in time to see Ragland deal with the surprise attacker. A lone cannibal.

'A scout,' Alex said leaning forward. 'I think they were hunting for whoever had taken down their gang when they didn't come back.'

Marly didn't make a move once he'd finished

but hadn't beckoned Ragland to tell his side of events, either.

'What did you take with you?' she asked after a pause.

Alex frowned. 'What?'

'I'm asking, what provisions did you take with you on your little adventure?'

'Er... I, er... took just a tin or two. Some wood. Flint. Other things.'

'Supplies for how long?'

Alex didn't speak right away, causing Marly to erupt.

'I said for how long!?'

Ragland looked at her, his eyes widening a little.

'Four days,' Alex said, sinking into his chair.

Marly put her face in her hands.

'You stole rations and equipment without sign-off. Do you know what sort of crime you've committed? And for what?'

'For the right reasons!' he protested.

Ragland decided to jump in. 'Listen. Marly. Maybe cut the kid some slack. I think he got a little scared from the incident with Kit.'

'I'll give him something to be scared about,' she said, pointing a finger. 'You've betrayed my trust, Alex. I gave you that job as head watch on your promise to me. What was important enough to make it worth breaking? Huh?'

The teenager placed his hands on the table, eyes searching Marly's. Ragland saw pain there.

Clear remorse for his actions.

'We all know about cannibals, Marly. But it's been a long time. Most won't see the danger. Some of the younger ones refuse to believe they exist at all. But you and I know.

'I had a feeling that after Ragland killed their crew, they might come back looking for revenge.' Alex wiped his nose. 'This man saved her life. I love Kit. More than anything. I couldn't just watch him go like that, because something in my gut told me they'd be hunting for him.'

Ragland looked at Alex. It had been many years since he'd been on the end of such a selfless act. The last one in fact, had saved his life. This one, no doubt avoiding further trouble altogether. Maybe the kid was right? It wasn't unreasonable to assume that they were hunting whoever they thought responsible for the murder of their gang.'

Marly shook her head.

'Sweet Jesus, Alex.'

'I'm sorry, Marly. I really am.'

She ignored him, turning to Ragland.

'Much of what he said true?'

'I think so, from what I saw. Either I got very unlucky, or it's possible they were hunting.'

Marly got up from her chair and started pacing back and forth, her petite form vanishing and reappearing in the dim light.

'How? How could they have hunted you? Didn't you tell us you killed them all? Kit confirmed it.'

'I did,' Ragland agreed, lacing his fingers. 'I have a theory. It's not a nice one, but maybe Alex here can build on it.'

'Oh?' she asked.

Alex frowned at Ragland. 'What is it?'

'These cannibals. You mentioned that, in these parts, they've grown organized. Care to expand on that?'

'I can jump in there, cowboy,' Marly interrupted, holding a hand up to Alex. 'Back in the early years after the fall, this area had been lucky. Just on the other side, and even along the Appalachian ridge, fights went on every day. Factions and gangs of kids, digging in their heels.

'It quietened down eventually, many of those who survived starved or got sick and died. A small band of us were from Bakerstown. Me, Claire, and Rahul are the founders of what you see now, I guess. We lived here before and got together to defend it from those who wanted to take what wasn't theirs, but also to welcome those who needed refuge.

'Eventually, we started to hear about a gang who were snatching people near the woods, killing and butchering them while they slept by their campfires. That sort of thing. It was hell. For a while, we were terrified to leave this place. It was then that we decided to fortify, and within a few years, we were completely barricaded from the outside world.'

'Like it is now?' Ragland asked.

Marly shook her head, licking her lower lip.

'Not quite. A year after the wall went up, we lost a lot of good folk.'

'They came,' Alex interrupted, his eyes haunted in the low light. 'The cannibals stormed the gates, tearing them down. It was all we could do to hold them back.'

'We weren't combat-trained,' Marly continued for him. 'But their numbers were smaller than they are now, and they were driven mostly by a shared hunger and desperation, and we got the best of them. Not before we lost a lot of our own though.'

'How does this story factor into what's happening now?' Ragland asked. 'With what Alex has said, they grew in numbers and got organized?'

Marly nodded.

'That's what we have heard and guessed. We've not seen many since. Only rumors of sightings now and then from traders, but always a long way from us.'

'But you have your suspicions that they're growing?' Ragland asked.

'Yes. Some of us.'

Ragland raised an eyebrow. As he did, the tightened skin pulled at the wound on his ear. The wet ooze of blood dribbled down his neck. A souvenir.

'Some?'

'Just a year ago, Alex here decided to gate-crash the local town meeting. He mentioned everything we have tonight but topped it off with a cherry most couldn't stomach to swallow, let alone bite.'

'What does that mean?' Ragland turned to Alex, who had sunken further into his seat.

'I suggested that the cannibals had developed a sort of society to rival our own. That they weren't all just dumb eating machines like the feral ones, and that there were smart ones in charge and that we should prepare for them if they ever came our way.'

He held up his hands as Marly shook her head.

Ragland listened with interest. Clearly, they hadn't heard of Norms and Zoms, but the kid had nailed it without knowing the titles they'd been given in other states. Still, the term "society" was a stretch. More like a few loose and scattered communities from what he'd seen and heard.

'So, have you seen it with your own eyes?' he asked, wanting to ascertain how the kid had come to his conclusion about the two tiers.

'I have. Once. The bastard smiled at me, from a distance. I was out one day, checking the ridge with an old pair of binoculars. I could make out his face. Behind the smeared blood. Tattoos all down his body. He had one of the feral ones on a leash and winked at me.'

'Winked?'

'Yeah,' he said. 'Winked.'

'That would have been a Norm.'

'A what?'

The drifter went on to explain about Norms and Zoms and told them he had rarely seen a gathering of them larger than five.

'Doesn't mean Alex isn't right about larger groups, I've just never seen it myself.'

The two locals digested that information for a minute before Marly clapped her hands.

'Alright, that's enough for one night, boys. Alex, go on home and get some sleep. Now, you sir, the Creaky is still free if you want to stay the night but make sure you shower before you bloody up the sheets.'

'Actually, I might need to see Claire.'

Ragland peeled back the bandage to reveal the bite wound on his ear. Marly winced.

'Well, I guess I can forgo any further sleep then,' she barked, marching with speed from the room, leaving Alex and Ragland in her wake.

CHAPTER 15

The town doctor, Claire, was rubbing her eyes as she opened the door to her offices. Marly simply gestured to Ragland and when she saw the state of him by the candlelight, Claire made a low hissing sound.

'You're back? You're like a bad penny! Not going to make this a habit, right?'

'I don't plan to, no.'

'Thanks Claire. I'm going back to bed,' said Marly. 'I take it you remember where the Creaky is, Mr. Ragland?'

'Sure do, thanks again.'

Ragland followed Claire through the waiting room to her office. He noticed that, aside from the absence of leaflets and computers, everything still looked remarkably similar to the way a family doctor's did in the days before the Fall.

'Place looks good,' he said.

'It wasn't always like this,' she said, closing the door behind him. 'Sit.'

'Yes ma'am.'

Claire tied her hair back in a ponytail, frowning at Ragland.

'Don't ma'am me.'

'Okay,' he said, forgiving her abruptness. He'd have been cranky too if someone woke him in the middle of the night.

'So, cowboy, how did the other guy fair?' Claire asked, peeling the bandage back to inspect the wound. It had stopped bleeding, and the teeth marks made a clear semi-circle encompassing most of the upper part of the ear, parts of it torn right through. 'You're lucky you still have it.'

'Yeah, he didn't fair so well, it was a goddamn cannibal.'

'Oh? How many?'

'Just the one.'

Ragland didn't know if it was the flickering lamplight, but he could have sworn he'd seen a shadow of a smirk on the doctor's face.

'How did you let that happen? I mean, if it was just one?'

He clenched his jaw.

'Snuck up on me.'

Claire stepped back from Ragland and reached into a cupboard. She pulled out a swatch of fabric, and a glass jar filled with clear liquid. Upending the bottle onto the cloth, she leaned in and dabbed his ear without warning.

Ragland flinched.

'Jesus, what is that stuff?'

'Moonshine.'

'Moonsh—Ow!'

Claire added more to the cloth, cleaning the wound on his ear with thoroughness. Ragland winced and sucked in a breath.

'Be quiet, you big baby. I'm almost done.'

He gritted his teeth, breathing a sigh of relief when she finally finished and went looking for some gauze. After a minute of rattling drawers and tossing their contents around, Claire returned with a small dish of greenish cream.

Ragland raised an eyebrow.

'What's that?'

'An ointment to stop infection.'

He watched her scoop out a blob with her finger.

'It doesn't look good.'

'Well, did you think we stockpiled a decade's worth of antiseptic cream? It's perfectly fine, no one's died from it yet. Made from goldenseal.'

'Goldenseal?'

'It's a plant. A leafy green that tends to grow further south. We've cultivated our own here. Saved a fair few folk here from losing limbs or worse. Sepsis doesn't play around.'

Ragland was impressed, noticing for the first time that one whole wall of her office was lined with cabinets filled with ointments and medicine that also appeared to have been made locally.

'Resourceful. I could learn a thing or two.'

'Even an old man like you?'

'Yeah, even an old man like me,' he smirked. 'I'm thirty-four, just so you know.'

'Still, the oldest we've seen. Where do you come from?'

Claire started to apply the green paste to his ear. It felt cool and soothing, and the sensation robbed his thoughts from the question. His exhaustion didn't help; the adrenaline from the fight had worn off, leaving him exhausted.

'No comment?'

'Oh, sorry. South. I'm from the south.'

'South?' she said, showing him a mocking smile. 'Just south, is it cowboy?'

'Yeah, why not?'

Another huff.

'Hmm. Keep your secrets then, old man. Let's close this up.'

She finished the application of the goldenseal paste, grabbed some of the gauze and fresh wrap, and cut a few small strips off with a pair of scissors.

'Don't move,' she said, as she began to dress and wrap the wound.

Ragland obeyed, hoping her focus on treatment had let him off the hook. But, as she stepped away to admire her handiwork, she brushed her hands together and folded them under her armpits.

'Come back day after tomorrow for a dressing change. So, you've been a whole lot of trouble in just the few days since you showed up. What's the deal?'

'Deal?'

Claire's patience with his ambiguity hit zero, he could see it. She pointed to the door and looked down at the floor.

'Go on. We're all done here. You can be someone else's problem.'

'Thanks for patching me up,' Ragland said, as he grabbed his backpack from reception where he'd dropped it.

'It's okay,' she said, pushing the door open and holding it for him. 'Try office hours next time, huh?'

'Will do,' he said, tipping an imaginary hat as he went through.

Outside he inhaled a lungful of cold, fresh air. His ear felt better already, the pain having subsided to a dull throb.

Up above the hills, he spied the moon sinking low behind branches. If he had any luck left in the tank, he might catch a few hours' sleep at the Creaky Motel. Shouldering the backpack, he took a quick glance back at the dark windows of the doctor's office, bit his lip, and went on his way through the sleepy, dark streets of Bakerstown.

Sunlight was streaming through the windows of the Creaky when Ragland woke up. All things considered, he didn't feel too bad as he sat on the edge of his bed. His leg muscles were sore from the run back, but his bandaged ear had gone from a dull throb to just feeling kind of heavy.

He thought about his next move. The overwhelming urge to get back on the road fought with a growing notion that maybe it would be better to hunker down in Bakerstown until he had more of a bead on the cannibal threat. He was sure Marly's earlier offer would still be on the table, and he was happy to help out to earn his keep.

He went round back to where he'd had the shower on his last stay. A second shower in a week was unthinkable, especially given how cold the last one was, so he settled with lifting the lid of the barrel, splashing cold water on his face and smoothing down his hair.

Feeling rejuvenated, he wiped his hands on his jeans and went out into the street. It was still relatively early, and few people were about. He decided to head to Simon's rather than disturbing Marly after her interrupted night.

He'd walked most of the way when he spotted Simon speaking with a man on horseback outside the café. The man bent and helped the Canadian take a sack that was laying over his saddle. Ragland hung back, not wanting to intrude, but the interaction came to a quick close, both men shaking hands before the rider turned and rode by Ragland, headed towards the gate.

Ragland gave the rider a cursory nod as he passed.

Out-of-town delivery? It made sense. Settlements over the years had redeveloped trade. So far, he hadn't seen a distillery, so he could only surmise that Claire had gotten the stash of moonshine from a neighboring settlement.

'Morning,' Simon called. 'I didn't expect to see you again. No offense.'

He smiled.

'None taken. Need a hand?'

Simon busied himself with the mysterious sack of goods and nodded to some crates stacked next to the wall on the sidewalk.

'Sure. Why not. Good way to earn breakfast. I'm guessing that's why you're here, right? Folk love those honey oats.'

'Just happy to help, but those oats *were* damn good,' Ragland replied, bending and lifting one of the crates up, taking care to use his legs to take the strain. It would be easy to blow one's back out—the thing weighed a good thirty or more pounds.

He followed Simon in, through to the back where he was stacking a walk-in pantry. Ragland was surprised to see small containers of ice littered about, preserving other goods, and even spied jars of milk amongst them.

'How did you manage that?' Ragland enquired, placing the crate down and stretching, checking out the ice with his fingers.

Simon smirked. 'Old wild west trick. It's why

we keep Jennie around.'

'Jennie? Sorry, I can't remember—'

'The chronologist here. She keeps track of all books and records.'

'Right.'

'So, we found a way to store ice during the summer,' he explained, following Ragland back out to the street to collect the last of the food. 'We carve up the ice from rivers and haul it back here. There's a cave not far. We used that at first. Then, Jennie read about how they would dig great big holes and cellars back in the 1800s and cover the ice in straw to keep it cold enough through the summer.'

'Jesus,' Ragland said. 'That's impressive work.'

The two big men finished stocking the pantry, or what served now as a walk-in refrigerator, in quick time and stepped back into the main café/bar area.

Ragland took a seat at the nearest table while Simon navigated the kitchen, pouring oats into a large pot before filling it with milk and water.

'Come to think of it, I heard about an ice cave just west of here. It's a week-long hike, but...'

'We did too. But it's too far, and we can get ice locally without any risk. Besides, it'd melt before we got it back.'

'True.'

'No bother, eh? Look at us now.' Simon's smile was broad and lit up his entire face.

Ragland watched Simon cook and busy

himself with kitchen prep for the day, in between stirring the big pot. He briefly considered mentioning the cannibal business, but it wasn't his style. He didn't gossip, and if anything needed to be announced, he'd leave it for Marly to do the announcing.

Simon had served up the oats, and he was about to take his first spoonful when Marly came through the door, the morning sun bathing her in its warm, yellow light to ensure the entrance was a memorable one.

'Morning, Simon. Morning Josh.'

Ragland jolted at the use of his first name. He'd gotten used to others referring to him by his surname, and it'd stuck. Over the years, he'd fallen into the habit, whenever prompted, of giving his surname.

As unaccustomed to it as he was, it sure beat *old man*.

'Morning,' he said, taking a quick spoonful of his breakfast as she sidled up to him.

'When you're done with breakfast, can I have you for a few minutes? Now that you'll be a Bakerstown resident for a while, I think it's time we see where we can put you to good use.'

Ragland caught the edge of Simon's smirk and raised his eyebrows at Marly.

'Resident?'

'Cut the crap, old timer, you're staying put.'

His refilled spoon paused halfway back to his mouth. He'd already come close to making the decision to stay for the winter. He let Marly's bold certainty push him over the line.

'How's Alex?' he asked.

Marly flashed her eyes briefly to Simon, then back to Ragland, hands going to her hips. 'He's fine. All taken care of.'

'Right,' he said, looking down at the glistening streaks of honey in his oats. 'Best get this porridge down me then, don't want me passing out of hunger while you work me into the ground.'

'Excellent,' Marly nodded. 'I think I know exactly where to put you.'

CHAPTER 16

'Cabbages?' Ragland asked, fiddling with his beard as he surveyed the small farm they'd made for themselves on the edge of town.

'You got it in one, old man. That back of yours is not going to give up on us, is it?' Marly quipped, grinning and sharing a laugh with a few of the other townsfolk, all in overalls and jeans, getting down and dirty in the mud.

Ragland held out his hand and she placed some well-worn gardening gloves in them.

'I'm sure it'll be fine.'

'Good. And if I hear you've been slacking,' she joked, after pointing out the row he'd be working on. 'I'll haul your ass back through the gate myself.'

'Roger,' he said, crouching down at the first cabbage, grabbing it with both hands and beginning to pull.

Before he could yank it free from the earth, a kid no older than fourteen stopped him. He wore dungarees and a brown cap backwards on his head.

'No, like this.'

Ragland stood up and the kid stepped forward, flattened the large outer leaves to the ground, then wrapped his right hand around the main head, tilting it and slicing the stalk with the short knife in his other hand.

The boy tossed it into the empty wheelbarrow next to Ragland's row, then moved to back to his own row.

'Thanks kid,' he said and got a smile in return.

Turning back to his own line of cabbages, he noticed a few of the farmers nudging each other and laughing.

Grumbling under his breath, still not quite able to comprehend the turn of events, he pulled his new knife from his boot and tried his luck with the next cabbage. Nothing to it, he thought and plonked it down in the wheelbarrow.

By midday, he was warmer than he'd felt in days and had discarded his jacket hours before. Now, with his sleeves rolled up, he'd gotten so involved with the work that he missed the call for a lunch break.

A small hand slapped his back, and Ragland peered up at the offender. It was the kid who had shown him the way of the cabbage.

'What?'

'We stop for food.'

'Already?'

The kid nodded.

'Sure. We got a lot more to do. Kale. Broccoli. Beets. Potatoes.'

'Kale? Christ I'd rather eat…'

'I think he gets it, Odin. Leave the poor man alone.'

The voice came from a black woman, her hair tied back by a piece of cloth.

Ragland nodded to her, which she returned in kind. He stood up, pulled off his gloves and walked to the end of the row and across to a small table. It was laden with plates of thick cut bread, and a large ceramic crockpot.

'Hey there,' said the woman who had chided Odin. 'New here? Name's Viola. Don't mind Odin, he's our special boy. He likes to talk. Always been that way.'

'No bother to me. Kid seems a solid worker, helped me out at the beginning there. I'm Ragl… Josh.'

He saw Odin tap his arm repeatedly, then shuffle along to grab a piece of bread, which he placed against his lips for a moment, as if enjoying the texture.

'What do you mean special? Something wrong with him?'

'Oh no,' Viola replied, grabbing a bowl next to the large pot. 'Nothing wrong. We've read into it, and we think he has a mild form of autism. He struggles in the classroom, too.'

'Is that why he's out here with you folk?'

'In part.'

'He's not a fan of school then?'

Viola shook her head, picked up a ladle, and scooped the steaming hot chicken broth into a bowl. Ragland's mouth watered.

'Not quite,' she said. 'Comes and goes. Some days he doesn't mind the indoors. Somedays, he can't stand it. But since he was young, he's been great with his hands. Not always the farm. We get him to help on the building, too. Or sewing. Rahul has even taken him in as an early apprentice. You met Rahul yet?'

Ragland rolled his eyes, taking the ladle from Viola and serving himself a generous portion.

'I have had the pleasure.'

'Oh, you have, have you?'

'Is he like that with everyone?'

'Just strangers,' she said. 'He's protective. One of the first to set up Bakerstown way back. Guy has done the hard yards.'

He nodded. Perhaps he had been too quick to judge Rahul. After all, he was a stranger in a world grown more paranoid about the nameless.

Viola grinned.

'You won't have hurt his feelings. Rahul's one of the toughest here.'

'Hell yeah, he is.'

A stocky guy a few inches shorter than Ragland had spoken. He pushed past one of the other harvesters and began ladling the soup into his bowl like he hadn't eaten in a week.

'This is David,' Viola said, her voice tightening.

'He's one of our hunters.'

'Best in Bakerstown!' he roared, placing his soup down to feign shooting an arrow from a bow.

Ragland held out a hand for him to shake, but he either missed or ignored it, instead grabbing a slice of bread, dunking it into the soup and then into his mouth without missing a beat.

'Incredible!' David said, around the food in his mouth. 'Simon does it again.' He seemed to notice Ragland again. 'So, you're the new one?'

'Yup,' Ragland replied, shuffling along with Viola to grab a piece of bread.

'Killed those cannibals a day south?'

'Yep.'

David laughed.

'You don't talk much, do you? What's up with that?'

A man much taller than Ragland rocked up to the table, grabbing his soup, followed by another two very muscular-looking guys, all wearing thick winter jackets and carrying guns, axes and bows.

'Maybe he doesn't like you, David,' one of the men said. He was a tall black man with a deep voice.

'Ah, can't be that, Travis. Just can't be. Everyone likes me.'

Viola snorted.

'You may be good with a bow, David, but you sure are full of shit.'

The men, including Travis, laughed. He shot them a menacing look and the laughter petered out. Turning, he noticed Ragland watching him and the scowl swiftly morphed into a humorless smile that was somehow more menacing.

This time, David held out a hand.

'Nice to meet another hunter.' He gestured to the men. 'This is Travis, Viola's brother. Big boy here is Matthew. Some call him Blackbeard. Can you see why? Haha and yeah, this is Sang-Hoon. Don't worry, he's Korean, not Chinese.'

Travis thumped him, and Viola hissed.

'Come on, man.'

'Ah!' David held his hands up in mock apology. 'Sorry. He's a good boy. He's one of the good ones.'

Sang-Hoon held out a hand of his own to Ragland.

'Just call me Sang, friend.'

'Friend?' David scoffed. 'You only just met the asshole.'

'He saved Kit,' Sang replied.

'And? Kit is always getting into trouble. Why should he get the blowjob welcome party? I mean, he could be anyone, right? No offense. Say, what's your name again? Joshua, right?'

Ragland had practically crushed the bread in his hand as flat as pitta.

'That's right.'

'Right. Okay, well, good to meet you, Josh,' he said closing the space between them until his face was inches away from Ragland's. 'We'll keep in touch. You see, we're a bit like protectors here in Bakerstown. We keep an eye on our own.'

Viola had heard enough, judging by the hand on her hip.

'Cut that shit out, David. Travis, why do you hang around with this jerk?'

'He's got a point, sis.'

David laughed, stepping away from the newcomer and thumped Travis on the shoulder, causing his soup to slosh onto the ground.

'Yep. Come on. Let's go eat. See you around, Joshua.'

The four men left, Sang the only one to give Ragland a half-smile. They strolled over to horses hitched up by a tree and walked back toward town, still holding their soup and leading their horses with them.

Ragland turned to Viola.

'Care to explain why I haven't met that crew before?'

'They were probably out hunting,' she said. 'Best you keep away. If you think Rahul doesn't like strangers, you haven't dealt with the Baker's Boys.'

'Baker's Boys?'

'Mhmm. It's what they call themselves.'

She and Ragland sat down and began to eat their meal in silence. He was hungry enough to let the topic hang for a moment, eager to fill his stomach and forget about it.

Once he'd mopped the last of the soup up with

his flattened bread, he wiped his mouth. 'They some sort of local gang?'

'They seem to think so, but no, more like a militia. Yes, David's an asshole, but generally they mean well. Of course, they can get carried away... looking for purpose, I guess.'

'Aren't we all?'

Viola gave Ragland a quick glance, then smirked.

'You're a man of mysteries, aren't you?'

'Don't know about that.'

No sooner had they stacked their empty dishes into a box next to the food, when Marly appeared, Kit at her side. Ragland could tell by her face that sleep and food had worked wonders. She wore a mustard beanie over her dark hair and a meek smile.

'Hi all, how's the work?'

A chorus of nods and choice words from all the farmers greeted their mayor. Marly seemed satisfied, as she walked over to Ragland and Viola.

'How's everything going?' Marly asked.

'All good,' he said, then nodded at Kit who gave him a half-smile.

'He's not slowing us down too much, if that's what you're getting at, Marly.'

Viola and Marly both chuckled, Kit still watching Ragland.

'Good to hear. Well, I just wanted to pop by. We've got another keen pair of hands who wants to muck right in. That good with you, V?'

'It sure as hell is. How're you feeling, Kit?' Viola asked, getting up and putting a hand on her face affectionately, checking her over.

Kit smiled.

'Much better. Like, totally different.'

Marly raised her hands up and clapped. 'Alright then. I'll leave her in your capable hands. If you could swing by with the yield numbers later, that'd be great.'

'Sure thing,' Viola called back, Marly already a few strides toward the road. 'Oh, check on David and the boys, will you?'

'Why's that?' Marly shouted.

'They're down Jack's, probably. Getting their game seen to. You know what they're like.'

Ragland saw Viola tilt her head towards him. Marly seemed to get the gist of what her friend was saying and waved.

'Loud and clear, V. See you later.'

'What was that all about?' he asked.

She took Kit over to the field, finding another pair of gloves for her. 'Never you mind. Lunch is over. These vegetables don't pick themselves.'

That night, as he readied for bed as weary from the hard day's work as he'd been in a long time, he was disturbed by a light knock on the door.

It was Marly and Alex.

'I've decided to send a team of three on a scouting mission to see exactly what we might be facing if these cannibals decide to pay us a visit.'

'I see. Who would that be?'

'Young Alex here, he knows the territory as good as the hunters, and two of them. Travis and Sang.'

'Just scouting?' he asked, looking at Alex.

'Yeah. Just scouting…'

'I made it clear that they are not to engage, just find their location and numbers if they can, and then get the hell back here.'

'Good. Sounds like a plan.'

Marly looked at him carefully and he wondered if she was waiting for him to volunteer. Truth was, he was enjoying the farm work and having somewhere to call home. He was in no rush to hit the road again, especially in the company of others.

'Okay then,' she said, after a pause and stood up. 'Just thought you'd like to know.'

'I appreciate it,' he said, and then to Alex, 'Don't take any chances out there.'

CHAPTER 17

The next three days passed without trouble for Ragland as he helped the rest of the townsfolk make sure the approaching winter didn't freeze their food in the ground.

Each morning, a step outside the Creaky Motel seemed to greet a deeper chill than the day before. His morning routine led him down to Simon's to enjoy a half measure of coffee—fresh merchandise from a long cart ride down to the southwest.

Ragland hadn't had coffee in years, and Simon mentioned it was a delicacy for them in these parts too. It took a long time for the supply team to travel, but despite the risk, it had always worked out well so far. Simon explained they didn't just come back with coffee, but rice and other old-world trinkets and bits and pieces, too.

'Our traders go well-armed,' he explained one morning. 'They take weapons and things to trade; Rahul is making quite a name for Bakerstown steel. If things get nasty though, well, they know how to handle themselves. And coffee sure boosts the morale around here.'

Ragland was inclined to agree. On the fourth day, he'd really gotten into the swing of things, meeting Viola and the others down in the dirt to pick potatoes now that the cabbage and kale had been farmed.

With half a week under his belt as a Bakerstown citizen, his face had grown familiar to the local folk, earning the occasional nod and wave from some. He got on well with the butcher, Jack, and stopped for a chat with him whenever they passed each other. He even had the pleasure of sharing an all-too-brief talk with Clint, the teacher, who, even though he was at least ten years younger than Ragland, was knowledgeable about the old world.

But his heart had been softened by the farmers. Odin especially, who had taken a liking to him and always found a way to make sure he was next to Ragland when they were picking.

Viola hadn't missed it. On the fifth day, just after lunch, she giggled on the way back to the field, nudging him.

'Might want to start calling yourself Thor.'

'Why's that?' he said, slipping his gloves back on.

'Odin has grown fond of you very quickly. Must be your calming influence, I guess.'

Ragland looked over and spotted Odin pressing his hands into the dirt and watching the earth pour off his fingers. Then, once it had all returned to the ground, he did it again. Then the kid looked up at him and smiled.

'Maybe he does, but wasn't Odin Thor's father?'

Viola laughed again.

'Probably, sorry, Norse mythology isn't my strongest topic...'

On the sixth night, with the sun tucked behind the hills and the inky-black sky studded bright with a billion stars, the townsfolk had gathered at Simon's Bar, for a harvest supper to celebrate the end of the season. They filled the sidewalk with wooden tables and erected additional torches and firepits.

Marly had extended the invitation to Ragland, who felt just as comfortable after a long day in the field as spending the evening alone in his shack, getting shut-eye.

'Not on my watch,' she had said, jabbing his chest with her little finger. 'You did good this week. Plus, Simon has a surprise. You won't want to miss it.'

Simon's surprise turned out to be a large batch of beer brewed right in Bakerstown. It had been the best-kept secret for months. Normally the lubrication on offer at the supper was mulberry wine or moonshine, so it created a buzz of excitement, with the sea of faces smiling. Before anyone could take a good sip, Marly raised her stein into the air, surrounded by her people.

'To Joshua Ragland. For making Bakerstown

his home—at least for a while—and for some mighty fine work on the farm. Here, here!'

A chorus of cheers erupted, and everyone clinked their steins and drank as if dying of thirst. Ragland tipped his gingerly, not having had an alcoholic drink since he was 22.

'You didn't have to say that,' Ragland said, savoring the sweet, hoppy taste.

'Oh, I sure as hell did,' Marly replied, nudging him. 'Not too bad for an old man, you know?'

They both smiled. Simon, busy at the bar, nodded to Ragland and shouted over.

'Like it?'

Ragland raised it up as a salute.

'It's great.'

The big man went back to serving his friends and family. From behind the same crowd of people, David materialized and ambled over to Ragland. He looked between him and Marly, as if contemplating his choice of words.

'You sure you should be toasting this guy, Marly? We don't know a goddamn thing about him.'

'I recall you were always a troublemaker back in the early days, during the fighting. But I gave you a second chance. And a third. Still here, ain't ya?'

Ragland bit into his cheek to stop himself from smirking. David hadn't seen the quick reply coming.

'That's not the same thing,' he stuttered.

'He's proven himself. He's worked hard. Earned his keep. You did the same, David.'

Out from Ragland's left, Jack the butcher appeared, rubbing his hands to keep warm and eyeing up the bar for a beer.

'Just got Rufus and Charlie all set up on watch. Is there a problem here?'

David shot him a withering look, taking a large gulp of his beer, letting the drips slick his chin.

'What do you make of the old man, Butcher?'

Annoyed at being spoken about as if he wasn't there, Ragland kept his cool, not moving an inch, but watching David's body language for any sign of aggression. No one else had noticed anything over the noise of the crowd.

'He saved Kit. What else is there to say?'

'So he says,' David replied.

Marly and Jack jumped in at the same time. Jack asked what the hell that meant, and Marly told him to relax and ease up on the drink. It had been a long time since any of them had taken in any volume of alcohol.

But Ragland's deep voice broke through their retorts, drawing David's attention.

'Listen, there's clearly something you're not happy about. That's fine by me. You don't have to like me, and I don't have to like you. So, there's Nothing stopping you from heading back to your buddy.'

He nodded in the direction of Matthew, the one they called Blackbeard, who loitered near the back of the bar.

David took a step forward. The two stared at each other, tension suddenly palpable in the air. Ragland placed his beer down on a table and drew himself to his full height, his hands slack by his side. Just as David squared up, the sound of piano filled the room.

The tension melted away as the bar started to bounce, people dancing and spinning each other around. With barely any room to move, David and Ragland were quickly jostled apart and swept into the mix. The man's stare conveyed more than words ever could to Ragland. It was a look he'd seen in men before. The look of a killer.

CHAPTER 18

The headache the following morning was almost worth it. Ragland peeled himself out of bed in the early hours before the sun had rose, throwing on his jacket and gloves, before meandering his way through Bakerstown in search of nothing in particular except for fresh air and respite from his spinning head.

Ragland's wandering took him back to the gate, where Charlie and Rufus were still standing watch, the low mumble of their voices barely audible from the ground.

'Mind if I join you boys?' he asked, craning his neck.

Two heads appeared, dark splotches against the moonlit sky. There was a brief conversation.

'Sure,' Rufus said, tapping the ladder. 'Come on up.'

Ragland climbed his way up and hoisted himself onto the wooden walkway. When he stretched to full height, he towered over the two teenagers. Rufus' eyes widened and Ragland smiled to put him at ease before turning to look out over the trees—textured smudges in the dark—highlighted by the three-quarter moon.

His warm exhale produced a cloud of vapor.

'You have one of those hangover things?' Charlie asked, leaning on his bow which was almost the same height as him.

'Something like that,' Ragland replied.

Rufus chuckled.

'Alex gave us a little beer. Haven't felt like that before. So that's what you old folk used to drink before the fall?'

'Hey, kid, I ain't old,' he said, pointing at his head. 'You see any grey hair?'

'No offense,' Rufus shrugged. 'But you're the oldest person we've seen, literally ever.'

Charlie backed him up.

'It's true. Sorry dude.'

Dude? Ragland pressed his thumb and middle finger into his eyes and rubbed them. It did nothing to alleviate the pain, so he gave up and looked down at their water flask.

'Mind?'

They shook their heads, still grinning, and watched as Ragland took a few thirsty gulps, spilling some onto his beard—a tangled beast that could do with some taming.

He handed them back the flask, gripped the edge of the fence, and watched the world in silence for as long as it took to let the nausea and spinning subside. The first tinge of dawn crept over the top of the hills, slowly illuminating the dark woods in the orange, yellow and rust shades of late autumn. It was a pretty sight.

'Is it true?' Rufus said, around a yawn. 'That you, er... you know, fended off, like, twenty cannibals on your own and saved Kit?'

Ragland raised an eyebrow.

'What?'

Charlie thumped Rufus in the arm. 'Not cool, dude.'

There it was again. *Dude*. It sounded foreign to his ears; he hadn't heard the word in years and to hear it from a pair of kids in a small Pennsylvania settlement a clean decade after most of the population had been wiped out, amazed him. Especially when they would have been about five years old at the most during The Fall.

'What have you heard?'

They both started to speak at the same time, which only frustrated Ragland more. He put up a hand.

'One at a time, boys. What have you heard?'

Rufus looked at his friend Charlie, who nodded. He went onto explain where he'd heard the rumors. It sounded to Ragland like a classic case of embellished Chinese whispers. Just talk and town gossip that grew in grandeur every time it passed from one person to another.

'Okay.'

'So, it's true? You really did that?' Rufus said, his eyes wide.

Ragland shook his head.

'No. A quarter of that. And it's not like the stories out there. It's messy and it's hard. And you never get away clean. Rarely. Don't think about any grand adventures or trying to be a hero. Your friend Kit thought the same, and if I hadn't gotten lucky, you'd never have seen her again.'

Charlie and Rufus nodded, seemingly sobered, then looked over to the ladder, which was creaking as someone climbed it. Ragland turned, half expecting David's face, but it was Kit.

'So, am I, like, interrupting anything?'

'Nope,' said Ragland.

He watched the boys shuffle aside to give Kit room to climb up onto the crowded ledge that ran the length of the Bakerstown's southern perimeter. A perfect platform for recon, hangover recovery and gossip.

'I was just telling your friends that grand adventures out there,' he gestured out over the forest, 'aren't all they're cracked up to be. In fact, they'd be silly to go off without the right preparation or telling someone.'

A small smile creased her lips. She wore a thick puffer jacket Ragland hadn't seen before, jeans, and the same hiking boots as before. Was this a morning stroll or something else? She seemed well-slept and prepared.

'Does that make me silly?'

'Yes,' Ragland said without hesitation.

She rolled her eyes.

'Harsh, old man! But fair.' He was relieved that their awkwardness after his departure seemed to have been forgotten. 'So, I've come up with a solution for that.'

He eyed her.

'Don't get any ideas about going out there again.'

'Oh, for sure. At least, like, not yet. I figured I just needed a bit of training, you know?'

'Training?'

'Yeah, so I can kill the cannibals when they come.'

Ragland groaned, Charlie and Rufus looked back and forth between them, clearly excited at the prospect.

'This conversation is over.' Ragland nodded to the boys, and climbed back down the ladder. Once on the ground, he made it about twenty paces up the street before Kit caught up.

'I'm only asking for you to train me. Don't you think that it makes sense?'

'Sure. If you want to get yourself killed.'

Kit huffed, jumping in front of Ragland and crossing her arms.

'You're not fooling anyone, old man.'

Ragland stopped, tilting his head back and silently counting to ten. When he looked back at Kit, he saw a bitter determination. An expression he'd seen plenty of times years before. His hand went up subconsciously to touch the onyx pendant but stopped himself.

Kit had noticed.

'I'm not her, you know? Like, I'm my own person.'

'You're not going to stop, are you?'

Her eyes were resolute, and he would have bet money that she'd picked a up lot of her ways from Marly.

'Nope. Not until you agree to train me; *especially* if you buy half of what Alex has been saying.'

Ragland noticed movement further down the street and narrowed his eyes as he peered over her shoulder. A figure disappeared into the shadows as quickly as they had appeared. He wasn't sure if it was paranoia, however from the person's build, he thought it might be David.

'Fine,' he conceded, splitting his attention between her and the place the mysterious lurker had disappeared. 'We'll meet on the far end of town, near the fields. Bring a bow and some arrows.'

'Yes! You won't regret it. So, like, when do you want to start?'

'Now.'

Kit paused, not quite believing him, then darted away at a run, down one of the side streets, toward the home she shared with Alex. He began to walk again, perhaps spooking the lurker who materialized from the shadows briefly before disappearing around a corner.

Hooded though they were, it was David, he

was almost certain.

Fully awake, the ebb of his hangover subsiding, Ragland walked to the corner, giving it a wide berth in case of ambush, and looked up the street.

Nothing. He was gone.

What is that man's gripe? Ragland puzzled.

No matter. Clear headed without last night's infusion of alcohol, he decided that if David started trouble, he'd go to Marly and set things straight. He was the stranger in town, not David, and the last thing he needed, with the possible arrival of a horde of cannibals, was to provoke the town into kicking him out.

CHAPTER 19

When Kit arrived, she had the bow and arrows as requested but argued that maybe they should move straight to hand-to-hand combat.

'I already know how to shoot an arrow. Didn't I catch you two nice turkeys?'

'Sneaking up on a fat wild turkey and sticking it from ten feet is different to shooting at a person, especially if they are running at you waving an axe or a blade.'

She couldn't argue with his logic.

'Alright, show me your form,' he said.

The two had found an open piece of land by a tall cedar; the earth was filled with roots and therefore had never been farmed. Ragland had marked the tree with a piece of flint, chipping away some of the bark to make a circular target about eight inches across. Then, after much protest that she could shoot from further, he'd convinced her to stand only twenty feet away.

She lifted the bow and nocked the arrow, drawing it back to her cheek and aimed at the cedar.

'Okay, stop! That won't do. Let me show you.'

She rolled her eyes and passed it to him. Ragland lifted Kit's bow and pulled the bowstring back, pulling until it ran dead-center from the tip of his nose and down the middle of his chin.

'See how it runs straight, nose to chin?'

'No one shoots like that,' Kit protested, chewing at her thumbnail. 'They hold it to their cheek.'

'Well, they're doing it wrong.'

'All of them?'

Ragland dropped the bow and looked back at her.

'Yes.' Then rubbed his eyes. 'No. Not technically. Do you want to learn proper form or not?'

'Well yeah, I kinda like, don't wanna die, you know? Or almost die. Not like before.'

He passed the bow back to her, along with one of the three arrows she had brought along with her. They had been handcrafted by someone in the town, judging by the wood of the shaft and the not-so-clean fletching. The tip, however, was sharp and purposeful.

'Here, you go. I want your left arm bent slightly, notch the arrow and pull back to your chin like I showed you.'

'Alright, gramps.'

She laughed, copying his instruction.

'Okay, I think I'm ready,' she said.

'Then loose.'

'What?'

'Shoot the damn arrow, kid.'

And she did. It sailed through the air, hitting the tree trunk with a deep thunk, missing the mark completely, a good half foot below the rough circle. Her sound of exasperation made Ragland smirk. It was only her first go, and she'd landed it in the tree. Most would have done worse.

'Okay,' he said, walking up to Kit and kicking her feet with his. 'Set these apart and stand more side-on. Try to aim a little higher there, too. Here you go.'

Ragland passed her the next arrow. This time, Kit's attempt made it within three inches of the mark. She spun around on the spot; her mouth open.

'Oh, my God. Did you friggin' see that shit? I'm a natural.'

'Steady on,' he smirked, raising a hand. 'Plenty more to learn. Take another shot, then collect the arrows for another round.'

He sat on the grass as she went to retrieve the arrows. He half expected her to call him for assistance, as they were embedded deep in the wood of the cedar, but as stubborn as him, she worked and pulled at them until she had collected all three.

Of her next three shots from forty yards, three were on target, one just missed.

'Not bad kid, not bad at all.'

'Not bad? I am friggin' awesome!'

'Well, don't get too carried away. You had skill before, but now that you have the correct technique, no turkey will be safe.'

'Your technique helps, I guess,' she conceded.

'I want you to practice more on your own this afternoon. See if you can get some more arrows, maybe have a friend doing retrieval so you don't wear yourself out. Do ten from thirty feet. If you get them all, then move out to forty. When you can hit the target ten times in a row from forty feet without a miss, you're ready.'

'Easy-peasy.'

'Do you remember what I told you about the second arrow when you're being rushed?'

'Yep. Don't try to shoot, just use it as a stabbing weapon.'

'Good. Now we can move on to self-defense in close quarters.'

Ragland picked some soft ground, away from any protruding roofs, and faced Kit, rolling up his sleeves.

'Next, we're going to learn what to do when the fight gets a little closer.'

'What, like kung-fu?'

Ragland raised his eyebrow. 'No. Not exactly. I want you to walk up and try and punch me.'

Kit's face changed.

'Huh?'

'Punch me. Try to, at least.'

'Are you, like… are you serious?'

'Haven't got all day, kid.'

She positioned herself, clenching her fists, then charged forward, hurling a knuckled blow toward the left side of his face. Ragland stepped to the left at the last moment, grabbed her arm, and yanked it down gently. With the momentum of her missed punch, Kit went flying, sprawling into the ground.

'Hey!' she said, coughing and getting back up, dusting the dirt from her coat. She unzipped it and tossed it aside. Ragland did the same. They would start to build up quite a bit of heat from the workout.

The corners of his mouth went up.

'That all you got?'

Kit tried again, falling foul to the same trick. On the third go, the same. But on the fourth, Ragland stepped the other way, into Kit and remained still, his arms outstretched. Her body collided into his, sending her stumbling backward.

'Hey, what gives? I thought you were supposed to be showing me how to kill and stuff?'

'I am.'

Kit rolled her eyes, kicking the grass.

'Yeah, right. You're just being a jerk. I can take it, you know. Just show me the moves.'

'These are the moves. It's not about spinning kicks and uppercuts. It's about evasion and protecting yourself. You can't kill anyone if you're dead.'

'Fair point, I guess.'

'Come at me again, but this time, do it slowly, and I'll show you why.'

Kit bared her teeth, moving the hair from her eyes and clenched her fists again, ready to fight. She stepped in, slowly this time, and threw a half-hearted punch at Ragland. Matching her speed, Ragland stepped left from the punch, drawing her arm in the same direction as her momentum, and jabbing his fingers to her ribs.

'Look what I've done here.'

Kit stopped, lowering her head around to look at his stiffened fingers.

He prodded her side.

'If I had something sharp, it'd be over. I could do it here, here, or even here.'

Ragland prodded various points of her ribs then let her go. She looked disheartened as she straightened her shirt.

'Fine,' she said, finally. 'So, show me what I'm supposed to do.'

'First off, kid, you're not meant to go on the attack. You wait. You bait them if you have to. Let them go for the attack first. My dad always said that you never attack first, but if they ever start something, you always end it.'

'Very wise and shit, ain't ya?'

Ragland shook his head at her little dig.

'Wax on, wax off...' She raised her eyebrow. 'Never mind. Anyhow, he was right. Now, let's get to business.'

For the next hour or two, until their stomachs grumbled for a breakfast they'd skipped, Ragland taught Kit how to duck away from an array of different punches, how to lock an arm, and how to throw a proper punch.

By the time he was done, Ragland was sweating, even though the day wasn't hot. Kit looked like she could go for another hour.

Grabbing up their equipment and jackets, the pair headed back into town, Kit thanking Ragland for the training, before turning left from the main avenue. He fancied a cool off under the shower before eating and headed toward the Creaky Motel, which had somehow become his home. It was the first home he'd had since the early days hiding out from the invaders in abandoned houses, sometimes for weeks at a time.

When he reached the Creaky, he stepped in, threw his jacket on the bed, and reached over to the cabinet for the bar of soap and towel Marly had provided.

The crack across the back of his head was sudden. It dazed him, and he sprawled over the top of his chest of drawers, the soap skittering across the floor. Dazed, he put a hand up to the back of his head, his fingers coming away slick with red.

'Son of a bitch...' he cursed, starting to get up before another heavy blow came across his back.

A pair of large hands grabbed him from behind, hurling him into the wall. The whole building shook as Ragland crashed to the floor and got to his hands and knees, looking back at his assailant.

David.

He looked like a man possessed—eyes alert, face red, fingers twitching. Behind him was Blackbeard. Ragland got up slowly, feeling the back of his head again.

'You don't want to do this, buddy.'

David pulled a knife from under his jacket and held it up to Ragland.

'I think I do, asshole.'

David came at him, swinging the blade in quick swiping motions. Ragland backpedaled, and his attacker missed most of his attempts before finally catching Ragland on the arm. He cried out and gripped the wound, blood oozing through his fingers.

'Stop,' Ragland panted, bending over slightly and holding out his blood-soaked hand.

The local closed in to finish the job, deceived by Ragland's phony surrender, throwing all his weight behind the thrust. The drifter saw it coming a mile off; he side-stepped, caught the knife arm and rabbit punched David in the ribcage. He was rewarded by a sharp yelp of pain and the thug spun out of his grip, clutching at his side. His knife arm wavered as he tried to catch his breath from the unexpected blow.

'Oh, you are fucking dead old man... oomph!'

Ragland hit him hard. It was a good old-fashioned rugby tackle, his shoulder catching the local in the midriff and sending them both hurtling into Blackbeard. The force of the crash tackle sent them bursting through the door in an explosion of wood and splinters.

Cries of surprise and shock met his ears, and looking up, he spotted Marly in the distance, running towards them as he wrestled David for the knife. Blackbeard rolled away when he saw the mayor, but David was still fighting for control of the weapon.

'Stop!' Marly cried, as Ragland finally shook the knife free of David's hand and pushed his forearm down onto his assailant's throat.

The blood-streaked Ragland looked up as Marly approached, her face blanched white with shock. Before any of them could say a word, the whine of a siren filled the air, accompanied by more shouts and cries of alarm.

What now? Ragland wondered.

'That's the warning siren at the gate,' Marly said.

The words were barely out of her mouth when Charlie sprinted into view and ran towards them. He stopped by Marly, bending over to catch his breath.

'The gates,' he panted.

Ragland eased the pressure on David's throat when the other man didn't try to make trouble, but he wasn't ready to let him up just yet.

Charlie's eyes widened at the bloodied state of the drifter and David.

'Who, Charlie?' snapped Marly. 'Who's at the gates?'

'Peter and Alex and the hunters. They said the cannibals are coming—a whole damn army of 'em!'

PART FOUR: LYNCH MOB

CHAPTER 20

Marly stood over Ragland and David with her arms folded.

He rolled off his attacker, who moaned and clutched his side.

'What's your prob...'

It was then he noticed the blood seeping through the pale fingers. Somehow in the struggle, David had been stuck by his own knife. The wounded man's eyes bulged when his hand came away covered in blood.

'You stabbed me, you bastard...'

Marly swore under her breath and Ragland's head spun.

'Marly-' interrupted Charlie.

'Not yet Charlie!' Marly snapped, kneeling down beside David. 'We need to get him to Claire. Can you lift him, Ragland?'

Ragland looked around to find David's sidekick Blackbeard had disappeared.

'Why not?' he said, feeling slightly peeved at the accusatory look in her eyes. He bent over and helped the wounded man to his feet and put an arm under his shoulders. David screamed and almost ruptured Ragland's eardrums.

'Got him,' he said, looking at Marly. 'This wasn't my fault you know...'

'Less talk. We need to go. Charlie, run ahead and prep Claire. This is a nasty one.'

Despite everything, Ragland would help the bleeding man to Claire so he could be stitched up, but he wasn't doing it for David, that much was certain. He and Marly set off into town, in the direction of Claire's office. The walk, while hampered by David's moaning and squirming, took less time than expected. Within eight minutes, they were at the front door, held ajar by a crimson-faced Claire.

Her eyes ran through Ragland like hot daggers, her jaw working overtime. Stepping delicately through the narrow doorway, he carried David through the reception, down the hall and into Claire's treatment room. There, he helped him onto a bed that was already prepared for him.

Claire appeared behind him, reaching for her stethoscope and pressing the circular end against David's chest after she and Marly had removed his shirt. There, for all to see, his stab wound oozed blood.

She went to the sink and washed her hands in silence, the room filled only with David's groans, before grabbing a cloth and cleaning his wound with alcohol and covering it in gauze to stop the bleeding.

'Marly,' Claire called, turning to the doorway where the Mayor had retreated. 'Could you grab me the liquor from the right cupboard, bottom shelf.'

'Sure,' said Marly, her face as pale as David's. She retrieved a large bottle of overproof rum, still labeled, and handed it over. 'That's some of your good stuff there, Claire.'

'I know. But it's the best stuff to ease the pain quickly.'

Ragland watched Claire looking for a cup for David to drink from. Already feeling in the way, his thoughts were interrupted by Claire's withering gaze.

'You can go. You're no use here.'

Ragland nodded.

'What did Charlie tell you?'

'That you're bad fucking news.' A pause, still watching the gauze to check for blood. 'No. He said it was an accident, but I don't want an excuse. As far as I'm concerned, you're bad news. Please leave, I need to work here.'

Marly nodded at Ragland, reaching out for his arm.

'Come on.'

As he went through the door he paused.

'Claire. Where did Charlie go?'

'He went back to the gate,' she said. 'There's something going on.'

'Thank you.'

Back outside in the street with Marly, Ragland

noticed how soaked-through his shirt was from David's blood. There was no time to change.

'I need to get to the gate, Marly.'

A heavy sigh escaped her lips.

'Go, see what the fuss is about. Rahul will help you deal with it. We'll deal with this later,' she said, then turned and headed back to Claire's door.

'Marly?'

The Mayor stopped and turned to look at him.

'What?'

He found he didn't know what to say. He couldn't help but see the disappointment in her face—the woman compelled to protect her town had encouraged and given refuge to a stranger. And since then, chaos and danger had followed his every move.

'Sorry,' he mumbled then ran off towards the gate.

Walking rapidly, arms pumping, Ragland navigated the side streets to the main avenue. There, in the distance, at the main gate, a small crowd had gathered at the perimeter fence.

From his left, Simon appeared, walking just as fast and with a towel over his left shoulder. He nodded to Ragland and regarded his bloody clothes when he got close.

'Should I ask?'

'Best not,' Ragland said.

'Right.'

When they arrived, his bloodied clothes a frightening sight for those gathered, a few familiar faces turned to them and called over. One such person—Rahul—charged through the crowd after spotting Ragland's shirt.

'The fuck is this, outsider? You bring the cannibals down on us?' he barked, causing a few townsfolk to gasp and murmur.

Simon stepped between them.

'Steady Rahul, he's here to help.'

'My ass. I'll help him right now.'

Rahul brandished a hammer he'd no doubt carried from his smithy. Ragland couldn't shake the image of a crazy Thor. As sullen and petty as his first impression of Rahul had been, he couldn't deny that he was a menacing figure.

'Where are they?' he said to Rahul. 'Marly sent me.'

After glaring at the drifter for a moment longer, the swarthy Rahul nodded over his shoulder to a shelter with a water trough and a few benches. The crowd separated and allowed Ragland through, Simon at his back. Alex, Sang and Travis were sitting in the shade, still catching their breath and drinking water.

Alex stood and stumbled over to Ragland. He looked exhausted.

'There is a pack hunting us, at least twenty.'

'How did they spot you?'

'We were spying at night. We were careful but missed one of their peripheral guards, Sang wounded him but he raised the alarm. We made it out of the area okay, but they sent some after us.'

Ragland swore under his breath.

'You should have led them away, kid.'

Alex lowered his head and Ragland had to remind himself he was barely into his twenties.

'Don't worry about it now. How far behind are they?'

'Probably a half hour if we're lucky.'

'A pack of twenty you say?'

Alex nodded.

'Shouldn't be too much bother,' said Ragland, turning to look for Rahul.

'There's something else.'

The drifter turned back to him.

'When we found the main camp, I was able to sneak in when it was dark and get real close to the leader's campfire. It was him and a group of the other Norms. I think they might have been like a council or something-'

'How many?' Ragland interrupted.

'In the council? I think…'

'In the camp.'

'I didn't count them.'

'Take a guess.'

'At least five hundred. Mostly Zoms.'

Ragland's jaw tightened.

'But that's not what I need to tell you. They were talking about hunting down a tall man and "the pretty meat bag" he took from them.'

Kit… and you led them right to us? He wanted to ask.

'How could they know?' he asked instead.

Alex shrugged.

'Maybe there was one you didn't see when you saved Kit?'

Ragland didn't think it likely, but there was no other logical explanation.

He turned to Simon, who had been watching the interaction with a worried frown.

'Can you tell Rahul we need people on the wall with bows and guns ASAP. And someone needs to get word to Marly that we're going to have visitors.'

'What do you want me to do?' asked Alex.

CHAPTER 21

Barely were the words out of his mouth when the siren split the air for the second time that day.

They looked at each other and then moved out from under the cover. Ragland looked up just as Charlie poked his head over the rail.

'Strangers! And they don't look friendly. I count twenty-one.'

'I'm going up,' he told Alex.

The blacksmith appeared.

'Rahul, do you have more bows and people who can shoot them?'

'We won't need more,' said Rahul, pushing him away from the ladder. 'I can shoot, so can Alex, Sang and Charlie and Rufus too. We have a stash of bows and arrows on the wall. Come on you two.'

Ragland waved the hesitant Alex and Sang after the surly blacksmith.

'After you.'

By the time he was to the top of the wall, all three men, along with Charlie and his fellow sentry Rufus, had bows drawn and aimed over the wall. Ragland heard harsh laughter and taunting from the pack outside.

As he approached the rail, Rahul jabbed a finger at him.

'I'm watching you. If you give a signal or say something to your buddies out there, I'll cave your face in.'

'I don't doubt it, Rahul.'

Twenty yards from the gate, the cannibals were assembled in a group, a rancid gathering of dirty flesh and blackened teeth. They were armed with a variety of spears and clubs. One man stood out from the rest.

He was taller and more upright than the Zoms around him, and on his forehead had the livid, pink scar tissue of a carved pentagram. But what really set him apart were his eyes. They found Ragland and zeroed in on him with a focus and intelligence that the others did not possess.

He smiled, revealing a line of teeth sharpened so they resembled those of a shark. Ragland drew himself to his full height and gestured to the archers either side of him.

'Wrong town friend. Best turn back.'

The cannibal leader's laugh sounded like gurgled spit. It proved infectious, and the rest of his pack joined in.

'No,' he said. 'I don't think we'll leave just yet. You have something that belongs to us. Where is the pretty piece of meat you stole?'

Alex growled and before anyone could prevent

him, he loosed an arrow that embedded itself in the eye of the cannibal shuffling from foot to foot beside the leader.

The pale creature spasmed briefly, then fell back dead.

The leader didn't flinch, or in fact even look at his fallen comrade. His smile widened.

'Was that meant for me?' he scoffed. 'You need some practice boy.'

As the cannibals laughed, a furious Alex fumbled for another arrow, but Rahul, apparently satisfied at Ragland's handling of the situation so far, lowered his bow and put a restraining hand on the boy's wrist.

Somewhat unnerved at the unafraid complacency of the leader, Ragland hid his disquiet by joining in the laughter.

'No, it wasn't meant for you. First was a warning. Second will be final word,' he said.

To reiterate his message, Rufus, Charlie, and Sang all turned their aim on the leader, pulling their strings taut.

The cannibal's smile faltered momentarily, before he nodded.

'Okay. Well, we'll be back Mister, but your chance to hand over the pretty meat bag is gone,' he said, sneering.

He made a loud clicking noise with his tongue, and in unison, his mates turned and scampered off towards the woods shrieking, *MEAT!*

He gave one last smirk at Ragland and turned

to follow. When they had all vanished into the undergrowth, Ragland let the bowstring slack and placed it against the rampart.

'What now?' Charlie asked, as they lowered their bows.

The old man looked back into Bakerstown.

'This town needs to prepare for a fight. A big one.'

'A war?'

'Yes,' Ragland nodded, looking Alex dead in the face. 'And I don't think it's ready.'

'You know nothing about our town,' growled Rahul. 'Besides I think they are full of shit. Marly will decide what's best for this town, not you.'

***

'Who says there was any cannibals there!' shouted one of the gathered Bakerstown citizens.

'Hoax!' screamed another. 'I don't trust him! He tried to kill David!'

A voice of reason challenged them.

'I heard 'em! Only a matter of time before those cannibal fuckers come back. You heard what they did to Kit.'

Rahul had disappeared when they'd reached the bottom of the ladder and now Ragland and Alex fought their way through the crowd. They were accosted by the heavy hands of agitated residents.

'What did they look like?' A woman no older than twenty asked Ragland, her face plastered with sweat despite the cold.

'Like killers,' was all he could say.

He raised his arms and fought through the tide to the edge, where the shouted questions chased him up the main avenue.

Behind him, he could hear the booming voices of Alex and Simon, both big enough to hold a few or so back and to encourage them to go back to what they were doing. Grateful again, he made a beeline back to Claire's. There was only one item on his agenda.

Speaking to Marly.

They had to begin arming the town now. Yesterday. And they would need to bolster their wall defenses too. Ragland shuddered at the thought of what would happen if they came back in force and breached those gates.

He closed his eyes as he walked, pressing his thumb and middle finger into them, a habit he'd developed whenever he was stressed many years ago. When he blinked back the light, the figure of a girl with long black hair and a splotch of a face as pale as snow, rushed towards him.

It was Kit, of course.

'Oh, my God,' Kit gasped, her hands going to her mouth, her eyes drawn to his bloodied clothes. 'She was right. Oh, my God.'

'No time, kid. Where's Marly?'

'She, er... she's back at the Doctor's office. With Claire. Trying to fix up David... you fucked him up bad. Rahul is there too but he wouldn't speak in front of me.'

'Right,' he said, breaking into a march.

'Hey, wait! You better be careful—they are really pissed with you.'

Kit followed Ragland back through town to Claire's office, only to learn Marly wasn't there. Claire had shut the door to the treatment room when they arrived, making sure he didn't butt heads with her patient, David.

She folded her arms.

'You need to leave,' Claire ordered. 'Now.'

Ragland held up his hands.

'Listen, I know I haven't made the best first impression here—'

'First impression?' she scoffed. 'What about a second? Or a third?'

'Claire…'

'Don't *Claire* me!' She jabbed a finger at him. 'I've got a guy in there with a hole in his guts. Just the other night I was sewing your ear back on! We haven't had incidents like this in over a year. Now all this in just a week?'

Kit stepped up.

'Claire. I wouldn't be here if it wasn't for him, we have to listen...'

'I get it,' the medic said, with her arms still crossed. 'But it doesn't undo what's he's done here.'

Ragland shook his head. He didn't have the time now to mend this particular bridge.

'Forget it.'

Without another word, he left the office, throwing open the door with a little too much force, and disappeared down the street.

Ragland, now on autopilot, wandered around Bakerstown thinking over his next moves as he sought out Marly.

He couldn't understand why she wasn't actively looking for him. Surely the others had told her about the threat from the cannibals? He had to convince her it was serious. They needed an urgent meeting to arm and prepare the town.

Scuffing his boots along a sidewalk some hours later, his eyes cast over the painted facades of old stores and the stencil-covered windows of offices and old cafes now converted or unused, and a feeling of hopelessness came over him.

Something in the mood of the town had changed. He saw it on the faces of passersby. Some looked wary and worried. Others looked fine. Happy, even. As if they hadn't heard about the events of the morning, or that they didn't matter. It staggered Ragland how something so obviously real could be cast aside by some as a hoax or as something trivial.

These people had perhaps had it too easy for too long.

Eavesdropping on idle chatter in the streets, he caught snippets of these notions. Squabbles about what happened outside the gates and whether it was exaggerated by the newcomer and the others. Fewer, suggesting that perhaps Marly was underestimating the threat or had gone soft in the head.

Marly wasn't in her home and no one he asked had any idea where she was. Ragland decided to head to Simon's; for the first time in an age, he felt like he needed a drink of something stronger than water.

Simon slid a cup towards Ragland and filled it up with a dark liquor from the cupboard behind him. Ragland held it up to his nose and took a quick sniff.

'It won't kill ya,' Simon laughed. 'But it packs a punch.'

Ragland raised the cup.

'Your health.'

He swallowed it in one gulp, feeling it run down his esophagus like liquid fire and settle in his stomach, leaving his eyes watering.

'Wow,' he rasped

'Told you, eh?' said Simon, throwing a dishcloth over his shoulder. He rolled up his sleeves and leaned over the bar, his eyes darting back once or twice to check no one was listening. 'You're not mad.'

Ragland raised an eyebrow and met his gaze.

'Never said I was.'

'But you're feeling it, eh?'

'Maybe,' he replied, and looked over his shoulder. A couple walked by the window, giving him a furtive glance, and quickened their pace. 'Word got around that quick, huh?'

'About you stabbing David? Oh yes, sir.'

'And you still poured me a drink?'

Simon smirked.

'Well, I never took to the guy, myself. And I figure there's more to it. Can't see why a man would save a kid, work the fields, only to shank some asshole one fine morning. Unless, of course, you know him from before?'

Ragland shook his head.

'Never met him until I came here.'

'That settles it then.' Simon took out the liquor bottle and poured both Ragland and himself a short measure before twisting shut the bottle cap.

'Thanks,' Ragland said and swirled the dark contents pensively. 'What about the cannibals? According to some, I'm still in contention for the Crazy Bastard or Biggest Liar of the Year award.'

Simon didn't respond right away. He eyed his own drink for a minute. Ragland could practically hear the cogs whirring in his head.

'Had the same thoughts myself before they showed up this morning.'

'Right.'

'I guess the town needs a wake-up call. Not everyone has it as good as us, right?'

Ragland nodded. That much was true. He'd certainly navigated his fair share of ramshackle dwellings and wild settlements on his adventures. Places that almost endorsed human suffering. Bakerstown was definitely the gold standard of the settlements he'd come across in the After Days.

His eyes bored back down into his whiskey. Now with what felt like the town turning against him, he wondered if he'd ever bother with human beings again when he moved on. After all, what had his efforts gained him here except suspicion and an attempt on his life?

'Hey, sir, you alright there?' Simon waved a hand in front of Ragland's face.

'What? Oh, yeah. Lost in my own head. So,' he said, licking his lips. 'What are we toasting to?'

Simon raised his cup and clinked it with Ragland's.

'To not being crazy bastards.'

'To not being crazy bastards,' he chimed in, and swigged the liquor back in one go.

Not giving it time to settle, Ragland rose from his stool and threw on his jacket. 'Do *you* have any idea where I might find the Mayor? I think she's avoiding me'

'Try the school,' Simon said. 'She's there most days at this time.'

'Thanks. And thanks for the drink. Seems like less and less people here like me every hour that goes by. I appreciate the ones who do.'

Simon nodded and held out his hand. They shook and Ragland headed for the door.

'Good luck with Marly. You're going to need it

if she's decided to go against your advice. The woman can be as stubborn as a mule.'

'Great,' Ragland said, and shut the door on his way out, the winter wind biting at his exposed skin. 'Just great.'

CHAPTER 22

Ragland knocked on the main door to the schoolhouse but there was no answer. He could hear the buzz of the children in a room about thirty feet down the hallway, so he followed the noise. He stopped outside the open door and peered in.

The pretty Asian woman he'd seen from across the lawn on his first day in Bakerstown was in front of a small class of the local kids, her hand animatedly pointing at the multiplication tables on the blackboard behind her.

A sign over the door read Ms. Erica. Remembering Marly had mentioned they let class out at two o'clock, he waited patiently for the class to be dismissed.

He only had to wait twenty or so minutes until a chorus of wooden chair legs scraped across the floor and a stampede of hurried feet headed for the door. Ragland stepped to the left as they poured into the hallway.

The kids, oblivious to his presence, charged down the hall and into the sunny afternoon.

Once he'd sensed the way was clear, he knocked and took a few steps into the classroom.

Erica eyed him as she tidied a stack of papers on her desk.

'Yes?'

Ragland was taken by her green eyes. She stopped what she was doing when he didn't answer right away.

'Can I help you?'

'Sorry. Name's Ragland.'

'I figured,' she said, turning to the board and beginning to erase the numbers.

'What can I do for you? A little old for basic math, aren't you?'

Ragland smirked.

'I guess I am. I'm looking for Marly. Simon told me she'd be here.'

'Might be,' she replied, then put down the board eraser and started moving around the classroom, tidying the desks of the children.

'It's urgent I speak to her,' Ragland pressed when nothing more was forthcoming. Sensing she could be an asset in influencing a response to the cannibal threat, he took another couple of steps. 'This town is in trouble.'

'Is that so?'

'Yes.'

'Perhaps you could teach creative writing next week?' she grinned at him, her smile pulled extra wide to hammer home the condescension, in case it was missed.

Ragland sighed. Clearly, he had misjudged her.

'Please. Just tell me where she is.'

'No.'

Someone cleared their throat at the door and in stepped a portly man Ragland recognized immediately. It was Clint, the other teacher.

'Clint!' said Erica. 'Perfect timing. Could you show this bearded troublemaker the front door?'

Ragland recoiled from the insult, puzzled by her passive aggressive demeanor. Why were these people so defensive?

Clint looked Ragland up and down, then waited for him to speak.

'I'm just looking for Marly,' Ragland asked, making it known how frustrated he was. His patience now hung by a thread. 'It's urgent.'

'Right,' Clint replied. 'What for?'

'Come on Clint,' Erica interrupted, slamming a book down. 'Can't you see he's trying to cause trouble? Just get him out of here.'

Clint shrugged and motioned to the door.

'Best you be going,' he said, almost apologetically. 'Come on.'

Ragland didn't move, he'd finally had enough.

'Do you two give a shit about those kids?'

'Don't you dare,' Erica snapped, stepping into his personal space. 'We keep these kids safe from the likes of you.'

'Not for very fucking long,' Ragland said. 'If I don't get Marly to convince you sorry bastards to prepare for an attack, you'll all be dead before

Christmas.'

'What?' Clint said. Ragland glanced at him; the teacher's head was tilted to the side like a curious dog.

Erica rolled her eyes.

'The cannibal thing?' She smirked. 'They don't have the numbers or the wherewithal to attack us. We're well armed and well protected and guess what? We've managed for nearly ten whole years before you came along! Show him out Clint, please!'

Ragland shook his head and leaned over Erica.

'You've all lost it,' he growled.

A large hand grabbed Ragland by the arm and pulled him back.

'Come on,' Clint said. 'We don't want any more trouble.'

'*More*?' said Ragland shaking him off easily. 'What does that mean?'

'Forget it,' the teacher said, his voice quavering. Ragland sensed his fear and knew that "trouble" meant the incident with David. His reputation had really soured in the space of a few hours and through no real fault of his own. The people of Bakerstown feared him now.

The notion hit him like a freight train. Perhaps that was it? He'd given them focus. A bad guy. Of course, they wouldn't care about the half-believed threat of the cannibals while a perceived threat was amongst them. It was the drifter they'd welcomed through their gate, who had stabbed one of their own, and who'd now become their villain.

Ragland's shoulders slumped and he allowed Clint to lead him out of the classroom. Halfway down the hallway, their footsteps echoing, Marly's voice called from the other end.

'Clint!?'

The big teacher stopped, turned Ragland around with him and called back.

'There you are,' Clint said. He gripped Ragland's arm more tightly, a warning not to try anything.

'What's going on here?' Marly asked, with her hands planted firmly on her hips as she approached the two men.

'Says he was looking for you. Were you expecting him?'

Marly's eyes moved between them both, then settled on Ragland.

'No, but since when does anyone need an appointment to speak to me? And why are you holding him like a naughty child? Let him go Clint, for God's sake.'

He dropped Ragland's arm instantly.

'Sorry, Mayor. He's just been pestering Erica about seeing you.'

Erica appeared in the classroom doorway, behind Marly.

'I can speak for myself, Clint,' she said arms folded. Marly turned and stepped back to include the teacher in the conversation. She seemed keen to address what had happened.

'Well?' Marly asked. 'What is the problem, and no bullshit please.'

'He's stirring up nonsense about the cannibals,' Erica said. 'Came barging in while I was teaching. Rude, undignified and uncalled for, Mayor, I really must protest.'

Ragland ground his jaw at the exaggeration.

'Barging in!? What the hell is your problem lady…'

'This ends here Erica,' Marly said. 'Now. I'll decide who I want to speak to, not you. Next time someone asks, you pull your head in and call me, okay? I don't need a receptionist.'

'Of course. I didn't mean t—' Erica stuttered.

'I know you didn't. Which is why I'm reminding you.' She took Ragland's elbow. 'Let's go for a walk.'

Marly led him outside into the crisp, bright afternoon.

'Don't let Erica get to you. She has a little thing for David—unreciprocated, thankfully for her—but that probably tainted her perception of you a little.'

They crossed the road to a store opposite the school. Behind the frosted glass, fresh flowers were bunched neatly in colored vases. Outside, in a few wooden baskets and crates, other selections rested in beds of compost and soil. With delicate movements, a young woman with curly brown hair snipped at a few branches and watered the base of others.

Marly—with Ragland just behind—stepped onto the sidewalk and bent down to inspect the seasonal flowers.

'Casey, you and Fred possess a magic I have yet to find a name for,' she marveled. Ragland had to admit, the array of vibrant colored flowers did impress.

Casey, the woman in the apron Marly had addressed, put down her trowel and responded in an accent so southern it caught Ragland off guard.

'That's just what we call God's honest hard work, Mayor,' she laughed, and hugged Marly. 'How are ya? What brings you by today? You didn't kill the violets I gave you, did you?'

'Of course not. They're very much alive and well on my dining room table. And still gorgeous. I've come to show my friend here your boutique.'

Casey looked over at Ragland, then craned her head up to meet his eyes.

'My gosh, you sure are a tall one, ain't ya?' She held out a dirty hand, all smiles and bright eyes.

'Nice to meet you. Name's Joshua Ragland.'

'Casey Jones,' she replied in her southern drawl. 'Originally from Mississippi, if you can't tell by my sultry tones. Freddie's in the back there, sorting out the compost.'

Ragland nodded, noting she hadn't flinched when he'd said his name.

'Mind if we go on in and say hello?' Marly asked.

'Go ahead,' Casey beamed. 'It's always mighty nice to see y'all.'

So, they did. Giving her another nod, Ragland followed Marly into the store, the walls stacked high with plant pots and flowers just like the ones outside. A rainbow of color.

'Wow,' Ragland breathed, as he inhaled the fragrances. 'I didn't expect this.'

'Oh, we do just fine in ol' Bakerstown,' a deep voice boomed from somewhere at the back of the shop.

Ragland craned his head and spotted a young man with a receding hairline, who was probably no older than twenty. He was bent over a plant by the counter. He stood up to greet them, his jeans muddied worse than Casey's.

Fred held out a hand. 'Nice to meet ya,' he said to Ragland. 'My, you must be the oldest man I've ever seen. No offense. How old are you, if you don't mind me askin'?'

Marly shook her head.

'Really, Fred?'

'I'm just askin'!'

'It's fine,' Ragland replied, used to being a curiosity to most survivors. 'I'm thirty-four. I get it a lot. I was one of the oldest when the virus hit and killed most of the adults off.'

Fred chortled.

'Bet ya been asked that a few times since the

fall, right?'

'Right,' Ragland confirmed. 'Give or take a thousand.'

Fred laughed again and rubbed the top of his bald head.

'That old and you still have more hair than me!'

They all laughed.

'Anyway,' Marly pressed. 'It was nice seeing you. Give my love to the kids and I'll see you tonight.'

'Right you are, Mayor,' Fred nodded.

Back outside in the street, Marly took Ragland by a few more spots, reminiscent of his first tour of Bakerstown, just over a week ago. He waited for her to raise the issue of the cannibals but finally realized it wasn't going to get discussed if he didn't raise it.

By the time they were done, and the sun had sunk into a thick smudge of clouds over the hills to the west, Ragland pulled Marly aside opposite a row of houses at the edge of town.

'I don't suppose there was a meaning behind all of that.'

'Actually,' she said. 'There was...'

'Marly, the threat out there is real and you can't be complacent. I know you love this town. Which is why I know you'll protect it. If Bakerstown wants to see another spring, it needs to prepare itself now.'

The Mayor's shoulders sagged, making her

seem many years older than what she actually was, a girl in her mid twenties. She climbed up onto a nearby fence, sitting on the top and resting her feet on the bottom rail.

'We can't, is my point.'

'What?' he asked, as he zipped up his jacket.

'You saw them. My people. Bakerstown. Most of them are just good honest people. We all are. Many of them didn't fight to keep this place. Only a handful of us did and only *we* have blood on our hands.' Marly looked down and rubbed a thumb across her left palm; even in the faint torchlight he could see the scar.

'We want it kept that way. Many of them have never fought, never taken a life. We can't afford the chaos that hysteria and war-panic might bring, especially when many know they can't defend themselves.'

'But they can!' Ragland shouted. 'If they can hold a bow, a club, or a gun, if you still have them, they can fight!'

'No,' she said, tears in her eyes. 'They can't. And I won't have them, either.'

Ragland couldn't register the words. It took him a minute to process. 'But you'll be slaughtered.'

'By the words of a few, and from a threat unconfirmed,' she said and climbed down from the fence. 'Let me worry about this town, Joshua. I am its Mayor, and I'll find a way so that we won't need to fight...'

CHAPTER 23

Early winter snow drifted and fluttered down from a steel-grey sky. Ragland—perched against a row of hitching posts—spent the morning after his disappointing conversation with Marly thinking about his next move.

Just how could he convince the town to prepare for a fight, when the Mayor thought there was another way. He had half a mind to call it quits and leave.

But he knew he wouldn't.

His fingers found the onyx stone on the leather thong around his neck.

He surveyed the faces of those walking by, wrapped up to keep warm, their eyes cast to the heavens in wonder at the falling snow.

No, he couldn't leave, because he'd regret it for the rest of his life. He needed to speak to Alex.

Making sure his makeshift poncho was tightened under his chin, he began walking to the gate. Ragland spied the man he was looking for astride a chestnut horse loping slowly toward him five minutes later.

It was a beautiful specimen.

'Morning,' Ragland called up to him on his saddle and nodded.

Alex smiled.

'Morning, old man,' he said, with a glint in his eyes. Snow day happiness? 'Hey, wanna give me a hand?'

'Sure thing.'

Ragland took the reigns from Alex, which left him hands-free to climb off the saddle and unload the saddlebags. The sleeve of his winter coat rode up, and for the first time Ragland noticed a long scar on his wrist, the rest of it hidden under his shirtsleeve.

He didn't want to ask about it just yet, so he steered the horse over to the hitching post and tied it ncatly.

The horse whickered and bobbed its head. Ragland smiled warmly, reached up with a hand and rubbed its face a few times.

'Gorgeous. Does he have a name?'

Alex heaved the saddlebags over his shoulders.

'*She* sure does. Barbara.'

Ragland raised his eyebrow and then bent over to look under the horse's belly.

'I see. Sorry, I guess I thought someone was feeling the cold.

Alex chuckled.

'So, Barbara? How did you come up with that?'

'Found a stash of comics in the library. Batman comics. Jenny let me have first dibs. Kit's a fan, too. It's kinda how we hit it off. Sorry, I'm er... I'm rambling.'

'Jenny?' Ragland asked.

'The chronologist. Keeps inventory of all the—'

Ragland nodded, patting Barbara's neck.

'I remember now. And why Barbara?'

Alex smirked. 'Batwoman's alter ego Barbara Gordon. Couldn't resist.'

'Sure. So, what you got there?'

'Oh,' he said as he adjusted the weight of the saddlebags again. 'Just some food supplies. I'm just dropping them off and then will take Barbara here to the stables. Looks like it'll be snowing on and off now for a while.'

Ragland looked back up at the sky. 'You think?'

'Oh yeah,' Alex replied. 'We get a lot of snow here quite early. Have done for the last few years.'

'Does that get difficult? For hunting, I mean?'

'Not really. David and Sang are the best hunters and never have a problem. But you have downed one, so who knows.'

'About that...' Ragland started, but Alex held up a hand.

'Listen, it's okay. I know what David's like. If he ended up with a knife in the belly courtesy of you, then there must've been a good reason for it.'

Ragland relaxed. Since he first met him at the Hunting Lodge, Alex had been warm and approachable. He hoped it would help him now, when he told him of the idea that had taken root in his mind.

'Listen, I wanted to speak with you.'

Alex frowned.

'What about?

'The cannibals. I spoke to Marly, and she's not seeing sense. She doesn't even want to talk about defense.'

'I know.'

'Then what's being done about it? Surely enough of you saw what I saw to make it clear you need to do something.'

Alex slid the saddlebags down on the floor and stood closer to Ragland, to avoid being eavesdropped on by the scattering of townsfolk nearby.

'I've been making traps with Sang. We both know what's out there and know we can't convince Marly to fight.'

'It's not enough,' Ragland said without emotion.

'I know.'

'Who else will listen? We need to move fast.'

'Less than half,' Alex replied and looked left and right. 'Rahul is always suspicious. Simon has a good head on his shoulders, and you've met Clint.'

Ragland rolled his eyes.

'I have. Not sure about him, a bit too easily bossed around.'

'But what can we do?'

'Rally. We need to get the word out. Find others

who want to fight. Who want to bear arms.'

'Most people don't know how,' he said. 'Most came here once the fighting was over. David and his boys can fight, but for obvious reasons I don't think they'll listen to you…'

'No,' said Ragland, hoping that the injury to David would keep him on his back while they worked this out.

Ragland kicked a stone down onto the road, disturbing Barbara. He patted her neck again and brushed off the dusting of snow on her mane.

'Listen,' he said. 'Get these supplies off. I'll take Barbara down to the stables and ask around. We need to do something. Where's Kit?'

'Okay but be careful. I've heard lots of talk about what happened between you and David and a lot of it isn't friendly to you. And Kit? She'll be at the farm, I guess. She likes the cold, so she'll be out in it. Crazy, I know.'

'Okay.' Ragland nodded, untying Barbara from the hitching post and turning her around. He had no intention of riding her—adding suspected horse thievery to the growing list of grievances against him would not help matters.

'Alright then,' he finished, nodding to Alex. 'Round up who you can. Tell them we meet tonight at sunset, right here, got it?'

'Got it.' And the two men left, feeling energized by their mission, no matter how futile it seemed.

Ragland soon found the stables on the east

side of Bakerstown. He couldn't help but be impressed by the recent construction. It was big. A good fifty feet wide and forty feet high and didn't have the rickety look that so many of the town's contemporary additions did. At the front were a large set of doors big enough to squeeze a Mac truck through, and on either side of it, sheltered storage for hay.

Beside one of these storage-holds, using the wooden awning to hunker away from the snow, Ragland spied a young kid chewing on a piece of bread, leaning on a shovel.

At the sound of Barbara's hooves, the kid turned his head. He was a grubby-looking one, with dirty blond hair hanging his eyes. He wore a pair of red overalls and thick winter boots.

'How's my girl?' the kid cooed as he waltzed up, taking the reigns from Ragland without a word.

'She's alright,' Ragland decided to reply. 'Just handing her over for Alex.'

'Got you doing the errands?'

'Just a quick favor.'

The kid nodded, unfazed, and patted Barbara on the nose, which she seemed to enjoy.

Not wanting to appear rude, Ragland held out his hand.

'Ragland. New around here.'

The kid took it and blinked a few times.

'You that guy that tried to kill David?'

'Look kid, if I *had* tried to kill him, he'd be damn well...' Ragland heard the strident tone in his voice and his voice trailed off. He took a deep breath. 'No I didn't try to kill him. He's fine. Hopefully he's learned a valuable lesson.'

'M'okay,' the kid replied with a shrug. 'My name's Jerry Walker. Good with the horses.'

'I can tell.'

And Ragland meant it. Jerry looked fifteen at most. He was short, dirty and disheveled, but looked extremely at ease with Barbara.

'Let's get her in and fed,' Jerry announced, and Ragland followed them in.

Inside the barn, a series of partitioned stalls ran down either side, filled with hay and horses, including a chestnut with a distinctive white mark on its forehead. He recognized it as David's mount.

'Gorgeous, ain't she?' Jerry said to Ragland after he tugged his gaze from the horse.

'She is,' he replied. 'A Beauty.'

'Want to take a horse out?' Jerry asked.

Ragland felt weird about the kid's sudden sense of trust. Perhaps he was paranoid, but something about it didn't seem right.

'No.'

'Then what can I do you for? No offense, but if you ain't here for horses, then I need an idea. Sorry.'

Ragland decided to throw caution to the wind. He had little time, and they'd need every able person ready for when the time came.

'Ever seen cannibals outside the walls?'

'Nope.'

Jerry paused. He'd been busy tending to Barbara, who now stood behind a closed gate, nudging at Jerry's hand to feed her.

'Heard about them ones at the gates. Is that true?'

'It is. Why, has someone said otherwise?'

The kid shrugged as if to suggest the answer to that was obvious.

'Half the folks think it was all some prank from Alex. Some say it's a hoax.'

'Who does?'

'I ain't telling,' said Jerry, turning back to tend to Barbara.

Frustrated, Ragland grabbed his shoulder and swung him back around.

'Listen Jerry, this isn't a hoax. The threat out there is real, and no one here is ready to fight. Would you fight if you had to?'

Jerry looked up at him with wide, fearful eyes.

'What do you mean?'

'I mean, if a horde of cannibals came through those gates, would you be ready to fight them?'

'You let go of my brother!' A whipcrack of a voice sounded from behind him.

Ragland let him go and when he turned, found himself confronted by a feisty young woman of about twenty and behind her a burly man of about the same age with a well used baseball bat cradled in his left hand. An older, whippet thin but tall man of around twenty-four appeared alongside them with a machete.

'I think it's time you left,' she said.

Ragland eyed off the men, who had stepped around her. From their determined faces he could see they were ready to do what they had to. The girl looked just as determined, and he noticed she also carried a weapon, a knife with a long thin blade.

The corners of his lips curled up.

Maybe there are some ready to fight after all...

He nodded and turned back to Jerry.

'Whether we want to or not, kid, we get called to fight for those we love. Just like your big sis is doing now. See you around.'

He left the barn, giving the group a wide berth.

'No hard feelings,' he said to Jerry's sister. 'We were just talking. You should ask him about it.'

She didn't respond and he felt her steely gaze pricking at his back, all the way back to the road. A few other residents had gathered to stickybeak and cast their own looks of judgment Ragland's way.

Time, evidently, was not on his side. He felt it. There was growing tension in the air and most of it felt like it was centered on him. The people of Bakerstown wanted him gone, and maybe as soon as tonight.

CHAPTER 24

'Let me,' Ragland said, when he came across Claire struggling with a large box of supplies on the sidewalk, as the snow fell.

'I don't need your help,' said Claire, standing up and stretching her lower back. She looked exhausted

'I know,' he replied, bending over and hoisting the box into the air. 'But I'm giving it anyway. By the desk fine?'

Several emotions warred on her face before she finally gave in.

'Fine. Sure. Just by the desk is fine.'

Smiling at his small victory, he carried the box through the door and into the main reception area, which had already been loaded with a few much smaller boxes and bags of equipment.

'Last supply run before the winter?'

Claire shrugged, choosing to work some smaller items out of their crates rather than engage in conversation.

Ragland didn't give up.

'How's David?'

'Great, considering you tried to murder him.'

'Claire, I met him in kind. Had I not, you'd have been burying me six feet under.'

She stopped what she was doing and blew a loose strand of hair from her face.

'What?'

'You didn't figure to ask him what happened?'

'Oh, he told me. I know David's an ass, but a heated argument never warrants a knife to the gut. Never.'

'Is that what he told you?' Ragland raised an eyebrow, incredulous someone so resourceful and smart could buy into such horse shit.

'Sure. I believe him.'

'Seems he missed out the bit where he broke in to the Creaky with his buddy and jumped me. You know the knife was his, right?'

Claire stopped what she was doing. She had her back to him, so Ragland couldn't gauge by her face what she was thinking. He decided to test her patience.

'Do you still have it? The knife?'

'It's in my office.'

She turned and looked up at Ragland as if weighing up his side of the story. Then, she frowned and marched down the corridor to her office. He followed.

By the time he reached the doorway, Claire had plucked the knife from a drawer. It was still caked in blood, likely put aside after the incident without a second look.

The old man leaned against the frame of the doorway and folded his arms.

Claire turned the knife over and peered closely at it.

'Shit.'

Ragland stepped into the office and, shaking her head regretfully, she handed the knife to him, handle first.

'What is it?' Crowley asked after turning the knife over and failing to spot anything.

'Look at the handle.'

Ragland looked more closely this time and noticed the vague scratching of two letters. D and H.

'His initials?'

Claire nodded.

'David Henderson. Full name. No other DH in Bakerstown.' She sighed. 'I owe you an apology.'

'No, you don't.'

She looked at him sidelong.

'Yes, I do. Don't be an ass. I know when to admit I'm wrong.' She took the knife back and tossed it back into the drawer.

'Nobody's perfect, Claire. Not even me.'

A smile briefly lit up her features. He had made progress.

'But listen,' he continued. 'I didn't just come here to set the record straight. It's not about whether you like me or not.'

'Oh really? Do tell...' She narrowed her eyes at Ragland.

It struck him, then, in the half-light of a lantern on her desk, how pretty she was. Behind her, snowflakes danced passed the window and he wondered briefly if it would be appropriate to tell her what he was thinking.

Not the time… he told himself.

'No. I came here because out of everyone I've met so far, you seem to be a voice of reason that Marly might listen to.'

'This is about the cannibals?'

'Yes. She won't fight… or even tell me what she plans if they come back.'

'If it's true that they'll be back, there's no way we could fight or hold them back. I agree with her.'

'But do you believe me?'

Claire approached Ragland, peering up into his face to search for a hint of a tell. Her blinkered expression told Ragland she couldn't come to a satisfying conclusion.

Instead, she stepped back and shrugged.

'Honestly, I don't know. I don't know you and nor does the town.'

'Does Alex's word count for nothing?'

Claire froze and a look of anger crossed her face.

'Really?' she said. 'Alex's word? No, it doesn't.'

'What do you mean?' Ragland asked, genuinely puzzled.

'No one's told you? The last time Alex kicked off about a threat from a settlement two days' walk away, we sent a scouting party and lost... lost one of them.' Her voice cracked on the last word. She turned and pretended to tidy her desk. 'So, you know, people don't really trust Alex. Took him a whole year to make it up to Marly and be given the watch command.'

Ragland felt foolish for having blindly trusted him, and equally terrible knowing he had been responsible for getting one of their folks killed chasing a shadow. Still, that didn't change anything now.

'He's right this time,' he said.

'Marly will find another way.'

Ragland sighed and pinched the bridge of his nose.

'This isn't right,' he said. 'For Chrissakes, they've been at the gates and told us they'd be back. I can't believe how many of you are turning a blind eye to this!'

'Woah, Cowboy! Calm down. We just mended a bridge back there.' Seeing how worked up he was, she softened her tone. 'Fine, let's take some fresh air and go and speak to—'

Claire stopped and cocked her head to the side.

'Did you hear that?' she asked.

Ragland listened intently and heard it too, a low buzz in the distance. A second later it became clear what the sound was.

'Is that people?' he asked.

'Sounds like it,' she said. 'And a lot of them.'

By the time Claire and Ragland had reached the main avenue, they could see in the distance a large gathering by the school. Several dozen at least, some of them holding up torches against the flurry of snow and encroaching twilight.

Claire tugged the coat tight around her.

'What the hell is this?'

'No idea, but isn't that David?'

Claire followed Ragland's pointed finger and groaned.

'That ass. I told him to rest or he'd open up those stitches. I'll kill him.'

The pair walked toward the crowd, and as they did, David spotted Ragland, and his voice boomed, grabbing the attention of everyone.

'There he is!'

The mob turned and almost as one, rushed them, angry faces and lunging hands enveloping them. Claire yelled and tried to intervene, but she was tossed aside as they grabbed Ragland. He grappled with a few of the men trying to pin him down, punching one and elbowing another, but he was quickly overwhelmed and hit in the face and head several times before he was subdued.

Kicking and protesting, five large men, including two he recognized from earlier at the barn, pulled him towards David and held him. David climbed to the top step of the store they were congregated in front of and gestured they should stand the prisoner on the step below so the mob would see him clearly.

'The man of the hour,' He declared after a theatrical pause. 'A trespasser no longer welcome.'

'Come on, David,' Ragland grumbled, his face aching from the loose fists he'd caught. 'Stop this. Where's Marly?'

'Where's Marly? Well, Marly don't have the balls to do what's gotta be done with you, Ragland. We folk of Bakerstown have had enough, and we've voted. And Marly will have to honor that vote, if we value a free world. Do we value a free world?' he shouted to the people, who responded by yelling in agreement.

'Let me through!' Claire called, struggling through the crowd before drilling the ringleader with a fiery gaze. 'David you idiot! A show of hands is not a vote, and this is just a lynch mob.'

With a furious gesture, David had Claire grabbed and marched back the way she had come. She kicked and screamed all the way.

'You asshole,' Ragland said.

'Fuck you.'

David clenched his fist and drove it into the side of Ragland's head, drawing blood at the first punch. The crowd cheered and bayed like animals.

Ragland raised his head once it had stopped spinning and spat some of the blood in his mouth onto the dirt. His ears rang, and through the hair hanging over his eyes, he saw more people arriving and, encouragingly, they were protesting to the crowd. He saw Alex, Simon, Viola, and a clearly frightened Kit, but the rest were caught up in a frenzy. For now, his would-be saviors were helpless and he was on his own.

'Now! As I was saying. We voted and it's a hanging we'll be having today!'

David basked in the power as the crowd roared and reached behind him, taking something from Blackbeard. He thrust his hand into the air, and gripped in it was a rope with a hangman's noose.

Cheers and baying drowned out the protests of the few in Ragland's corner.

BOOOM!

The shotgun blast behind the mob sent people scurrying with cries and screams of surprise. Then silence reigned for a few seconds as the crowd parted to allow a stone-faced Marly, shotgun in hand, to pass through.

She pumped the shotgun and chambered a new round.

'Back off. All of you.'

From a baying mob to a group of chastened citizens, they obeyed immediately. David lowered the rope, his face red with anger.

'Stop, Marly! The town voted. They want him strung up for attempted murder! Look!' David lifted his shirt to show the place where he'd been stabbed. It was a gruesome sight, now weeping fresh blood through rudimentary stitching. There were gasps and angry grumblings as the emotions of the crowd swung back his way.

'And by your own knife! I wonder how that happened?'

All heads turned towards Claire, including Marly's, as the medic shook off the two men holding her arms. The cold wind and falling snow were forgotten as they waited for her to say more.

She made her way back to the front, and stood between Marly and David, her eyes avoiding Ragland altogether.

'I saw the markings on the knife. Your own blade. Why were you there, where he sleeps, with your hunting knife?'

Murmurs rippled through the townsfolk. Ragland eyed Claire, thankful now that they'd made amends. She may have just saved his life.

'It's my property! I always have it on me. I went there to talk—'

'Enough!' Marly yelled, raising her shotgun but refraining from squeezing the trigger. 'This ends now. We did not build this place to act like animals and lynch people. Especially a man who saved one of our own.'

'And tried to kill another!' cried someone from the crowd. They were met with shouts of agreement.

'Christ, people! Were you not listening!' called Claire but acquiesced to Marly when the Mayor held up her hand for silence.

'So, you would hang someone without a trial?'

Marly continued, tipping the cutter hat she wore against the onslaught of snow. 'That is not how we do things in Bakerstown. David, I will look further into this, and I better not find out you're lying. Release him.'

The men holding Ragland glanced at David who nodded, apparently resigned to the fact his chance to deal with Ragland was lost, and they let him go. The Drifter shook them off and stepped off the steps, spitting blood into the dirt and wiping the hair from his face as he joined Marly. For now at least, she was still their leader.

'Gentleman,' he offered, mock saluting to the thugs.

David scowled.

The Mayor spun around, regarding the rest of the mob, shotgun now lowered over the forearm, trigger finger resting outside. 'Now get. The show's over. Go on.'

They dispersed, some looking shamefaced, some looking angry, but none stuck around. Finally, the only people left were he and Marly, David and Blackbeard, and the others who had come to Ragland's defense.

'Come on,' snapped David, to his oafish sidekick. 'I've had enough of this shit!'

'We'll be having more words about this David!' Marly called after him. The man paused and looked back at her, his hands clenched and unclenching.

Finally, perhaps thinking better of mouthing

off, he spun and walked on.

'Thank you, all. Things were getting hairy there for a moment.'

The others closed around him.

'No drama, although I'm sure glad Marly came along with her shotgun,' Simon said, clapping him on the shoulder.

'Goddam fuckers!' said Kit. 'You shoulda finished the job on him.'

'Settle down Kit,' said Marly, easing her way in front of Ragland.

She looked up at him as if trying to find words. They didn't come but he couldn't mistake the look on her face for anything other than regret.

'You want me to leave, don't you?'

'I'm sorry, Joshua. I really am. I don't think there's much of a choice,' she said, patting his elbow with her free hand. 'I need to nip this in the bud to clamp down on any influence that David might have gained from that performance.'

'No!' said Kit and Alex in unison.

'It's David who should be banished, not the old man!'

Ragland put a gentle hand on Kit's shoulder.

'It's okay Kit. Marly's right. Trying to expel David could set something in motion that's more dangerous than the cannibals right now.'

He looked at Marly.

'I'll leave first thing in the morning.'

CHAPTER 25

Kit drew back her foot and kicked the empty can of beans as hard as she could. Ragland watched it sail, over the bed and into the wall.

'This is bullshit,' she cursed as she stomped around the Creaky Motel.

He had been awake when she knocked on his door just as dawn was lighting the eastern sky, and now after twenty minutes of railing at the unfairness of it all, Ragland caught a glint of sunshine through the window.

Morning had arrived, and the people of Bakerstown, except Kit and a handful of others, would not tolerate his stay a moment longer.

He finished packing his gear, including a new bow and quiver of arrows that Rahul had sent over the night before. It had surprised him, given their previous encounters, but Marly explained that the smith was no friend of David's. Once he'd been given the full picture by Claire, he had insisted on the parting gift.

'Aren't you even going to try and talk her out of it?'

'No, kid. This is the best option.'

Kit huffed and crossed her arms.

'I fricking hate them. They're so blind! This town used to be better, Gramps, I promise you. It was never like this.'

'I believe you,' he said. 'Everyone goes soft with comfort and routine. Gives people like David a chance to thrive. Hopefully Marly deals with him.'

'Yeah…'

Ragland donned his thick winter jacket, zipped it up to the throat and fed his arms through the straps of his backpack. In his left hand, he took his new bow and slipped it onto his left shoulder, leaving both hands free.

'How do I look?' he said, grinning.

'Well, you know, like the old man who frickin' saved my ass,' she said, then turned away abruptly.

'You alright, kid?'

'Yeah. Just, like, dust in my eyes or something. Shit.'

Ragland shook his head. He hated that he had to leave like this and seeing her get upset hurt him more than he'd like to admit. Reaching up, he placed a hand on her shoulder.

'Want to walk with me to the gate?'

Kit turned, wiping her left eye and not fooling Ragland for one second. 'Sure.'

Taking one last look at the ramshackle hut he'd slept in for less than two weeks, Ragland peered about at the emptiness of it. The old bed. The rickety cabinet and the beaten up wooden chair. It was cold, musty and dusty, but he'd grown weirdly fond of his temporary home.

'Listen, there's one thing before we set off,' Ragland said, clearing his throat. 'I want you to have this.'

The old man untied the worn leather thong hanging around his neck and handed it to Kit. She eyed the onyx pendant, slowly reaching out and grasping it. She stared at it resting in her palm as if it might come alive.

'Your sister's necklace?'

'Mhmm.'

'But, why?' she looked up at Ragland, eyes wide, searching for the motive that drove him to part with his most precious possession.

'I figured there must have been a reason why I've survived for so long in the wild by myself. Figured, I had her looking over me.'

Kit didn't speak. Instead, she held it up close, turning the black stone over in her hands. Then, with care, she tied it around her neck and laid it down on her shirt.

The sight made his chest tighten and unanticipated tears stung his eyes.

'Looks good,' he coughed into his hand and turned quickly to the door.

'Dust?' she asked, with a bittersweet smile.

'Something like that,' he said and threw the door open.

The walk through Bakerstown felt eerie. Some of the townsfolk, those that rose early, stood on the sidewalks and watched silently as he walked by.

Ragland and Kit didn't speak and apart from the crunch of frost on the road, all was silent. The snowfall had stopped overnight, but the altostratus clouds overhead promised a fresh dumping of powder soon.

They arrived at the gate to find Marly, with her shotgun in case of trouble, Simon, Viola, Rahul, and even Claire. Rahul busied himself with Charlie to ease open the gates to the wild beyond.

With Kit still by his side, Ragland went to Marly and shook her hand.

'Keep them safe, Mayor.'

She offered him a weary smile that didn't instill much confidence.

'Will do, old man. Thank you, again, for Kit and for the work you did. I know what happened with David was… well shit happens I guess, and you got the raw end of the deal, and I'm sorry.'

'Forget it. You can't please everyone or be everywhere. It's done.'

Marly nodded.

'Good, well I'm glad we met.'

'Me too,' Ragland said, shaking her hand again. 'Me too.'

Ragland continued with the others, getting a laugh from Simon and a warm hug from Viola, who said she didn't give a hoot about what the town thought, and he was always welcome back at the farm.

From behind them, Odin appeared at the last moment, throwing his arms around Ragland, before ducking away as if burned.

'Good work, mister! Come back soon!'

Viola put an arm around the kid's shoulder and Ragland ruffled his hair.

Next was Simon.

'Stay safe,' said the big Canadian as he pulled him into a bear hug.

Last was Claire, who just a day before would have sent him on his way with a kick in the pants. She stepped forward, took his hand, and stopped suddenly, lowering her head. Ragland, confused and still with her warm, soft hand in his, looked at the others for guidance, awkward and unsure about what to say or do.

Finally, lifting her face, Claire wiped a tear from her face and nodded.

'Sorry, for being so harsh on you Cowboy. Take care.'

Without another word, she let go and began to walk back into town, with Odin chasing along behind her.

'What was that about?'

He only got shrugs and confused looks in reply. Accepting he wouldn't get an answer, Ragland watched her for a few seconds, suddenly wondering what could have been if the circumstances had been different.

Burying the thoughts quickly, he adjusted his gear, and took one last look up the wide avenue into Bakerstown. In the distance, hunkered but not hiding in the shadow of a building, he saw David. The thug waved a hand then turned it and flipped him the bird, a faint smile on his face.

Ragland ignored the petty gesture from the petty man and turned to the gate.

A hundred yards away the wilds of Pennsylvania waited for him. Kit was still with him as he crossed the threshold.

'Take care, kid,' he said pulling her into a hug.

'I will,' she said. Then as they pulled apart, 'You remind her of John.'

'Who?' he asked.

'Claire's man. He died early last year.'

Something fell into place.

'The scouting trip? Alex?'

Kit nodded.

'He didn't mean to... it just... but it might be why she's, like, been off with you and stuff.'

Ragland sighed.

'Explains a lot. Well, kid, this is it. Look after yourself, you hear? Keep that onyx safe, and it will do the same for you.'

'Roger that, Gramps. Try not to pull a muscle or whatever.'

He winked. 'I'll do my best. Say goodbye to Alex, I won't be going past the lodge.'

Ragland waved to them as the gates slammed shut.

Silence and solitude enveloped him. A familiar blanket, but one that felt a lot more threadbare than it ever had before.

Turning, he walked off east into the trees, the frost-bitten twigs and undergrowth crunching underfoot.

PART FIVE: EYE OF THE STORM

CHAPTER 26

The afternoon following his departure from Bakerstown, a snowstorm hit, leaving it impossible for Ragland to do anything but hunker down in his tent until morning. The storm had passed by dawn, but light snow persisted.

He ate some of the berries and nuts Simon had slipped him on his departure then went back to sleep. Even when he awoke again late in the afternoon, he would have happily stayed in the tent where there was some semblance of warmth, but his growling stomach wouldn't allow it.

With the knee-deep snow it wouldn't be easy to hunt, but first and foremost he was a hunter survivor and eventually crawled out of the tent to gear up.

Kneeling in the crisp powder, he reached down with a gloved hand and touched the faint impressions in the snow. Tracks. Small prints.

A Snowtail.

Taking out the bow Rahul had made him,

he tested the bowstring again to ensure it felt secure. Rahul's bow was much smaller and slender of limb than his manufactured one had been, and the string was less durable having been fashioned from sinew. It wouldn't last as long as the dacron string on his old one, but if he kept it dry it would make do until he could find a replacement.

Grabbing an arrow and nocking it, he followed the tracks, making sure to avoid twigs and branches that, if snapped, would alert the rabbit of his presence.

He thought about Kit as he stared off across a flat piece of forest ground, searching for the animal. Ragland's mind drifted with the snow, remembering the moment she had put the necklace on.

Even now, alone in the world without it, he didn't regret giving Kit the last memento of his sister.

His mind flitted from that melancholy memory to his forced departure from the town. Bitterness came with it. The town's willingness to blindly ignore a genuine danger outside its walls annoyed him more than he cared to admit. So did the fact that he had let himself fall into the trap of caring too much.

Ragland spotted his quarry as it bounced from behind a small bush and he raised his bow. He drew the bowstring taut and followed his target.

No, it was best he forget all about Bakerstown

and its inhabitants. Even Kit.

He loosed the arrow and it cut through the cold air, striking the rabbit and sending it cartwheeling in a cloud of snow.

Darkness was setting in by the time he got back to camp. Sheltered from the wind, Ragland nursed a small campfire into life and soon had the small game twisting and hissing over the orange flames.

When the rabbit was cooked to his satisfaction, he pulled out the knife Rahul had given him. It still proved sharp to touch and he prized the rabbit off the spit, and waited for it to cool for a few moments before slicing meat from it and eating ravenously.

The meat, though tough, tasted delicious. A hard-earned meal always did.

Halfway through his meal, Ragland heard the snap of a branch behind him. With memories of the ambush he had suffered in similar circumstances just a week or so before, he dropped what was left of the snowtail, grabbed his new bow and rose to his feet in one quick movement. With another arrow nocked and ready he began searching the darkness.

After what felt like minutes, but was in fact just a few seconds, a turkey burst from the tree line, stopped and stared at Ragland for a moment before turning tail and speeding off into the shadows.

Releasing his breath and chuckling, Ragland tossed the bow down and took up his food again.

'Goddamn gobblers,' he laughed and bit into the carcass with even more rabid focus.

The encounter with the turkey left him feeling on edge and, paranoia or not, the feeling of being watched settled on him. He left the fire burning after his dinner, and entered his tent. He had deliberately positioned the tent closer than customary to the fire to allow some of the meager heat to swell and circulate under the canvas. He suspected the benefit was more psychological than anything, but it made him feel cosier.

In the morning, when he opened his eyes, the first thing he noticed was the sagging roof. The second was the eerie silence of the snow-muffled world. He peeled open the tent and was met with several more inches of snow than had been there the night before.

Grumbling, he dug around in his pack and retrieved one of the single-most crucial items he had looted since the fall. Waterproof coverings for his legs, that would tuck nicely into his hiking boots.

When he was dressed for the day, the last old man clambered from his tent and wasted no time packing it away.

With his pack on his back and his bow over his shoulder, Ragland still couldn't shake the feeling of being watched. He turned his head and peered between the trees at the edge of the clearing but still couldn't see anything out of the ordinary.

'Too much time in that goddamn town Ragland,' he growled, before setting off again. 'You've gone soft in the head.'

When the sun was high overhead, Ragland settled and finished the leftover rabbit with some of the root vegetables Simon had packed for him. Thanks to the cold, the cooked food had kept well and satiated his hunger and need for nutrients.

At a tiny stream, he refilled his bottle and spent some time watching the ice thaw at the edges; the simple view and sound of the babbling water comforted him. After all these years he was still a sucker for the picturesque beauty of nature, and nothing could quite beat untouched snow in the woods.

Almost a full two and a half days out from Bakerstown, Ragland began to notice markings and signs in the forest that worried him. At first, he had ignored it as wildlife. But the noises and a half-scuffed print here and there were not random enough, and he began to suspect he was being stalked. Cannibals? If so it wasn't the moronic Zoms, it could only be the smarter ones, but only one or two at the most, or he was sure he would have seen them earlier.

Choosing to test his theory, he deliberately took a path through more difficult terrain, areas where a careless step would dislodge rocks or break sticks in the undergrowth.

Four hours of that yielded no reward and only served to tire him more quickly.

As the sun sank in the west he began to set up a new camp but remained more vigilant, making a quick kill and then setting snares around the perimeter that would alert him of anyone trying to get too close.

He went to bed again with a full belly of rabbit and slept so soundly that it probably would have taken a siren to wake him.

More snow had fallen overnight and it crunched under his boots as he cleared away the snares he had set, the sound muffled by the blanketed trees around him.

That brought to mind the traps that Alex had mentioned he and Sang had set. While he had traveled too far to encounter any now, he hadn't spotted even one as he moved away from the town. Unfortunately, he thought that the kid had pretty much wasted his time.

On the fourth day, Ragland again chose a path through the more treacherous undergrowth. His perseverance was rewarded about three hours after he set out.

The snap of a branch, accompanied by a low cry of surprise about a hundred yards behind him, saw him throwing down his pack and sprinting in an arc towards the location of the sound, an arrow already nocked and ready to shoot.

Traveling with great stealth, he slowed when he thought he was parallel to the position the noise had come from. He hunkered down behind a large cedar and peered through the trees to the west.

Two figures stood next to each other talking quietly, their hands and arms moving animatedly as they argued over something.

His stalkers.

They weren't cannibals.

In fact, they were clothed in pristine snow gear and boots and both carried bows, not the usual choice of weapon for cannibals. If not them though, who was it? He needed a closer look. It was easy to slip from behind the cedar and get to a large boulder another twenty feet closer.

Cannibals or no, they were a threat and as he peeked over the rock, he raised his bow and aimed at the closest of the two figures, pulling the string tight. He slowed his breathing, and prepared to let fly as the smaller of the two turned their head his way.

CHAPTER 27

'Christ!' Ragland rasped, relaxing the tension on his string immediately.

It was Kit. Anger at the near disaster surged through him and he shot to his feet and stormed towards them.

'What the hell are you two idiots doing!'

Kit and her fellow traveler whirled around, their eyes wide. As he suspected from the size and shape, her companion was Alex.

Both shrunk away from his ire as he closed the gap, their mouths opening and closing like fish pulled from water.

'Well?!' he roared, standing over them.

'We had to come find you,' said Kit.

'No,' Ragland growled. 'You didn't.'

'The town needs you, even if they don't know it,' Kit persisted.

Alex spoke up.

'Kit and I figured you would be looking for them. Hunting them.'

'Well you're wrong. I'm just picking up my travels where I left off and I'll avoid the cannibals if I can. You and your town should do the same.'

'You wanted us to fight them before, you can't give up on us, Gramps. Not yet.'

Seething with anger at how irresponsible they'd been to trek alone without enough people to put up a fight if they did come across trouble, he could barely speak.

He stormed past them, fists clenched.

Once he had put a few dozen yards between them, he turned and pointed back the way they'd come.

'I didn't give up on the town. It gave up on me. Now go home. Follow your tracks. Keep the fires low and maybe you get back in one goddamn piece.' Ragland shook his head, attempting to keep his composure. 'Kit. After everything? Are you trying to throw your life away?'

'Hey, man, that's not fair,' Alex said, stepping forward. 'This was a joint decision.'

'Ah,' Ragland laughed, throwing up a hand. 'Joint stupidity it is. Of course.'

Kit looked hurt. But if it meant she'd turn back with no argument, then he'd say whatever he needed to say.

Alex wasn't finished.

'I figured someone like you would understand.'

'Understand what?'

'That we risk our lives for people we care about,' said Kit, stepping in. 'I guess we were wrong about you.'

Her words cut deep. Before he could reply, Kit

reached inside her coat and plucked out the onyx pendant.

The breath in Ragland's lungs froze.

'This means everything but not if we just give up. I figured we three could find these assholes so we know when they begin their move. We have a better chance of making the town see sense if we know when they are coming.'

Ragland couldn't take his eyes off the black stone. The muffled silence around them seemed to cut off the rest of the world. A single snowflake drifting onto his nose stirred Ragland from his reverie.

'I still think this is reckless,' he croaked. 'You two aren't built for the wild like I am.'

Kit tucked the stone back inside her coat and smiled.

'Lucky we're together then, right Gramps?'

Sensing the tension had dissipated, Alex looked around, searching the trees.

'Hey, where's your gear?' he asked.

'Back there,' Ragland said and pointed a thumb over his shoulder. 'I left it by some rocks. Heard you coming from a mile away.'

'Not surprised. The terrain nearly broke my ankle.' Alex suddenly smiled. 'I suppose that was —'

'Deliberate? Absolutely.' Ragland finished, and then regarded them silently.

He was silent so long Kit started to wonder if he'd had a stroke. She was about to say so when he spoke.

'I guess I can hang around a little longer, but once we know when they're heading to Bakerstown, I'm on my way again, understand?' They both nodded, Kit doing her best to suppress a smile. He lowered his brow. 'Kit, you know better than anyone how quickly things can go south. You both do exactly what I tell you, when I tell you, got it?'

'Got it,' they both replied in unison.

Ragland paused again, hands on hips and looking at the snow on his feet, wondering if he was doing the right thing. Misgivings aside, he felt like he had unfinished business with the town and the people in it, so for now, yes it was the right thing.

'So,' Kit prompted, adjusting her backpack, a hopeful glint in her eyes. 'What's the plan?'

'My gear.'

Ragland turned and walked back towards where he'd dropped his pack. The two followed him

'I've been looking out for signs, but so far, nothing. I think they'll be coming from the east again. So we'll head that way.'

'And then what?' Kit asked.

'Then,' the Drifter explained, navigating a fallen tree. 'Once we find a sign, we track them. We look for where they're holed up. We assess their numbers, then we wait.'

'Once they move, how long will we have?'

asked Alex.

Ragland reached the spot he'd hidden his backpack. He bent down, strapped it tight over his back, and re-adjusted the bow on his shoulder.

'You found them two days out, right? If they haven't moved yet, and we can maybe thank the snow for that, we'll be three on foot against at least two hundred of them. I know you estimated four to five hundred, but I don't think they'll all be fighting. Anyway, I figure we can beat them there by half a day.'

'Shit,' Alex said under his breath. 'That's not much time.'

'We might get lucky,' said Kit. 'Maybe they changed their mind after you told them off at the gate.'

'I looked into his eyes,' he said. 'They'll be back. And not just for you or me. Bakerstown is a human meat farm—that'll be too much for them to resist. Marly won't be able to negotiate with them, unless it's to sacrifice some of her own people to buy a short reprieve. If she does that, they'll be back again and again for years until there is no one left.'

'How do you know?' Alex asked, falling into step with Ragland.

'Trust me. It's not the first time I've seen...' Ragland paused to swallow a bad memory. 'Just trust me.'

He noticed Kit and Alex exchange looks before

he turned his attention back to their snowy path southeast.

They paused for lunch when the sun was high in the sky. Ragland didn't allow them a fire.

'How far have we come you think?' Kit asked, washing down some jerky with a gulp of water.

Ragland shrugged.

'A few miles.'

'What are we looking for?'

'Anything. Remains of a campfire. Blood. Bones. Come on, let's get moving, I want to make camp at sundown.'

They tromped for four hours until the afternoon light began to dim. Ragland began to look for a good spot to make camp.

Concentrating, he almost missed the whisper of shock from Kit. To him, it had sounded like a bird on the wind.

Kit repeated the words, only louder.

'Oh, God...'

'What is it?' Ragland stopped their party and frowned.

She was as pale as the snow on the ground, her eyes staring between the sparse trees at the crest of a low hill a few hundred yards distant.

Ragland's blood chilled and he was thankful when Alex grabbed Kit and pulled her close to him, hiding her face from the horror.

'Stay here,' whispered the old man, dropping his backpack and unslinging his bow. He indicated they should hunker down behind a fallen tree. 'Don't make any noise.'

Cautiously, Ragland climbed the small incline using the trees as cover.

As he approached the top, he kept his eyes averted from the horror that awaited, and instead surveyed the area for signs of company. The snow was pristine, there were no prints or other signs of recent activity.

Satisfied they were alone, he stood up to full height and climbed the rest of the way, finally giving his full attention to the unfortunate soul he found there.

The body was that of a young man, nailed through the wrists to a rough pole that had been staked into the ground.

He had been flayed and gutted, strips of muscle cut from the legs and arms. There was nothing clean or symbolic about the scene, it was just a brutal butchering. Both the nose and ears had been removed, no doubt as mementos.

It was also a warning, intentional or not, that they were not the only ones hunting.

'Cannibals,' he murmured when he got back to Kit and Alex. 'We need to move.'

'Figured,' said Alex. 'Does that mean their camp is near?'

'I don't think so,' Ragland replied. 'I didn't see any signs that there had been more than a handful. Maybe it was just a hunting party.'

Kit pulled away from Alex's chest, a hand to her mouth.

'Holy shit,' she said. 'What the fuck?'

Ragland couldn't agree more with the sentiment.

'You're not going to like a theory I have,' the old man grumbled, hands on his hips like Marly as his eyes scanned the woods.

Kit looked at Alex, who looked at Ragland.

'Just tell us.'

'Fine,' Ragland said. 'I think its possible they anticipated something like our mission and that they are out hunting.'

'What?' Kit gasped. 'No. That's not possible, right? We'd have seen or heard them?'

'Maybe not. After all they probably don't know *who* they are hunting for, just that someone is looking for them. We can't underestimate them, and we have to assume that they'll find out tracks. In which case, they *will* be hunting us.'

'So what are you saying,' Kit said. 'That these cannibals are sophisticated?'

Ragland nodded. 'You saw the man at the gate and Alex also spied on them at camp. They're not all brain surgeons, but they are being led by the Norms. Cannibals, but cannibals who are intelligent and calculating.'

'Then why have we only just learned about it? Goddamn, man, this doesn't feel right.'

Ragland shrugged.

'Well no offence, but your town is pretty sheltered and seem to have their world view shaped by a handful of people who have never been outside the gate. There's more of the Zoms, so naturally if your people did encounter them, they probably never saw the hierarchy up close.'

'Right.'

Kit shuffled from Alex's arms and straightened her backpack.

'So,' she said. 'What signs did you find? Were they here recently? Could we track them?'

The reply caught him off guard. Kit surprised him more and more. Bakerstown was lucky to have her. Then he smiled.

'The body's well and truly cold. I think its been at least twenty-four hours. That means they could still be close, so we have to be on high alert.' Kit shuddered at the thought. 'I did find one print in the dirt under a pine. It was headed north.'

'North it is then, I guess?' Alex said putting his arm around Kit's shoulder again.

Ragland nodded.

'North.'

CHAPTER 28

Ragland felt the possibility of being hunted was, in some twisted way, a little poetic. He'd spent so long in the new world being a hunter that he'd almost forgotten what it had been like to be prey.

But it had happened before.

Having seen out the period after the infection until the Chinese army was driven back across the Appalachians by the retrovirus, the young survivors alone and hungry, without any form of government or authority, had scattered or banded together.

Some of those groups were savage. Killing at will over food or territory. For a time, Ragland thought that was how it would be forever, but then during his travels, he heard of a stronghold in Albany, New York where, rumor had it, the son of the last president ruled.

Doubting the veracity of the rumor, but tired of being on edge and avoiding the gangs of marauding teenagers, Ragland decided some order was what he needed and set out for Albany. He didn't know what he'd find, but there was nothing else for him.

He traveled as inconspicuously as possible, mostly at night and on back roads, but avoiding people all together was impossible. Because he was alone, he was often assessed by opportunity seekers to be an easy target. Sometimes he could avoid conflict, but sometimes it was inevitable.

One such incident had taken place three miles from the border of New York, when three straggly teenagers armed with blades and axes had confronted him.

'I killed all three of them,' Ragland said, as he stoked their campfire on the third night. 'The first time I took a human life and I had to take three. I never arrived in Albany. I decided after that incident that it was best to avoid people altogether, so that's when I began wandering.'

They'd found a small cave-like structure, which sheltered them enough from the wind and helped hide the fire, though not entirely. It was a risk, but extinguishing it for complete stealth would ensure they wouldn't wake up in the morning.

Alex and Kit sat opposite him on an old log, sticks of squirrel meat forgotten in their hands.

'How old were you?' Kit asked.

'I was about twenty-five, or twenty-six. I can't recall exactly. The early years kind of blend into one.'

Kit hung her head. 'I might beat that Gramps. I'm not even twenty but I might have blood on my hands before Christmas. It's so screwed up.'

'It is,' Ragland nodded. 'There's no good age when it comes to killing. But if you're doing it for the right reason and only when you need to, then it's... *righteous*, I guess.'

'Do you think I'll be able to go through with it when the time comes?' she asked.

He paused a minute and pondered the question while he chewed squirrel meat.

'You have it in you. Most do. It's just a matter of time and circumstance.'

Alex raised his eyebrows.

'Man, that's a bit dark?'

Ragland shrugged.

'Maybe, but it's true. Maybe if things hadn't turned out like they did with you getting on the radar, it might have been different.'

A gloomy mood fell over the camp for the rest of the night. Once they'd eaten and set traps, Ragland put out the fire and they took to their tents and slept.

Ragland dreamt he was wandering through Bakerstown. The streets were filled with corpses that he couldn't avoid stepping on. Every now and then in the mess he would see a familiar face. Simon. Marly. Jack the butcher. Erica. He had a sinking feeling in the pit of his stomach, *Where was Kit*? Finally he saw the school in the distance and knew this was where he would find her.

His foot squelched on something and when he looked down he saw Claire's face under the sole of his boot. In horror he lurched away towards the school only to find there was a tree in front where none had been before. It was a tall cedar and pinned to it with arrows was Kit. She was facing him, her mouth open in a silent scream, her eyes bloody sockets.

Ragland sat bolt upright. Panting heavily he scrambled out of his tent on hands and knees and took in gulps of fresh, cold air.

'You okay?'

Ragland brushed his long hair away from his eyes and saw Alex already awake, checking on his backpack.

Ashamed to be caught in such a vulnerable state, he climbed to his feet.

'Fine,' he growled.

Alex nodded with a doubtful look on his face and went back to packing.

The nightmare set the tone for Ragland's day and, in a foul mood, he tore his tent down a little impatiently and stuffed it into his pack. He was ready to move when Kit surfaced.

'About time,' he barked.

'Jesus,' she yawned and rubbed her eyes, before moving out of the way as Alex wordlessly began to pull down their own tent. 'Relax Gramps. I'm up, aren't I?'

'Barely. Get your shit packed and let's go.'

Ragland turned his back, not wanting to see Kit and Alex exchange looks or whisper their opinions. Instead, he took a short northward walk away from the camp and waited.

After just five minutes, the pair appeared on either side of him. Kit's eyes softened when she saw Ragland's face. He looked older this morning, the faint lines on his face a little more noticeable, his eyes haunted.

'Sorry about before,' she said, even though she'd done nothing. 'I had a nightmare. It was pretty frickin' bad.'

Ragland's eyes widened but he had no intention of mentioning his own bad dream.

'Forget it. We're all tired and cold. Let's just keep going. We can't be far now.'

The land they walked became an incline, easy at first but then steeper until it led up a hill to a sharp crest.

The branches thinned and the ground started to level out near the summit and they slowed to catch their breath before eventually reaching it.

'Wow,' Ragland said. 'Beautiful.'

'Yeah,' Kit replied. 'Seriously awesome.'

From the crest, the land sloped down into a small valley. It was steeper than the other side and treeless, but not impassable. From their vantage they overlooked snowcovered treetops for as far as the eye could see.

Alex was silent, but when Ragland checked on him, he saw the kid was appreciating the vista as much as he and Kit. Only, he wasn't really a kid. Neither was Kit. Not kids like they would have been before the Fall.

Still, he couldn't think of them any other way, and because of that he felt a responsibility to keep them safe. The nightmare was probably a manifestation of the weight of that responsibility, but its effects had faded as their hike progressed. Now a sense of empathy washed over him like a gust of warm air. It served to focus him on the task at hand.

They started down the hill and were still two hundred feet from entering the trees when Alex stopped and pointed into the distance.

'Look there, is that smoke?'

Ragland squinted and could make out a thin white plume masked by the glare of a low sun on the horizon. It was hard to see, but Alex had caught it.

'Good spotting!' Ragland said, and thumped him on the shoulder. 'Very good eyes.'

Alex beamed and Kit stood on tiptoes and kissed him on the cheek.

'Nice work, Babe.'

The adoration on her face struck Ragland and he knew it wasn't just puppy love but a real thing the two shared. Kids like these would be the future and he felt more than ever that he had to keep them alive.

'Right,' Ragland said. 'This is where we need to be extra careful. This is a recon only. No engagement. No heroic shit. Got it?'

The pair nodded.

'Good.'

'So, like, what're we gonna do for evidence then? Get close, sketch a picture and show the town we were right?' Kit offered.

Alex chuckled, and Ragland allowed himself the ghost of a grin at her humor.

'If only that would work. Sure do miss my old smartphone.'

Alex and Kit looked blankly at him.

'Forget it. We're going to get something they can't ignore. A count of their numbers. Maybe evidence of their ferocity.'

'A hostage, right?' said Alex.

'No,' Ragland said. 'Too dangerous. We're going to get ourselves a trophy.'

'A trophy? What, like we cut off one of their heads and take it back?' Kit asked.

'No! Jesus, kid, if you people had tech I'd say you were watching too much TV. No, not a head. We're going for one of their necklaces.'

Kit looked confused and touched her pendant.

'Oh,' Alex said. 'You mean the ears. The string of ears they make from the ones they cut off their victims?'

Kit's face paled.

'Sorry,' said Alex.

'It's sick,' she said, and took a deep breath. 'Why do they do it?'

'Why do you think?' Ragland rasped, checking his bow and securing it back onto his shoulder.

'Tallying their kills. Trophies?'

'Both. Let's go.'

The three began their careful descent down into the trees and turned in the direction they'd seen the plume of smoke. Once in the trees, the sense of danger set in and prickled at the hairs on his arms the deeper into the forest they went.

They all stumbled a few times, the deep snow hiding the roots and rocks in their path. After an hour they came to a freshly trodden path. The snow and mud had been trampled by many feet and swung in a slight north-westerly direction. Kit shot Ragland a look of trepidation.

The cannibals were moving in the direction of Bakerstown.

'There must be hundreds of them,' Alex said, kneeling down to inspect the footprints.

'Yes,' said Ragland. 'I'd say it's the bulk of the group you saw on your scouting mission, but not all of them.'

'Is there still time?' said Kit in a strident voice. 'To get ahead and raise the alarm?'

'I don't know,' Ragland said. 'But three of us can move quicker than hundreds.' He unslung his bow and broke into a light jog. 'Come on.'

CHAPTER 29

By nightfall, Ragland, Kit, and Alex had caught up with the cannibals who had set up camp.

They were now near the northern boundary of the former national forest they'd been walking through, and the problem soon would be the open land beyond.

Ten years had not been long enough for the forest to claim back the former farmland and roads it gave way to. Once out of the forest they would be more exposed to the weather and at risk of being spotted by the cannibals they followed.

When they had the location of the camp, they moved a mile away and set up their own camp in a dry creek bed sheltered by a steep bank. Clustered tightly around a small fire, Ragland passed around morsels of the small rabbit he'd shot an hour before they stumbled upon the cannibal camp. They made short work of the meat.

'Do either of you two know these parts?'

Both shook their heads.

'Not really,' Kit shivered, as she bunched up close to Alex.

'I haven't been this way before,' he said. 'But I suspect it will be bloody cold as we'll be a bit more exposed.'

'It will. I'd hoped to be much further south by now if things had…' He glanced at Kit. 'Been different, but winter this year has surprised.'

He reached over for another stick to throw on the fire and grimaced, holding his lower back for a minute.

'You okay?' Alex asked.

'Yeah,' he said, thankful that the glow of the fire hid his red face. 'I know I might be old to you, but I'm still in my prime. I'm just exhausted.'

'We all are. You grab some shut eye, I'll take first watch.'

Ragland shook his head, earning him frowns from the other two.

'Not me, kids. I've got to get us that necklace.'

Kit sat up straight.

'Like hell you are, Gramps. Are you friggin' insane? You think you're just gonna waltz on in. All howdy and stuff and just, grab a spare necklace of ears?'

Ragland couldn't help but smile. She was a little more cantankerous than his sister had been, but not by too much. The reminder cheered him up.

'No. They'll be settling down for the night, but there'll be some out and about foraging or scouting. I plan to find one of those and take them quietly.'

'I'm coming with y—'

'No, Alex. You're not.'

'But—'

'No,' he barked as he reached for his pack. 'You stay here and keep Kit safe.' The girl bristled and he quickly corrected. 'Keep *each other* safe. Make sure to keep the fire as low as you can. Before I go though, I need something to pep me up.'

Kit was scowling as he pulled a tiny pouch and what looked like a small steel pot from his backpack. While they watched he poured the contents of the pouch into the pot and topped it with water. While he couldn't make out what the dark powdery substance was by the low light, Alex smelled it immediately.

'You have coffee?!'

Ragland nodded.

'Simon had a small supply left in his pantry and gifted me some.'

'He must like you,' Kit said softly, her scowl somewhat softened. 'Coffee is mad rare. We only get some of it because of the long trade journey Marly sends south every spring.'

'Not surprised,' Ragland replied, as he held the pot over the flames. Without a percolator or filter, he'd been told to boil it and filter through a small mesh paper Simon had given him.

He poured the coffee through the filter into his tin cup, and did so for Kit and Alex too.

Then, he raised his steaming cup to theirs.

'Here's to…' he started.

'Coffee,' Kit finished for him, and taking a big gulp. She grimaced in pain as the hot liquid burnt her mouth, but managed not to spit any out before it was down.

'Damn that was hot,' she said through watering eyes and then she blew furiously trying to cool it quicker.

Alex laughed and shook his head.

Hot or not, she threw hers down while they were still sipping their way through theirs. Done, she placed the cup down, closed her eyes, and let out a long breath.

'God, I love that shit.'

'Yeah,' Ragland said. 'I can tell. Maybe let it cool a little next time so you can actually taste it.'

He finished his a few minutes later and as he stood up, he could already feel the caffeine kicking in.

'Okay you two. Stay put. Keep warm but keep the fire low. I won't be long.'

They nodded.

'Are you taking your bow?'

'No Kit, this calls for stealth, and the less I carry the better. My knife is all I need.'

She nodded but didn't look convinced.

'Back soon.'

'Don't die,' said Alex, immediately regretting his choice of words. Kit thumped him.

Ragland moved off into the trees without

comment.

Twenty minutes later, he was within a hundred yards of the cannibal camp. They were just beyond the edge of the forest, sheltered from the worst of the weather.

Crouched low in the darkness of the forest he rubbed his hands to keep the circulation going. He watched and surveyed the camp just like he had before rescuing Kit the first time.

It was big and well run—it had to be for them to be able to move so many people in such an organized fashion. Thankfully, it didn't look to be the full population Alex and his spies had found. This group looked to be about a hundred and fifty, but from what he could see they were armed to the teeth.

This then was their army.

As ramshackle and rudely armed as it was, he hadn't seen a large fighting group like it since the Chinese red army had departed.

'Not good…'

The plume of warm breath faded like a ghost in the cold darkness.

He would have no hope of just sneaking into the camp to find what he wanted. His only option as he'd mentioned to Alex and Kit, was to wait for an individual or small band to break off and enter the woods to forage or take a piss.

That would be his move, but even now he was doubting that obtaining the trophy and taking it back would convince the people of Bakerstown they were in imminent danger. The longer he sat there in the cold, the more he began to think it was nothing more than a hare-brained scheme.

No, Bakerstown would only fight if the threat was bashing down their gates. Literally. If they didn't wake up and defeat, or at least fight the cannibals to a standstill, they would only grow stronger and like a plague, move on to the next town, and the next, and the next.

Much more was at stake than Bakerstown.

He was on the verge of calling the mission off and thinking about how to explain it to Kit and Alex when he spied a pair of cannibals saunter away from the firelight, into the woods and only a hundred feet from his position.

These two were dressed in decent winter gear and didn't have the shuffling appearance of Zoms. As he moved through the trees, rounding their position to come up behind them, he did spy a group of Zoms, their ankles chained one to the next, with the two on each end secured to trees. These were ugly and malnourished, almost unrecognizable as human beings, and he realized with shock that the two Norms were guarding them.

Were they deliberately starving them? The inhumanity of it hit him hard but it was when he deduced why that he felt sick to the stomach. Shock troops. They would unleash this group first and crazed with hunger and whatever treatment they'd endured their whole lives, they would rampage through the streets of Bakerstown like a mobile meat grinder.

With a fresh resolve, Ragland found the two men laughing and swearing as they emptied their bladders side by side.

He lunged at the one on the right, burying the knife into the back of his neck and severing his spinal cord, ripping it out as he grabbed the second in a headlock, and clamped a hand over his mouth.

The cannibal struggled and thrashed around as he tried to escape Ragland's grip. He couldn't, and inevitably the Drifter's blade opened the exposed skin of his throat, unleashing a gout of crimson. Ragland held him until it was over then let the body crumple next to his pissing buddy.

Taking a quick breather, he rolled them both over and cursed. Neither wore a string of ears.

It was a good time to turn around and head back to the others, but something about what he'd seen stung him deeper than he could explain, and now, cocky from the easy kill and just for the bloody hell of it, he wanted to get one up on the bastards, by sneaking into their camp and stealing something from right under their nose.

He looked down at the bodies and a grim smile slowly dawned on his face.

Five minutes later, with bloody stripes painted on each of his cheeks and wearing the white coat he'd stripped from cannibal number one, he sheathed his knife and walked confidently toward the camp, holding the small axe his victim had been carrying loosely in one hand.

CHAPTER 30

Ragland cast furtive glances as he went, but no one seemed to have noticed him yet.

A razor-sharp focus, courtesy of the adrenaline coursing through his system, had kicked in. He would find a necklace, put it around his neck, and then get the hell out of dodge.

He was heading into a quieter part of the camp when a heavy hand fell on his shoulder.

'What's that trinket ya gone found yaself there, brother?'

Ragland was silent for a moment, searching his brain for a response that wouldn't get him killed.

'Hey, fuckhead, I just asked ya a question.'

The hand was joined by another and Ragland found himself spun around and looking up into the face of a gigantic bald man. Recognition washed over Ragland. He knew this gigantic savage from somewhere.

The giant's eyes narrowed.

'Found it out in the woods,' Ragland said, holding up the axe.

'Oh yeah? Whose blood is that?'

Ragland shrugged.

'Don't know, but sure tastes sweet...' he said, raising the axe blade and licking some of the cannibal blood from the edge.

The big cannibal stared at him a little longer before cracking a laugh.

Other cannibals stepped forward, curious about the conversation. Ragland, nauseous at the coppery taste in his mouth, wished he was back up behind the hill with Kit and Alex.

'You must be hungry to be licking cold blood off a blade.' The cannibal slapped him on the shoulder and moved off. 'Don't worry, you'll get your fill of meat when we take that town.'

Ragland watched him go as the feral cannibals chained up to the trees heard "meat" and began to shriek the word over and over. He barely noticed because it had dawned on him where he knew the face from. This man was the living, breathing image of the gigantic Zom he had killed the first time he left Bakerstown.

Gigantic twins. One a mindless freak, then this specimen, who was even more terrifying because of his ability to think and speak.

Ragland focused on controlling his breathing as the others around him dispersed or followed the giant.

Subdued by this interaction, he went back to scouting the camp when he noticed ahead another face he knew. The man he had turned away from the gate of Bakerstown a few days before.

The leader.

He was laughing and drinking with more Norms, including females, and greeted the giant loudly when he entered the firelight.

'Moose! Where have you been?'

'Taking a dump boss.'

This was greeted with howls of laughter. Ragland tarried just a second too long and the eyes of the leader fell on him before moving back to his circle of buddies.

Cursing quietly, the Drifter pulled down his hood and ducked into the shadow of a tree, waiting for a shout of alarm. He counted to ten and none came.

When he felt safe, he slipped out of sight down a path between two lines of tents. He came to another open area, this one not as boisterous or populated as the last, and began weaving through sleeping bodies. Spooked by the two close encounters, he was about to call time on this particular mission and begin to make his way out of camp when he spied, draped over a stick wedged into the frozen ground, a necklace of ears.

A lot of them.

He paused and listened, then glanced left and right, before reaching up and taking the trinket. The ears, mostly shrunken and darkened with age, were frozen solid, like rocks to touch. At one end were two fresher additions, blood still congealed at the edges where they'd been severed from their owner's head. The tops of the ears had been pierced and a thin wire threaded through them, before being joined in a tight knot.

It was one of the more gruesome things he had ever seen.

Now that he had it, he was unwilling to put it over his head and instead shoved it inside of his coat. He looked up and for the first time noticed that he was being watched. It was a girl of about seven sitting by a small fire. Her dark eyes were fixed on him.

That awful empty gaze spooked him more than the necklace of dead flesh, but he maintained his composure.

'Just getting it for him,' he bluffed.

She didn't say a word. Just kept on staring at him, eyes unblinking.

A Zom. Too simple in the head to even understand he was talking to her.

Ragland licked his lip, and looked past her. Just one fire ahead, and beyond its glow, he could see the long stretch of trees that would lead him back to his companions.

Ragland took a deep breath and started walking. He'd barely taken ten paces when a figure stepped from the shadows and blocked his path.

'Hello, brother.'

It was the leader.

He wore a winter jacket, jeans and boots. Ragland thought that if it wasn't for the carving in his forehead, the cannibal could have easily blended in with the Bakerstown folk.

As Ragland tried to find a way out of the situation he found himself in, he spotted movement in the shadows on both sides. Guards who, no doubt, would block his escape.

'There's nothing you can say that will help you friend. I never forget a face,' the leader said, as he crossed his arms behind his back. 'What brings you to our camp?'

Ragland didn't speak. Instead, he turned and lunged for freedom, only to come crashing into the chest of Moose.

'No, you don't, little lamb,' the giant cannibal said, grasping his upper arm and holding him in front of the leader.

A cold deeper than the winter's night chilled Ragland. This was it. He'd walked right into the lion's den and offered himself up as a free meal.

The leader stepped forward slowly and reached out, unzipping Ragland's jacket. There, he slid his cold, long-fingered hand in and plucked free the necklace of ears.

'Oh, dear. What is this, Friend?'

Ragland remained silent.

'No? Well, no matter.'

Ragland struggled against Moose's grip but the big man clamped down tight enough to make him wince. The leader and a few of his friends laughed.

The feral cannibals at the trees screamed "meat" in a blood curdling chorus. The leader raised his hands into the air, his sharpened teeth glinting in the firelight.

'Yes! Meat, my pretties.'

The chorus died away, and the leader rubbed his chin in a thoughtful manner.

'My loyal pack always speak true. It's our tradition. Our way of life. Meat. The best kind of meat. And you come to us on the eve of our greatest feast yet. An appetizer. Confirmation of our righteous path. Thank you stranger, for this gift.'

He grabbed Ragland's chin and inspected him, pinching his cheeks and prodding his body.

'Lean, but you'll do,' the leader said, and signaled Moose before walking past them and back towards his campfire. Ragland found himself lifted from the ground and hoisted over the giant's shoulder like a small child being carried by its father.

Ragland struggled as they followed the leader, but the grip of the gigantic cannibal was unshakable.

Near the fire, the leader motioned to a tree. Three minutes later he was tied securely to the rough bark of the trunk.

Triumphant, the leader came over Ragland and licked his bottom lip slowly as his grey eyes bored into him.

'What's your name, meat?'

'Go fuck yourself.'

The leader howled with laughter, then punched Ragland in the jaw. The sharp pain was accompanied by a flash of white that filled his vision momentarily, then his mouth filled with blood.

Disorientated from the blow, he spat out a globule of blood.

'Let's try that again. What is your name?'

Feeling as if it was already over, Ragland didn't see what he had to lose. So he smiled through the blood.

'Go fu—'

The second punch was somehow harder. It crunched into his lower jaw, flung his head to the side, and Ragland felt a tooth come loose. Raising his head, he adjusted his position against the tree and worked his tongue along his back teeth.

Sure enough, a molar had broken off. He spat it at the leader's feet.

'Ahh, a trophy. Thank you.'

The leader picked up the tooth and, smiling, put it into his coat pocket.

'I am going to enjoy eating you. Perhaps we'll filet and cook you while you watch?'

He plucked a hunting knife from his belt and took a step towards Ragland when a howl sounded from the woods opposite, followed by a whoosh and flames flaring up amongst the trees.

The leader spun around, distracted by the

commotion.

'Moose! Get everyone you have,' he ordered before stepping up to Ragland and putting his face mere inches away. 'Don't go anywhere, my sweet meat.'

Ragland watched him run off with the rest of his baying troops and looked around. His knife was on the ground, well out of reach.

He craned his neck to check the woods to the left and in his peripheral vision spotted a shadow racing up behind him. There came a thud, and a panting breath as fingers began to fumble at the rope.

'*Fuck fuck fuck,*' a voice rasped.

'Kit?'

'We've got to go. Alex said he'd delay them as long...' her voice broke and she fell silent.

After nearly a full minute of fumbling and slicing, the ropes fell to the ground. Ragland bent over and grabbed his knife before joining Kit behind the tree. She stood up, her eyes wide with fear and handed him his backpack. He took it and slung it over his shoulders, before taking the bow.

'Where is Alex?'

Kit shook her head.

'He didn't give me a choice.'

He gripped her by the shoulders.

'Where?'

Tears rolled down her face as she pushed him off, her eyes glowing in the orange firelight.

'He's... he's...'

A shout interrupted them and Ragland spun around to see two cannibals speeding towards them. Taking out his knife, he told Kit to run.

'I'll be right behind you!'

Throwing the knife from his right hand into his left, he ducked under the punch of the first cannibal and sliced him across the stomach. Ragland met the second cannibal head-on, knocking his knife-wielding hand away and sticking his own blade deep into the cannibal's eye socket.

His shriek of agony pierced the night.

Cries erupted, the leader's louder than the rest.

'Back to the fire! Our meat is escaping!'

The bloodcurdling chorus of the Zom cannibals screaming for meat again rose up, drowning out everything else.

The cannibal with the open belly had turned, unaware that his guts were spilling onto the snow, and came at him again. Ragland sliced his throat this time, and was gone before the body hit the frozen earth.

CHAPTER 31

Ragland and Kit dashed into the woods, their pace as hard and as fast as they could, the bloodthirsty horde behind them providing plenty of incentive.

Ragland deliberately had them running deeper into the forest but after ten minutes they arced towards the north. Miraculously the screams and yells behind them fell off and continued west, the cannibals clearly not skilled at tracking.

'I think we lost them,' said Kit, panting hard at the exertion.

'We keep going,' said Ragland. 'Once we're out of the forest we'll re-evaluate.'

Twenty minutes later they emerged onto a field where hard gusts of wind cut through their clothes like they were nothing.

'Keep going!' Ragland roared over the noise of the storm, his hand pointed toward a row of abandoned houses.

Their feet sunk into the fresh snow as deep as their knees in some places. Behind them, the glow of fire reflected across the field. Ragland glanced over his shoulder and cursed. Not as poor at tracking as he thought, although it was only a small group. There were shouts when they were spotted and he saw two split off and head back the way they had come. They would summon the rest.

Lungs on fire, Ragland helped Kit up over a fence and kicked in the back door of a house. Inside, out of the wind, Ragland ran through the kitchen to the living room. He tore a length of curtain off, wrapped it around his hand, and punched the big plate glass window.

Immediately, great flurries of snow filled the room. Ragland took the glass pieces and rushed to the back door, and started to wedge them upright between the floorboards.

'What're you doing?' Kit shivered, the strength and energy gone from her voice. Leaving Alex to the cannibals, and the seeming inevitably of their own capture and death, was too much for the young girl to handle.

'Buying time. It'll slow some of them down. We need every edge we can get. Come on, let's go.'

The two were through the front door less than three minutes after they entered and back out onto the street fighting against the wind. They turned into another yard, this one in the row of houses opposite.

Ragland vaulted a set of broken steps up to a long porch. Once at the top, he drew back his foot and kicked through the big double front doors of the two-story home and ran inside.

Kit was right behind him, her pants hard and sharp.

'We... we can't keep running. We've got... to... stop. This storm...'

Ragland shook his head, his eyes searching for something to use. Nothing became apparent.

'No,' he said and darted into the back room and toward a glass sliding door that led to the back garden. 'We have to move.'

'But the storm? What about Alex?'

Ragland turned and grabbed Kit and stared deep into her eyes.

'Alex is gone. If we stay or linger, we die too. Our only shot is to keep going, all the way back to Bakerstown.'

'But...' Kit choked, trying to hold back tears. The exhaustion aided in keeping them back. 'That's a day's hike.'

'I know,' he said and let go of her and looked through the doors toward the woods that backed onto the fenced garden. 'But it's the only choice we have right now. Are you ready? We'll make for the trees there and jog up to the next hill.'

Kit tucked some loose hair back into her beanie, and secured her coat.

'Ready.'

In just half an hour, Ragland guessed they'd covered two miles. It wasn't record-breaking, but in the conditions it was great progress. For now, they hadn't stumbled and his knees were still in good working order.

As the incline eased and swept over toward the top of the valley, they crested and dipped down toward the other side out of sight, then swung hard north west.

Above them, the sky was blotched grey-black, all of the stars hidden from view even though the snowstorm had eased off to a light fall. The distant howls of their pursuers had also dropped off, and as they continued their methodical jog, he began to hope.

After another half hour though, Kit stumbled and clutched at a tree, slowly sliding down until she was sitting on the snow. Ragland doubled back and knelt next to her.

'I. Can't. Do. It,' she said, in short harsh pants. 'It's too far.'

'You have to,' Ragland begged.

In the distance, he fancied he saw a brief wink of light between the trees. Cannibals, or a trick of his eyes, it hardened his resolve.

'Come on,' he said and helped Kit back to her feet. 'You're stronger than you think.'

'Alex always said so,' she said and wiped her face. 'Now he's gone…'

She started to sag back to the ground but he took her face in his gloved hands.

'Do it for Alex, Kit! Make his sacrifice worth something.'

She stared as if slapped and Ragland worried

that he'd gone too far. Kit eventually nodded, straightened her beanie and shook snow off her sleeves.

'For Alex.'

Their dangerous marathon lasted into the early hours, fuelled only by nuts and berries and desperation. Finally, the endless night ended when the distant sun broke light across the powdered treetops.

Ragland and Kit slowed to a trudging walk but continued towards home. When they passed a large fallen cedar on an established path, Kit told him they were a half-day away—a reward for their grueling run through the night.

They stopped an hour after sun up and ate the last of the rabbit from two nights before, washing it down with a few handfuls of snow.

Ragland's bones ached and the tip of his nose was numb. He knew without the warm blood pumping through their systems from the exertion of the flight they'd both be sporting a bad case of frostbite or worse.

He stood up again and Kit groaned.

'Can we rest for a just bit longer…' Kit said, eyes barely open.

Ragland turned back and peered into the distance behind them. He spotted a plume of smoke at least three miles behind them.

'We'll rest for five more minutes. I think they are doing the same, it will give us a chance to put more miles between us and them.'

She nodded without opening her eyes. He felt more for her then, than at any time since he'd met her. She just lost her partner and to compound the agony of the raw grief, she was on the point of exhaustion.

He sat close and let her rest her head on his shoulders as they shared their warmth. He didn't even realize he'd fallen asleep until he was startled awake by a gunshot in the distance. He clambered to his feet and helped Kit up, newly energized.

'Sorry I fell asleep,' Kit said.

'Don't be—me too. Let's move.'

Rejuvenated by their meager portions of food and the few minutes shut eye, Ragland and Kit set off at a jog.

After an hour, the regrettable happened, and he fell down hard when a rock he trod on tipped unexpectedly, rolling his ankle.

'Shit, are you okay?' Kit said, helping him up.

'I think so-' he started and promptly fell to his hands and knees again when his ankle failed to hold.

'It's not broken, I think I just sprained it,' he said and began to rise again. Kit held him down.

'Let me look.'

In a flash she had his boot and sock off and they inspected the damage. The joint was swollen, but not ridiculously so. Kit wrapped it tight with a bandana she pulled out of her pocket and he put his sock and boot back on.

'Thanks. Feels better already,' he said after taking a few tentative steps. 'But we won't be jogging the rest of the way to Bakerstown.'

'Fine by me,' said Kit.

Within a mile, Ragland had warmed up completely and barely felt the ankle as long as he maintained a steady walk and didn't try any fancy moves.

The last stretch to Bakerstown took the rest of the afternoon, and by the time twilight started to consume the sky, soaking the snow in deep purple, the weary pair were in sight of the gates.

Fifty yards out the siren started to blare and Ragland made out Charlie at the top, his eyes wide. The siren, an old wind-up job, continued blaring.

But the gate remained shut.

'Open the gate Charlie!' Kit called up to the boy as they came to a pause below the lookout.

Now that they arrived, the adrenaline of the chase ebbed and they both felt the cold and hunger begin to catch up on them. Ragland's ankle began to stiffen and he used his bow to support his weight.

Kit looked at him and he waved it off.

'It's fine. I'm just tired,' he said. 'What's taking them so fucking long?'

The siren began to wind down and they enjoyed the silence briefly before the faces of Marly, David, and a few others appeared at the top.

The gate remained closed.

'Where's Alex?' Marly asked, her voice uncharacteristically cold.

'He... he...' Kit started, but fell to her knees, the emotions she'd been bottling for the last sixteen hours spilling out as she bawled into her hands.

Before Ragland could finish her sentence, David did.

'He's dead, isn't he? Ragland, you son of a bitch. You did it, didn't you?'

Marly moved her hand, and the other men on the fence raised their bows as she waited for his answer.

'Kit, you move away from him...' Marly called.

At the end of the line of men, Ragland spotted Rahul, a rifle aimed loosely in his direction. The outrageous accusation and puzzling over what had changed between David and Marly in their absence had silenced him momentarily, but Ragland finally found his tongue.

'Marly what the hell's wrong with you?' Ragland said. 'Its nothing like that, these two came after me but we were attacked. They're chasing us now, less than a day behind! They got Alex, and they're—'

David pulled out a handgun, a big barrelled revolver, and pointed it at him. It seemed to come as a shock to Marly, her hand fluttering to her mouth. Whatever had changed between them, it was easy to see that David had more power or some hold over her that he didn't have before.

'Bullshit,' said David, as he cocked the weapon. 'I'm going to end you right here.'

'David-' said Marly.

Ragland knew the look in David's eyes and knew there was no way he'd be talked down.

There was only one thing for it.

As quick as a snake, Ragland drew his hunting knife, and in one movement grabbed Kit and pulled her to her feet as he stepped behind her, his blade against the pale skin of her throat. He swivelled her from side to side, making sure anyone thinking of taking a shot would think twice.

Kit went limp and held her hands out as people assembled on the gate cried out in shock, a hostage showing she was co-operating. He knew she understood what he was doing and why, but the act of last resort still left a bitter taste in his mouth.

He looked up at David.

'Let me in, or I finish her right here.'

PART SIX: WOLVES AT THE GATE

CHAPTER 32

The look in Marly's eyes as she followed David through the opening gates was like a punch in Ragland's guts. It was the gaze of someone who had been betrayed in the worst possible way.

With the knife still hard against Kit's pale and exposed throat, he took stock of the folk surrounding him, weapons drawn and with more on the way. They looked determined to take him if they could.

This wasn't a popularity contest. It was about saving the town and its legacy, and Ragland had to gamble and pray that Kit understood his gambit.

'Easy does it,' Ragland said, swinging Kit around as David darted behind him.

Marly hissed and put her hand up.

'David, wait!'

The veins in David's neck were protruding, his eyes wild and wide. So close to his end goal, he wanted to kill Ragland before Marly could talk the townsfolk out of it again. The Drifter could almost smell the copper in the air, even though a drop of blood hadn't been spilled.

'We gonna let the asshole get away with this, Marly?' said David, still circling. 'Let's just take him!'

Charlie looked terrified and glanced from Ragland to Kit.

'Please don't hurt her, Mister!'

He answered but his eyes were on Marly.

'I've got one condition.'

Already, a dozen men and women had arrived at the gate, holding a range of home-made weapons, of the bludgeoning and stabbing type, but also a few guns.

All for me? Ragland thought.

In truth, knowing they were willing to use weapons to defend themselves gave him a sense of relief, even though he wasn't the enemy they needed to be concerned about.

'I think we're past negotiating with you,' the Mayor said. 'Let Kit go, and we won't kill you.'

'Can't do that.'

'You have no choice.'

David took a step closer, and Ragland swung Kit around, pressing the blade harder against her throat. He whispered sorry into her ear.

Marly's hands came up again to warn David off, then she bowed her head in resignation.

'I have the leverage here, Marly. For once, be smart about this,' said Ragland, and he began moving Kit towards the gate, pivoting her every time one of the aggressors got too close.

'Fine,' the Mayor replied. 'What's the condition?'

A few angry jeers and shouts filled the street. They didn't care about reason or logic. They just wanted to kill him.

'That you hear what Kit and I have to say. You make a promise to act, and then you can do what you want with me. Clear?'

Marly looked around at her people, who walked as one group in Ragland's wake, eyes on his knife. A familiar face appeared, pushing through the townsfolk nearest him.

'Let him speak,' Simon said, his thick arms folded.

More angered cries, but another voice met Simon's. One Ragland had not expected to hear.

'I agree with Simon.' It was Claire. 'Let's hear what he has to say. We owe him that.'

'We owe him nothing!' screamed David. He pulled up his shirt to show the townsfolk. The numbers had swollen, and now more than thirty people milled about.

Soon, it would be the entire town.

'Look what he did. And now look at him. A knife to Kit's throat! He didn't save shit. She was just an opportunity for him. A means to a goddamn end! Ain't that right, Ragland?'

Voices of agreement were in the vast majority. The thick tension filled the air. Ragland felt it. His mouth was dry, and the rapid thuds of his heart pounded in his ears. Things were getting ugly very quickly.

'Why are you doing this Ragland?' Marly asked, her voice hopeless.

'Would you have let me in if I'd not grabbed Kit?' Ragland asked. She didn't answer immediately. 'Would you?'

'No,' she said. 'We wouldn't have.'

'So, it had to be done.'

'Did it?'

Ragland cleared his throat.

'The threat is real. It's out there. We all saw it. Kit saw it. Alex saw it. They're coming, and they'll be here by tomorrow—'

'Where is Alex!?' someone in the crowd yelled.

Kit squirmed in Ragland's grasp. He knew she wanted to speak, so he loosened his grip enough. David moved his feet apart as if ready to pounce.

'They killed him,' Kit croaked. 'Ragland's telling the truth. There are at least two hundred of them. Alex, he... he... saved us. We got away. If it wasn't for him, we'd both be dead.'

Ragland clenched his jaw. It was a lie. Alex had sacrificed himself to save Ragland alone, but Kit was smart enough to know this fact would possibly tip them over the edge into violence.

'He's making you say this, Kit,' David interrupted. 'We'll get you away from him. Just tell us... Ragland killed him, didn't he?'

'No, it was the cannibals. He caused a distraction and—'

'Stop it,' David said again. 'Don't protect this

man-'

'Shut the fuck up, David!' Kit screamed.

The outburst stunned the crowd into silence and David's mouth hung open.

'You've had, like, the worst vendetta against Ragland since he turned up. So listen to me. All of you. This shit is super fucking real. We don't have long and... *Nooo!*'

The blow to the back of Ragland's head stunned him and sent both of them sprawling face-first onto the road. Barely conscious, he realized he'd also dropped the knife and began to turn his head to see who had hit him when another blow finished the job.

Everything went black.

Ragland awoke. He had no idea how long he'd been out but the agony in his head was immense. It felt like his brain had swollen to twice its size, and he had to work hard to retain consciousness.

Before opening his eyes, he instinctively tried to move his hand up to touch his head but realized they were both restrained above him. Slowly his body sent him signals about his predicament. The biting of rope at his wrists. The frigid cold. The slick wetness on the back of his head.

Gritting his teeth, he slowly opened his eyes, blinking away a flurry of fresh snowflakes and squinting as he twisted his head left and right.

He was in front of the main gate. As much

as he could—restricted in his movement by his tied arms—Ragland tilted his head back to check their handiwork.

Over a supporting beam, the town folk had secured a hanging rope and had hung him by the wrists. Ragland wondered, then, why they hadn't just killed him or thrown him into some basement somewhere. Then he had a horrible realization.

They were going to use him as bait or a warning.

If he was telling a lie, he would continue to hang and die within a day from exposure. If he was telling the truth, he would be the first to be killed.

He wriggled and decided to try and turn himself. His feet were also tied at the ankles, but he found that if he extended them as far as possible, the toe of his boots just found purchase on the ground. As luck would have it, he had full mobility to spin but was simply met by the wooden surface of the gate inches from his face. He turned back again and noticed a figure a short distance away, hands in their pockets, watching him.

It was David.

'Well done,' Ragland said. 'You've just killed your town. Does your dick feel big yet?'

The forced chuckle introduced him to new agony as sharp pain lanced his ribs. He groaned loudly, twisting in his bonds. This drew a laugh from David.

'The folk did a real number on ya, Gramps. Deserved more, but Marly said we'd made our point.'

Ragland believed him. Now more awake, his body felt beat to hell.

'Look, David. I don't give a shit if you hate me, but just arm your people and get them ready. These cannibals aren't going to come knocking politely—'

'Shhh.' David walked up Ragland and pulled down on his legs. Ragland clenched his jaw as the rope cut into his wrists. It was all he could do not to give David the satisfaction of groaning in pain. 'No, we won't be doing any of that.'

Ragland noticed he had a new handgun holstered on his left side and a shotgun in his right hand. An uneasy feeling filled him then. What had happened?

'Where's Marly?' Ragland asked, worry overriding his pain. 'What have you done?'

David laughed, resting the shotgun back onto his shoulder nonchalantly. 'None of your fucking business. But we've got her holed up safe. That's all you need to know.'

'What are you trying to pull here, dickhead?'

A smirk.

'That's not the way to speak to the new Mayor, now, is it?'

'What?'

'That's right, asshole. Baker's Town is under

new leadership. Letting you live was the final straw for a lot of people and when I called a vote... well as you can see, we're under new management. Her last order was to hang you like a pinata. I wanted to kill you straight up, but I figure it's going to be a lot more fun watching you go like this, so we decided to leave you hanging.'

'Where's Kit?'

'Oh, don't you worry about Kit,' he said with a sly smile. 'She's safe and sound, unlike Alex. Shame about him, I guess Kit will need a shoulder to cry on.'

'I don't like that tone.'

'Too fucking bad,' David spat. He stepped close enough to Ragland so his whisper could be heard over the wind. 'She's all grown up now. Maybe I'll be the lucky one to make an honest woman out of her...'

Ragland thrashed against the rope and David stepped hastily away.

'Settle down Gramps. Do me a favor, be alive in the morning and I'll tell you all about it.'

'You son of a bitch! Get back here!'

David laughed and pulled the gates open, slipping inside.

'Sleep tight old man.'

The thought of Kit being accosted by David kept him awake for hours but eventually, the numbing freeze of the night stole him from the land of the conscious.

Ragland slipped into darkness again, not knowing if he'd ever wake.

Muffled voices from above and around him began to rouse him from sleep, followed very quickly by the sensation of falling. Hands caught him and eased him to the ground. It was still dark, and Ragland couldn't make out who had cut him down.

'Jesus...' he heard a voice whisper. 'He's half-dead. We've got to move. Quick.'

'Rahul had better keep his word,' another voice replied. 'One, two, three, lift!'

Ragland felt his body grow weightless again as he was picked up. He tried to speak but nothing worked. His jaw felt as though it was locked, and his throat was useless.

'He will. Just move... we're screwed if we're seen,' said the first voice.

The second voice replied.

'Yep. Shit, he's heavy.'

Ragland listened to their voices for as long as he could but holding onto consciousness felt like trying to grip an icy ledge over a dark chasm.

Once more, he tumbled into the abyss.

CHAPTER 33

'He's waking.'

The crackle of a fire and its incredible heat enticed Ragland to roll over to face it. He winced at the aches this drew from his body, but fire or not, he still shivered uncontrollably.

'C-cold,' he muttered and drew the blanket tighter around himself and tried to roll towards the flaming logs again.

A hand grabbed him and rolled him back.

'Steady there, old mate. You don't want to be that toasty, believe me.'

Ragland coughed and turned his face up to see the smiling visage of Simon. He felt a wave of emotions cascade over him. Gratitude, relief, and then dread.

He sat upright with the cook's assistance. His head throbbed and his body was crying for rest, but rest would have to wait.

Lamplight and the roaring fire illuminated a few dozen faces. Townsfolk, crammed into what looked like a small living room, were resting on sofa arms, the edges of tables, and even on the floor.

All eyes were fixed on him.

'What's going on…?' Ragland asked.

He shifted in an attempt to get to his numb feet but gave up quickly. How long had he been hanging in the cold?

Ragland checked the windows and noticed a thick layer of snow along the windowsills. They had almost certainly saved his life; he was sure he wouldn't have survived another hour.

'A rebellion.'

It was Kit's voice. He looked around and she knelt by his side, putting a warm hand on his shoulder.

'David's gone too far, He forced a vote, but his goons had already threatened a lot of the people who would have voted for Marly. We're not backing a bully and with your help we'll focus on the cannibals, then deal with him.'

It wasn't the content of what she said that struck Ragland deeply, but the mature tone of it. She sounded different. Which, he figured, was just about right for someone who had come so close to death. Also, for someone who had lost someone important to them.

Ragland could see a steely resilience in her eyes. She wanted to fight.

He cast his gaze around the room and recognized many of their faces. Simon was next to him, sitting on the floor. Elsewhere, he spotted Rahul, Viola, the couple from the florist shop, and a fair few more he'd worked with on the farm. Sang was there too and that was a big deal considering he was a part of David's group.

He nodded to them.

'Thank you. For saving me. How much time has passed since I was...?'

Simon gripped his shoulder. 'Just a few hours. Any longer and you'd have been—'

'Dead.'

The response came from Rahul, the stern-looking blacksmith of the town who had been tough to align with. He trusted few, and Ragland recalled he'd failed to gain that before leaving. A stoic figure, Ragland gritted his teeth and rose to his feet. Reaching out to the equally tall man, he shook Rahul's hand.

'Last time I saw you, you were pointing a rifle at me... thanks for not shooting. I'm guessing this is your place?'

Rahul didn't take his eyes off Ragland. His thick brows cast a deep shadow over his brown eyes. He nodded.

'Sorry about that, it was a mad rush to the gate when you and Kit showed up. Not much time for thinking, or I'm guessing Marly would have played it differently. Yeah, it's my place. Serves our purposes right now, I figure.'

'So, where is Marly?'

'David has her under house arrest,' Kit replied. She stood, too, and crossed her arms. 'We need to stop David and his thugs.'

Ragland shook his head.

'There will be time for that, but not now.'

Kit frowned and shook her head.

'No, we don't know what they're doing to her —'

'You saw what I saw Kit. Saw what's coming. It'll be far worse, and we need to get ready now.'

'But how're we supposed to fight off cannibals with David and his supporters ready to shoot us in the back.'

Murmured questions filled the room. Finally able to feel his numb toes, Ragland stood and held up his hands for silence.

'I'll bait them.'

'Bait them? How?'

'Well, I'm assuming they've taken the school, right?'

Simon jerked his head up. 'How did you know?'

He shrugged. 'It's what I would have done. Central location, multiple rooms, second story.'

'And only two exits that can be guarded,' a man spoke up from the other side of the room. Ragland craned his head and spotted Clint, one of their teachers.

Beside him stood Erica.

'It's true,' Erica chimed in. 'And there's a stock of food there, as well.'

'Perfect,' Ragland said, surprised to see them both here. Apparently, Marly still had a lot of respect and support in the town.

'So, my plan is to bait David and his followers,

so they don't have a choice but to join us and fight the cannibals.'

Many questions were fired at him at once and he held up his hand.

'I'll show you.'

He turned to the fire, grabbed a few small ornaments from the mantlepiece, and began setting them on the floorboards.

'School. Gate. Stores.' Everyone crowded in and stared down at his crude representation of Baker's Town. 'Now, strategy is key with fewer numbers. You're going to have to dig deep, perhaps exhaust your supplies, but if you want to live, you won't have a choice.'

He met everyone's eyes and then was distracted by Claire standing in the doorway. Something unspoken passed between them, and she nodded.

'We need to set traps. Rahul, how many do you have?'

'A few bear traps and some wire snares I could set. With more time I could have done pit traps, too, but the ground is too hard anyway.'

Ragland nodded.

'Get everything you have. Set them in the grass and areas running along the main road from the gate. Once they breach the gate, we go medieval on their asses, and pour fuel, kerosene, oil, basically anything flammable over them and light it up.

In their panic to avoid the fire, they'll branch

out to the flanks, which is where the traps will come into play.'

Nods of approval met his plan, but Rahul held up a finger.

'We still don't have nearly enough for the numbers you spoke of. Not for two hundred? Sorry, old man.'

Ragland smiled.

'We won't need two hundred, but everything that can thin their numbers and make life uncomfortable for them is valuable. Now we need archers and shooters on the rooves on either side of the avenue. Start firing as soon as they are past the fire. Between the fire, the traps and the shooters, we should have them reeling. To top it off, we need people inside the buildings that line the street with any weapons they can get their hands on to clean up stragglers looking to flank hard on either side. Our objective, here, is to bottle-neck and hopefully do enough damage to turn them on their heels.'

'I need one person stationed about half a mile down the road. If I've judged it right, that army will be knocking on the gates within two hours, and we need a signal to know when they're close. Sang, can you do that?'

'Sure, what signal?'

Ragland pondered this for a moment.

'A gunshot?'

'No,' said Rahul. 'I have an old flare gun that will do the job.'

'Really? Okay. Even better.'

'What about you?' Simon enquired.

'I'll be here,' Ragland said, and pointed at a space between an upturned cup representing the school, and the line of items representing the buildings on Main Avenue. 'I will set myself across the way from the school and when we see the signal, I'll bait David and the others across onto Main Avenue and lead them towards the gate. If we time it right, they'll have no option but to join our fight.'

'I'm coming with you,' said Kit.

'No, it's too dangerous.'

'Exactly. If you bait them, what exactly is going to stop David or one of his goons from just shooting you?'

'I'll be able to-'

'Outrun a bullet? Put up a hand and stop it?' She crossed her arms. 'No, I'm coming with you, and I'll be sticking real close; he's mean and dumb, but even David's not stupid enough to risk shooting me.'

He saw there was no arguing with her, and the idea actually made sense.

'Fine, but you'll do everything I tell you when I tell you.'

'Sure thing, Gramps,' Kit said with a mischievous smile.

People whispered amongst themselves. Fingers pointed at the representation of Baker's Town. Ragland's eyes met with a few who looked vaguely confident, but most of them were just plain terrified. The heat of the fire at his back had done wonders to thaw out his joints.

He rubbed his hands together.

'We have to get moving now. Simon, get the fuel and set up the trap on the gate. Rahul, get the traps placed. Viola?'

'You called, dearest?'

Ragland smirked.

'Sure did. If anyone can rally people together for their positions on either side of the avenue, it'll be you. If you think he can be trusted, you should warn your brother Travis and tell him to watch for the flare. Only if you think he can be trusted not to spill his guts to David, though.'

She nodded gravely.

'Alright. Come on everyone, let's get to it, come on!'

Rahul's small house filled with the scutter of feet as people dispersed, readying themselves for what Ragland felt would be a bloody battle. Most of them didn't know it yet, but they were about to face the biggest test of their lives.

He looked back down at the representation of the town, checking to see if he had missed anything when Rahul handed him a 12-gauge shotgun that looked like it was fresh out of the box, along with a box of shells.

'Here,' he said. 'I've been saving it for a rainy day.' He paused. 'Or snowy.'

Kit sidled up to them and admired it.

'Wow, Rahul. This is, like, the prettiest thing I've seen. Did you give it a name?'

'No.'

Ragland pumped it just to ensure the chamber remained empty. He trusted Rahul, but he'd promised himself a long time ago to be almost religious with his gun etiquette.

'Very nice.'

'Hope you don't need it. But when you're done, I'd like her back—I'm attached to the old girl.'

Ragland chuckled.

'Thought you didn't name guns?'

'I don't. But this one has always been a "she".'

Kit nodded in approval.

'Nice.'

'Time to go, Kit.'

'Is it… as bad as you say?' Rahul asked.

Ragland nodded.

'Worse, Rahul, just do what you can.'

The blacksmith cracked his knuckles and gestured to his hammer leaning against the mantlepiece.

'I plan to.'

The sun, just beginning to peak over the horizon, was hidden behind heavy grey clouds. It aided Kit and Ragland as they skirted the edges of buildings, keeping to the shadows and out of sight. He had his bow over his shoulder and the shotgun in hand. Kit had her bow.

Before they had set out, Kit had urged Ragland

to have a mug of the coffee Simon brewed after they had decided on their course of action. He didn't have to be asked twice. The steaming black liquid worked its magic within a few minutes, and he felt energy wash away the ravages of the frozen night.

As they made their way up the main avenue, Ragland spotted their people on either side getting into place. They were quiet and efficient, and unless someone was specifically looking, they wouldn't notice anything out of the ordinary.

Ragland finally ushered Kit into the alley that cut through to Second Street and the vacant block opposite the school. In the shadows of the temporary shelters that were used to cover street stalls for the markets there every Saturday, they settled down to wait.

'I need you to know, things are going to get ugly,' he said to her.

'I know that old man. I'm still here, right?'

'Yes, but we might have to do some ugly things to get the rest of the town to follow.'

Kit took a deep breath.

'I'm not sitting back, idle, and letting Alex's sacrifice mean nothing. If that means we have to kill David or someone else I know, then so be it.'

'Good,' he nodded.

Ragland looked back to Main Avenue and spied shapes on the rooves of the stores and a couple of shadows in windows. The preparations seemed to be going smoothly. Kit leaned over to him.

'How are we going to lure-'

Almost as if she'd been overheard, the main doors to the schoolhouse opened and David stepped out with Travis and Blackbeard and another man whose name Ragland didn't know.

The men were talking quietly, their breath pluming in the cold morning air. Three doors down from where Ragland and Kit waited, a figure emerged from Jack's butcher shop. It was Viola. She stepped out onto the sidewalk and began walking confidently towards the four men.

She was within ten feet and had called out to her brother when a flare shot into the air, casting them all in a brief, crimson glow.

'What the hell…' he heard David say.

There was nothing for it. Now was the time. He turned to Kit.

'Okay. Let's make ourselves known. When I say run, we run. And we don't stop, got it?'

'Got it.'

With Kit following, Ragland stood up and strode into the middle of the road and bellowed at the top of his lungs.

'Should have made the knot tighter, David!'

Stunned, David, Travis, and the other two turned to the pair in the street, then David began fumbling for his pistol. Ragland raised his shotgun, and Kit her bow, an arrow nocked and at the ready.

The school door opened, and more of the townsfolk spilled out, all holding weapons and curious about the commotion. The flare faded out and Ragland fancied he heard roars and yells on the wind.

'Maybe you best finish the job!' Ragland called and pumped a shell into the chamber before firing over their heads.

David and the rest ducked for cover, some scrambling back inside. He saw Viola rush to Travis and whisper something harshly in his ear. There was no time to wait for his response.

'Run, Kit!' Ragland yelled and bolted into the alley with Kit hot on his heels.

'After them!' roared David.

CHAPTER 34

Chests heaving, and legs and arms pumping, Kit and Ragland tore through to Main Avenue. Kit's idea to stay close had been a good one; even David wasn't willing to take a shot for risk of hitting her. They would chase until they could get their hands on them. Ragland just had to hope that by that time, the horde would be on their way to the gate.

He needn't have worried. He heard the roaring and baying of the mad army a second before Kit called, 'They're already here!'

They rounded the final bend to the gate and in the distance, he saw Charlie and Rufus sending arrow after arrow into the baying crowd beyond the gate. Despite their best efforts, the gates were bulging inwards. Large pieces of it had been hacked away by axes, and in the jagged holes feral Zoms tried to claw their way through while their masters continued to work at the gate.

Clint, the mild-mannered teacher, came from nowhere and began hacking with a tomahawk at the scrawny arms reaching through the gaps. He was screaming with anger and had some success, leaving the ground around him splatted with blood and fingers and hands until a plank above him broke inward and a Zom, wild with hunger, squeezed through, landing on Clint's shoulders and tearing out his throat with a vicious jerk of its head.

Blood spurted into the air as the big man fell to his knees, the cannibal still on him, its mouth full of flesh.

'No!' Kit cried, sending an arrow clean through the air and into the cannibal's flank, eliciting a squeal of agony.

'Stop now!' yelled a voice behind them followed by a loud gunshot.

Ragland put his hands up and with Kit, turned as David and his enormous number of followers stalked towards them, clearly unaware of what was just around the bend, although, some looked curiously at each other trying to work out what the din coming from the gate meant.

Only a few had guns. If he didn't resolve this quickly his worse fears had come true and all of them would be fodder for what was about to come through the gate.

'They're here! Can't you hear?' Ragland roared, and began walking backwards towards the gate, as they rushed towards him.

Finally, in sight of the gate the group halted.

'Oh my god!' A woman screamed, pointing at the dying teacher.

'You let this happen David! But it's up to you all

now to fight.'

The blood had drained from David's face, and he flinched as an almighty blow impacted the gate. It was followed quickly by another, as a Zom slithered through the widening gap and bounded on all fours towards Ragland and Kit.

Kit's scream gave Ragland enough time to whirl around and fire the shotgun. It took the Zom in the throat, blowing its head clean off, the carcass crumpling into a heap at his feet, as the head rolled across the road coming to rest at David's feet.

One of the men vomited violently as their leader's mouth hung open.

'Believe us now?!'

'I...' he stuttered. 'This can't...'

Before he could get another word out another boom rocked the gate, this time sending what was left of the heavy doors crashing inward.

The gates of Baker's Town were breached and leading the charge into the town were the feral, deliberately starved Zoms.

'Now!' roared Simon.

'Move back!' Ragland shouted, as he and Kit ran back towards their erstwhile pursuers.

David and those of his group that hadn't yet run saw what was happening as Simon, Charlie and Rufus began tipping buckets of fuel and oil off the wall and over the invaders, dousing a dozen or more below.

The cannibals coughed, choked, and staggered

away as Simon dropped a wad of burning cloth onto the soaked ground under the archway.

With a whump, flames shot up and engulfed them all, pursuing the ones not immediately consumed like a vengeful monster. The air was filled with screams and the stench of burning flesh.

All too soon the flames died down and more cannibals of both types replaced the ones who had been neutralized.

'Shit!' Kit screamed and began firing her arrows.

'*Fight*!' Ragland cried at the top of his lungs and charged forward, blowing a hole through the chest of a cannibal making a beeline for Kit.

Another, this one tall and carrying a rifle, ran at him while raising the weapon, but Ragland beat him to the shot, blowing out his kneecap and smashing the butt of his shotgun into his face as he fell.

He had barely swung around when something heavy crashed into him from behind, knocking him to the ground and the air from his lungs.

'*Meat*!' screamed his scrawny but powerful assailant, his rotten breath warm and foul on Ragland's face.

It was all he could do to keep the man's serrated teeth from his neck as he wrestled fruitlessly, trying to free the shotgun.

His attacker smiled, as he slowly won the tussle, his teeth inching closer to Ragland's vulnerable throat when suddenly a piece of metal sprouted from his mouth, then vanished just as quickly. The cannibal gurgled then collapsed on top of him.

Ragland groaned, rolled the body off him, and stood up to discover a pale David holding a long bloody knife in his hand.

'Thank you...'

David didn't answer, he was now apparently occupied with a singular goal, and just turned to shoot and cut at more cannibals as they poured into the town. More fights were breaking out around him as David's followers, including Blackbeard and Travis, joined the fight for their town, mowing down cannibals with their guns.

To his left, he heard the sharp snap of metal followed by a horrible scream, and turned to see a cannibal writhing on the ground, clutching the stump of their leg, the remains, from the shin down, clamped in a bear trap.

A gore-covered Rahul appeared next to him, obliterating the face of another Zom with his big hammer before he pointed to the rooftops.

Ragland followed his gaze and saw Viola and a line of others, even Odin, readying their arrows.

It was time for the third prong of their defense.

'Fall back! Fall back!'

The townsfolk turned to run. Ragland turned to make sure they had everyone, and saw Charlie, Rufus and Simon sprinting from the shadows after coming back down the ladders. The flow of cannibals had slowed as they became more circumspect about the danger inside the gates, and the little group were almost to him, Simon in front, followed by Charlie and Rufus ten feet behind. The boys were whooping, clearly invigorated by the fight and their part in it when Rufus tripped over the arm of a charred corpse.

Charlie ran on before he realized then turned back.

'No!' Ragland screamed. 'Keep going. I'll get him!'

Charlie didn't listen, running back and reaching down for Rufus who looked up thankfully and took his hand. The expression on his face didn't change when the arrow thudded into the back of his skull.

Charlie screamed as his dead friend's hand slipped from his and Ragland let off a shot in the direction the arrow had come from. He reached Charlie and grabbed him by the scruff of the neck.

The hysterical kid fought him and tried to get Rufus up. Ragland's heart sank. He had anticipated casualties but seeing the familiar face of one so young dead on the ground shook him to the core.

'Charlie!' he shouted, tugging him.

The young boy, his face stained with tears, jerked himself away eventually, as another arrow whizzed by. Ragland pulled him along and they retreated up the up the avenue, weaving side to side to make themselves less of a target

CHAPTER 35

Ragland, Charlie, Kit, and a handful of others broke into an abandoned store, still a full block and fifty yards short of the school, and began shooting through windows at the cannibals running up the avenue.

The sight unnerved him, but it was a hundred times worse for the Baker's Town natives. Terror and the vigorous desperation to survive was etched on their faces but out in the streets, the cannibals armed and in survival gear—the norms who egged on the Zoms—walked with a fearlessness that felt inhuman. Even as volleys of arrows from the rooftops cut their numbers down, they continued on.

Charlie echoed his thoughts.

'They... they keep coming,' he whimpered. 'They're not human.'

'They are,' Ragland replied, as he blew away a Zom who strayed too near to the building. 'And they die like humans.'

There was a scream from a building opposite as a group of Norms kicked down the door. Kit took one with an arrow between the shoulder blades but the other three entered and more screams ensued.

A body crashed to the road and lay still on the sidewalk like a ragdoll, its head at an unnatural angle. It was Jenny, the archivist. There were cries of horror from the people around him.

Ragland turned to Kit who was ghostly pale, her eyes furtive and wild. The death of Jenny inspired fierce gunfire from the other locals on the rooftops and a handful still on the street including David and Rahul. The blacksmith swung his hammer like a demon, caving in the heads of any dumb or careless enough to come within range.

Momentarily the enemy was pushed back.

'We have to get to the school. Are you all ready?'

Most of them nodded.

'Then let's go. Keep low. Follow me.'

At the back of the store, he knocked open the door and the small band fled down the back alleyway to a vacant lot that was now used as a marketplace each Saturday.

They sheltered under the rickety canvas-covered stalls while Ragland surveyed their next move.

A lone Zom cannibal appeared ahead, and Ragland dropped it with an arrow into the eye. No more appeared.

'Go!'

Ragland led the way, plucking the arrow from the corpse as he went, and nocking it again as they emerged on Second Street. The school was now just a fifty-yard sprint.

'I… I don't think… I can…'

Ragland turned to see one of the younger townsfolk had fallen to his knees. He didn't recognize the man who stared out across the open street toward the school.

Kit put a hand on his shoulder.

'Callum. You can do this. Think about Mellissa. Think about your friends, Casey and Fred. They're all there, waiting for you…'

In the distance a shrill scream interrupted her, followed quickly by a burst of gunfire. The man flinched and shot to his feet, ready to flee.

'No… I…'

Kit slapped him hard across the cheek.

'Pull it together!'

The young man put a hand on his cheek and looked at her with wide eyes. Finally, he nodded, and Kit turned to Ragland.

'Let's do this.'

Ragland nodded.

'When I move, follow me and stay low.'

The group ran from under the shelter and across the open tarmac, their feet crunching on a scum of dirty snow. There were yells and screeches behind them. They'd been spotted and the chase was on.

Kit and Ragland paused to loose a few arrows

at the cannibals emerging from the abandoned marketplace they'd just left.

'Run!' Ragland urged, the schoolhouse now just a clear run across the square.

Battle cries behind them elicited screams and swearing from their small group and they broke formation and scattered, their sole destination the school.

Ragland was ahead next to Charlie, with Kit just behind them. The rest lagged behind, unable to keep up. As he flew over the icy lawn, Ragland turned his shoulder and charged into the closed doors, knocking them open with a tremendous crash.

He was met by the stunned expressions and raised weapons of the townsfolk inside.

'Wait! It's us. Get ready to barricade this door.'

Ragland turned and ushered everyone through, yelling encouragement. Callum was the straggler of the group and a good five paces behind the next to last, but his terrified face relaxed when he began to climb the steps to Ragland.

There was a crack of gunfire from further down the street and suddenly Callum lurched, clawing the air and stumbling through the doorway and into Ragland's arms.

His dead weight took them both to the floor. Screams and shrieks grew louder, and more gunfire blew splinters from the wall around the doorway.

'The doors!' Ragland screamed, pushing Callum off and dragging him into the corridor.

Simon and Kit slammed the doors shut while Jack and Erica slid a heavy side table against it. It wouldn't hold forever, but it would buy them time. Ragland faced his fellow survivors, all worn and exhausted.

Kit went to Callum and put two fingers against his throat before shaking her head. Someone passed her a shirt, which she placed over his face.

'What now?' Simon asked.

'We try and break down their numbers. Everyone with a bow, take to the top-floor windows and give them hell. Anyone else with a working gun, move desks out into the corridors for cover and stand your ground. Only fire when you have a clear shot.'

'And us?' Simon asked, raising the wood axe in his hand.

'When they come through, we'll engage them at close quarters.'

As if on cue, thunderous and persistent banging on the doors began.

There was a commotion at the rear end of the corridor and everyone tensed, Ragland stepping forward with his shotgun ready.

'It's just us!'

It was Marly and David, the latter coated in blood. Kit rushed forward and hugged Marly, who was holding her trusty shotgun.

'How..?'

Marly shot David a look that said there'd be a reckoning at some point.

'David let me out. No time for the whys and wherefores, now. What's the situation here, Ragland?'

'Guns on the lower floors. Archers in the top windows. Anyone with a melee weapon will hold back and assist with barricades and wounded. Until, of course, we all have to get our hands dirty. What about the back doors?'

David cleared his throat, his pride all but gone.

'Barricaded.'

'Great,' Charlie said from behind Ragland, his eyes on the front doors that trembled with heavy blows and had begun to buckle inward. 'So we're trapped?'

'This is our best bet,' said Ragland. 'Out in the open, they can separate us like cattle. It might have been different if we'd prepared, but…' He left the thought unspoken.

Marly looked down sadly at Callum's body and then to Ragland.

'I'm sorry.'

Ragland locked his eyes on her.

'Too late for regrets now. Let's just do what needs to be done and hopefully you'll have some pieces of this town left to put back together.'

'Right,' Marly said taking the hit on the chin. He knew it had stung, but she had the stern, narrowed look of someone keen to rectify her mistakes. So did David.

Where's Rahul?'

'I tried to bring him with me,' said David. 'But he's in some sort of battle lust trance. Last I saw he was charging towards the gate.'

Behind them, there was a loud crack and the doors pushed inwards a little. There was a short reprieve accompanied by thuds and thunks and the screams of the enemy as a volley of arrows from the top windows rained down on the cannibals trying to knock the doors open.

A burst of automatic gunfire put an end to the reprieve.

'Break down that fucking door!' roared a commanding voice. The doors bulged, finally exploding inwards, sending the table that had been pushed against it and other debris flying. Feral Zom cannibals scampered over the debris and launched themselves at the defenders.

Simon's axe met the first one, splitting the creature's head straight down to the neck. The cannibal fell and then they were all fighting for their lives.

CHAPTER 36

Ragland's face and beard were hot and wet with blood minutes later as he surveyed the scene. They had been forced deep into the corridor but had held off the onslaught. Around them and all the way to the front door, the floor was littered with the corpses of the feral shock troops.

While their swarming attack had been effective in the open, the Zoms had not been so effective against a determined well-armed enemy in confined spaces.

Bent over and heaving air into his lungs, he evaluated the other survivors and shared a brief look with Kit, who looked as tired as him and the rest.

The onyx necklace had been shaken free of her shirt during the struggles and the sight of it gave him strength.

'If you have any ammo left, reload!' he called, but a shadow darkened the doorway as he jammed two more shells into his gun.

Ragland turned and recognized the cannibal leader holding a military rifle loosely in one hand. His stance was non-threatening.

'Ahh the one that got away,' said the leader, in a sing-song voice.

Ragland held up his hand to indicate his group should hold fire—he was curious to hear what he had to say. Charlie missed the signal or ignored it and let an arrow loose from the stairway to their left. It embedded itself in the door frame barely eight inches from the cannibal leader's head.

He looked at the arrow and smiled.

'Tsk, tsk. I come to parley, and you shoot at me?'

Ragland slowly raised his shotgun until it was pointing at the cannibal's belly.

'Say your piece then.'

'Alright. Here's my offer. If you surrender now, I'll let the women and children live. You've lost one way or the other, but at least this way there'll be some survivors and we won't have to spend weeks plucking bullets from carcasses.'

Ragland replied by pumping his shotgun. Without taking his eyes off the leader he addressed the people behind him.

'Fall back down the corridor. To the gymnasium. I'll be right behind you-'

'No, Ragland. I don't think so,' David said, stepping up on his right. Simon, too, stepped up on his left, axe in one hand and a small snub-nosed pistol in the other.

'Yep. No can do,' he agreed. 'He'll have to come through all of us.'

Ragland didn't have time to argue, let alone ask the Canadian where the hell he'd gotten that pistol.

'Marly, Kit, take the others. Hold the gymnasium!'

'Ragland, we're not going-'

'Do it!' he yelled without looking back, his attention focused on the leader.

A gentle hand fell on his shoulder. It was Marly.

'Don't die for my mistakes, Joshua.'

Her use of his first name shocked him; it felt personal.

'I won't,' he said softly. 'Keep them safe.'

The leader laughed at the display of affection and calm words. Beneath his heavy brow, his eyes glinted with aggression and hunger for death. This man was ready to kill.

So was Ragland.

The cannibal nodded to someone just out of sight and raised his weapon.

'Fire!'

The corridor descended into chaos as bullets and arrows ripped through the space. Pulverized wood and plaster flew from the walls and ceiling. Ragland crouched behind a stack of overturned lockers. Simon and David did the same on the other side. The leader scurried out of the doorway after unleashing a volley of bullets, the first time Ragland had seen him show any urgency.

'I'm out,' called Simon. And others responded in kind. The drifter began to reload but knew a sustained push by the cannibals would probably overwhelm them.

Ragland heard screams of *attack* and *meat* outside as he pumped the shotgun. Swarms of armed cannibal men and women, a mix of Zoms and Norms, rushed in through the door.

'Retreat!' Ragland yelled as he and David fired into the frontrunners.

Four cannibals went down, slowing the others. David walked backwards, shooting, and following his retreating people.

'Hold the big one for me!' the booming voice of the leader called as he entered the hallway, his rifle at his shoulder.

David put down two more, but Ragland needed to reload.

'Keep going,' he called to David, as a bullet whizzed by his head.

He ran through the open doorway to his left. It was Erica's classroom. He shut and locked the door and rested his back against it as he pulled two more shells from the rapidly dwindling supply in his pocket.

Freshly reloaded, he pumped the shotgun and turned to face the small square window in the door. The leader was leering in at him. They fired simultaneously. The cannibal's round pierced the door in a spray of splinters and hit him in the thigh, while his blasted a large hole in the door catching the leader in the upper right arm.

Ragland reeled back, clutching his thigh as the door was kicked in. Another round hit him in the shoulder. He fell back onto a kid's desk as his shotgun clattered to the timber floor.

The drifter pushed against the desk and turned, wincing in pain as he put weight on his wounded leg, but he was determined to stand tall as he faced death.

The pentagram carved into the leader's forehead stood out starkly against his pale, pained face. His right arm was a bloody mess, but he had switched the rifle to his left and held it one handed, finger on the trigger. Ragland stared defiantly at the cannibal, who forced a smile as he aimed the barrel of the weapon at his face.

The dry click of the empty magazine saw the smile fade as quickly as it had appeared and with the reprieve, Ragland lunged at him.

The cannibal leader could do little to avoid Ragland, but managed to raise his knee and bury it into his side, knocking the wind out of him.

They fell to the floor with the leader managing to roll on top of Ragland, bringing his rifle around and jamming the still warm barrel against his throat, pressing it down with his good hand and the elbow of his mangled arm. Blood splattered Ragland as he attempted to push the weapon off his throat with his good arm.

It was no use. The cannibal had the

ascendency and his two wounds meant Ragland didn't have the strength to fight him off. Black motes began to swim in his vision as his eyeballs bulged. The gunmetal slowly crushed his larynx.

The leader's eyes glared at him, ravenous and determined, his bloodstained, sharpened teeth bared by his rictus sneer.

'Oh yes,' said the cannibal as he saw the light in his victim's eyes begin to fade. 'I'm going to enjoy eating your girl. The one you care for. So young. So lean. She'll be a meal to savor.'

Rage ignited in Ragland's fading consciousness.

With a supreme effort he rolled his hips, slightly unbalancing the cannibal and smashed his knee up between his legs. The leader screamed and the pressure on his throat eased. Seizing the moment, Ragland reached up, put a big hand over the back of the cannibal's head and pulled it down as he propelled his own head upward, his forehead savagely meeting it.

The cannibal's nose shattered with a loud crunch, and he fell off Ragland clutching his face, blood pouring through his fingers. The drifter clambered to his feet, his head reeling, and took a moment to steady himself.

Too late, the dazed cannibal grasped the threat of the man standing over him, and he used his good arm to try and get up but slipped on his own blood, falling to his side and holding up a hand for mercy.

'No mercy for you...' grated Ragland, before kicking the cannibal in the jaw with his steel-capped boot.

The gargled scream through his broken jaw was surprisingly loud and as he rolled away, clutching his ruined face. Ragland picked up the rifle, gripped it by the barrel, and smashed the stock over the back of the leader's skull.

The man collapsed face first into the floor, moaning. Ragland struck him again. The moaning stopped. Then again and again and again until the man's head was an unrecognizable, pulpy mess.

Ragland stopped finally, then leaned on the bloody rifle heaving deep breaths, wiping sweat and blood from his eyes. Distant screams and a gunshot sent a shot of adrenaline through him.

'Kit...'

Unarmed except for his knife, drained of energy, and wounded, Ragland staggered down the blood-soaked corridor to the rear of the school and the gymnasium. Bodies and parts were strewn everywhere, most of the dead were cannibals but a well of sadness opened when he saw the butcher, Jack, dead with a meat cleaver embedded in his chest. Next to him lay a girl he didn't recognize missing an arm.

Bastards...

The heavy double doors to the gymnasium were closed, and a skinny cannibal, naked from the waist up and with a badly broken leg, was struggling to push them open.

Ragland stepped up to him, put the knife against the back of his neck, and slid it between the wretch's C3 and C4 vertebrae. He fell to the floor without so much as a sigh and the drifter put his good shoulder against the doors and pushed, struggling to move the dead weight behind it.

He fell through the opening onto the dead bodies of the fallen cannibals and locals, then struggled to his feet as he took in the scene before him.

Up in the bleachers he saw Viola, her face drained and holding her bloody side. Next to her, David aimed at the small crowd on the floor of the gym trying to get a clear shot.

Ragland followed his gaze and saw a stunning sight. It was the giant cannibal whose twin he'd killed barely two weeks before. He was the eye of a storm. The bodies of townspeople and other cannibals alike lay around him like wheat that had been scythed. In one hand he wielded a baseball bat wrapped tightly in barbed wire, in the other an axe.

The cannibal was surrounded but had evened the odds rapidly. Near the basketball hoop, Ragland spied Kit, who like David was trying to get a shot with what looked to be her last arrow. Closer in was Marly, who swung an inadequate broomstick bravely but ineffectually. Simon,

Charlie, Blackbeard and several others harried the giant with handheld weapons.

'Give me a shot!' Kit yelled, but the remaining defenders darting this way and that to stay out of his long reach meant it was all but impossible.

Simon, to the giant's left, ducked beneath a swinging blow of his axe and lunged, burying his own small axe into the giant's left arm. The cannibal howled and swung the bat at the already retreating cook, striking him hard in the chest and sending him soaring and crashing into the front row seats.

'No!' Ragland cried.

Everyone froze and looked over at him as his wounded leg gave way. The cannibal shot him a shark's grin.

'Ahh, it's you again. Fight gone out of you, hey? I will enjoy this...'

The words weren't quite out of his mouth when Blackbeard, taking advantage of the distraction, darted in, slashing his knife at the cannibal's lower back.

The cannibal dodged it and turned, and with a downward swing of his axe cleaved David's lieutenant's head open to the bridge of his nose. The big Baker's Town local collapsed to the floor, his dead weight pulling the axe handle from the giant's grip.

Blackbeard's gruesome sacrifice gave Kit the opening she needed, and she released her arrow. It whistled through the air and struck the cannibal just below his left shoulder blade. He shrieked and spun around, pawing at the arrow as he looked for his tormentor.

He saw Kit and forgot about the arrow.

'You,' he growled. 'I'll eat you alive…'

Kit let her bow fall from her shoulder and pulled a knife from her boot as he charged. Marly tried to block him but he palmed her away, sending her hard onto her back and skidding over the polished floorboards, now slick with blood.

'Kit!' Ragland gasped, watching on helplessly.

The giant swung the deadly bat in a big, overhanded arc, but the nimble girl evaded it, stepping lightly to the side. The giant swung again, and she ducked away, the base of the bat missing her face by a mere inch.

David attempted another shot from the bleachers but missed and the giant swung again, and again, becoming frustrated at the elusive girl. Clearly tiring with the effort, Ragland saw blood dripping from his mouth and knew the arrow deep in his back had almost certainly pierced a lung.

Then, with a final lunge, Kit ducked under another wild swing of the bat and with a move Ragland had shown her, stepped in close to his unprotected flank and buried her knife to the hilt just under the giant's rib cage.

Like quickfire, she pulled it free and danced away, slicing his thigh as she went. David, Marly,

Ragland, and the rest watched in awe as the gigantic cannibal fell to one knee, clutching the open wound in his belly.

He lifted the bat one more time and swung weakly at his tiny tormentor. He missed and as he tried to catch his balance, Kit darted in and with a wicked, full-armed swing, sliced the man's throat open.

Kit rolled away from him as he dropped the bat and clutched at the mortal wound, the blood pouring from the wide gash and already pooling in a red lake beneath him. Five seconds later, like a felled oak, he crashed face first onto the floor and didn't move again.

Kit stood panting, her hands shaking as the adrenaline began to wear off, and looked over to the drifter where he lay prone on the bodies of the dead.

'Ragland!' she cried and ran towards him.

She was only three feet away when a hand surfaced from the pile of bodies and grabbed her ankle. Her mouth was a perfect 'O' of surprise as she fell, and the concealed cannibal lunged and grabbed her hair, ripping her head back to expose her throat.

Ragland saw the glint of a blade in its hand...

Kit flinched, but suddenly the cannibal squawked briefly and fell onto her, his eyes lifeless. There was an arrow embedded in the back of his skull. Confused, she turned to the doors as did the quickly fading Ragland and the rest of the survivors.

Alex, one side of his scalp and face coated in blood but looking as alive as she could ever remember, lowered his bow and looked around, slowly taking in the carnage.

'Alex! Kit screamed as she clambered out from under the cannibal and rushed over to him, nearly knocking him off his feet.

'Did I miss much?' he said, smiling and rubbing her back.

'A whole lot,' she said, pulling away and looking into his face. 'But I can't fault your timing.'

Ragland grinned through the pain; as far as surprised went, it didn't get much better than Alex appearing alive and well in time to save his love. He began to climb to his feet again when a wave of nausea knocked him back on his haunches.

'Shit! Ragland!'

Kit, with Alex trailing her, rushed over to him.

She knelt at Ragland's side, quickly inspecting his wounds.

'We need to find Claire!' she cried. 'He's been shot!'

'I saw her down the street, she and a few others are helping the wounded.'

'The cannibals?' Ragland gasped.

'Dead or fleeing. The fight went out of them when one came out screaming about the leader being dead.'

Ragland nodded.

'I'll get Claire,' he said, and gently squeezed Ragland's shoulder. 'It's good to see you again, old man.'

His mouth opened to speak, but instead his eyeballs rolled up in his head.

'He's passed out, hurry!' said Kit.

Ragland drifted out of unconsciousness once. The world was swaying gently, and Claire's beautiful face hovered above his.

'Well done, Cowboy. We've got you now,' she said with a smile, before everything faded to black again.

CHAPTER 37

Ragland sat on the wooden porch outside Marly's house, soaking in the afternoon sun. It was a clear day, but the faint smell of smoke tickled his nostrils. He ached all over and the bandages over and around his wounds pinched.

Both hands were wrapped tight around a mug of coffee, and he sipped the scalding black liquid gingerly.

Footsteps creaked behind him.

'Morning, sunshine. Touch and go yesterday. How're you feeling now?'

Marly sat down beside Ragland on the bench and took a sip of her own coffee.

'You reckon this is the last of Simon's batch?' Ragland asked, deflecting.

'Probably,' she said.

'Shame. How is he?'

'Bruised and punctured. Two broken ribs according to Claire, and he needed some stitches where the barbed wire tore his skin.'

Ragland shook his head.

'Must be a tough bastard; that would have

killed a lesser man. What about you? That was quite the hit you took?'

Marly lifted a thigh and patted her rump.

'Lucky, I have plenty of padding. Just a bump on my head.'

This drew a chuckle from Ragland, and he realized it was the first time he'd laughed in at least a week.

The two settled into an easy silence. After a few minutes Marly put a hand on his leg.

'I owe you… *we* owe you a debt Ragland. And an apology. You were right all along, and I was stupid to think we could negotiate our way out of a fight. We'll never be able to repay you.'

He shook his head.

'No need.'

'I mean it. I want to repay you.'

He sighed and looked down into the black liquid as he swirled it gently.

'Just rebuild. Live like you have been but be ready. We don't live in an ideal world anymore, no matter how much time goes by and makes you think its okay. There's death around every corner. You need to lead your people through it and not bury your head in the sand.'

'Well, the thing is,' she said. 'I don't see the town accepting me as leader again. They followed me all these years, put their lives in my hands, but my failure to see the danger of the cannibals, and letting David pull the wool over my eyes, means I lost their faith. David agreed to step down so there can be another, proper vote in a month, but how can I rebuild that trust before then?'

'One day at a time.'

He took a deeper swig of his coffee, turned, and was shocked to see tears falling down the Mayor's face.

'I was so desperate to believe the world outside didn't exist anymore...'

'Then I came knocking to remind you,' Ragland replied grimly. 'Don't blame yourself for wishing the world a better place. What's done is done.'

'I suppose.'

'They won't forgive quickly, nor will they forget, but if you're patient and follow your common sense you'll win them back.'

Marly wiped her face with the back of her sleeve.

'I probably don't deserve it, but I'll try. I believe in Baker's Town.'

'Good.'

They sat and talked until well after their coffee was finished. Marly told him about the clean up they'd started yesterday, piling the cannibal corpses and burning them through the night.

'What about the dead townsfolk?'

Marly's eyes misted again.

'They'll be buried over the next few days and then we're having a memorial for everyone in a week.'

Ragland nodded then rose slowly, using the crutch Rahul had fashioned him for his recuperation.

'Thanks again for having me. Your place sure beats the Creaky as a recovery room. I'm going to lay down again, doctor's orders you know?'

Marly laughed gently.

'Take all the time you need, I'm not kicking you out ever again.'

His shoulder healed more quickly than his thigh, but within a week, he was able to walk without the crutch and was only left with a slight limp.

'You're lucky the bullet flattened out when it passed through the door. It was messy but stopped short of bone and nerves,' Claire said, doing a final check of the leg wound which had crusted over nicely. He had made his way over to her office without the crutch. 'You're also lucky that the bullet to the shoulder went straight through the deltoid. Only missed your joint by a matter of half an inch.'

'Yep, lucky me…' he said wryly.

She laughed and turned away to throw the old dressings in the trash can.

'So, what are your plans?' she asked quietly, still facing away from him.

He didn't answer for a few beats, suddenly feeling like an awkward teenager.

'I guess, if you give me the go ahead, I'll head

out day after tomorrow.'

Her shoulders were stiff as she turned back around.

'Oh, sure. You're good to go if that's what you want.'

He didn't know how to read her. Her tone was offended but her words were encouraging.

'Okay, good. Claire-'

'Yep, good. Okay, well I have stuff to do.'

He shook his head puzzled.

'Okay, I guess I'll see you later.'

'Maybe,' she said flatly.

Odin, alongside David—who seemed to have had a genuine turnaround—fashioned a series of crosses to mark those who had fallen in defense of Baker's Town. There were too many for the small graveyard. Too many for such a small town to have to bear.

Rahul melted down scrap metal and cast nameplates for every single cross and when it was all done, Ragland walked the rows with all the townsfolk on the day of the memorial.

Marly's eulogy mentioned every one of the dead by name. She was eloquent and passionate, and there wasn't a dry eye in the house by the time she'd finished. Ragland knew with that one speech, she'd done a lot to restore the faith she had been certain was gone forever.

There was a large outdoor celebration afterwards. Beer and moonshine flowed but

Ragland made his way out of the warmth and light to walk the empty streets.

With his thick coat drawn tight, Ragland found the florist Fred sweeping snow from the door. The man nodded, but there was no smile forthcoming.

'I'm leaving tomorrow,' he said. 'I wanted to ask how you were.'

Fred shrugged, his gaze frozen on a patch of the road next to Ragland.

'Not great. Casey's gone. She was my world. I don't...' He stopped and his eyes welled up.

Ragland put a hand on the man's shoulder.

'I'm sorry for your loss, Fred. Whatever you do, don't stop what you have here. The flowers. We all need that something extra to give our lives color again, and you and Casey brought a lot of color to this town. Not just with flowers.'

'Yeah, you're right,' Fred said, wiping his eyes. 'So, where're you headed after? I don't suppose you care to stay behind?'

'No,' Ragland replied. 'My place is on the road.'

'Does it have to be? I know a certain someone who I suspect would like to see you stay...'

Ragland looked at him curiously.

'Maybe so,' he said gruffly, 'but Kit will forget me after a while. She's young.'

'Oh, it wasn't Kit I was talking about. Never mind me, I'm just being an old gossip. Have a good night.'

With that he turned around and headed back

inside, leaving Ragland with an eyebrow raised, staring after him.

After the discussion, Ragland made his way back to the noise of the celebrations. The question of Claire was playing on his mind, and he wasn't comfortable leaving the next morning on the note they'd finished on. Was it her that Fred had been referring to?

The first group he saw was a bunch of familiar faces; the ones he'd begun to think of as the leadership group of the town—a sore and sorry Simon, Kit and Alex, Marly and Rahul. Missing was Claire, Viola, still recovering at home from a shallow stab wound, and thankfully, David. Ragland wasn't ready to forgive past transgressions as easily as some of the others.

The group was in good spirits, fueled somewhat, he suspected, by alcohol.

'Joshua!' Marly called. 'Come join us.'

Still not in the mood for partying, he reluctantly joined them and accepted the tankard of beer that was thrust into his hand.

'Go on Alex. Tell us the end of the story!'

'Well, you kind of know the rest, I rode in on a white horse and saved the damsel in distress!'

There was laughter all around, but Kit who had observed Ragland's troubled face by the firelight elbowed him.

'Finish it properly.'

Alex sobered.

'Sure. Well, I told you how they captured me. I got clubbed over the head. When I woke up, I was slung over the back of a horse, and we were on the move. I guess I'm lucky they were after you almost right away, it meant they didn't have time to make a meal out of me.

'When they attacked, they left me near the rear tied to a tree. Stupid them, they didn't save any for a second wave, they just went all in. Cocky, I guess. It took me an age, but finally I worked my way out of the ropes and freed myself.

'The fighting was mostly done by then. Rahul was finishing off the last few with his big hammer... boy, what a sight! How many did you get Rahul?'

The Smith shrugged, a sheepish look on his face.

'Twenty-three.'

Alex whistled.

'Anyway, it was mostly done by the time I arrived, and Claire had already started helping the wounded. They sent me onto the school where... well, you know the rest.'

They fell into easy chat after that, the swapping of war stories essential to processing the trauma they'd all suffered.

'So,' said Marly, finally. 'It's late and I think it's time we wrapped this up. Joshua, are you sure you won't stay?'

He stared into the fire for nearly a full minute

as their eyes fell on him.

'You aren't stroking out on me are you, Gramps?' asked Kit.

He smiled.

'No. Thanks for the offer, but I'll be moving on tomorrow and this time it'll be for good.'

There was movement beyond the circle of the fire and Ragland looked up in time to see Claire walking away.

'Excuse me,' he mumbled and shot up from the log, heading after her.

'Claire! Wait, please!' he called, running to catch up to her.

She stopped but didn't turn around until he put a hand on her upper arm.

'So even after all this, you're still going?' she asked.

He nodded. Then did something that shocked him as much as it did her. He pulled her into an embrace and kissed her. Even more surprising, she kissed him back.

Long absent feelings rose inside him as they kissed and when they finally parted, both panting for breath he leaned his forehead against hers.

'Come with me...'

She pushed him gently away so she could look into his eyes.

'You know I can't.'

'Why?'

'I'm the town medic. The only one qualified.

You stay.'

'I can't. I'm a rambling man, Claire. I need to keep moving but I want you by my side.'

In a stalemate, they stared at each other before Claire finally spoke.

'Tell you what. You go and ramble around the countryside. But I want you to come back in a year. In the meantime, I'll train someone up. Kit has expressed an interest, so maybe her. That'll give us both a year to think about what we want. If you are tired of your wandering and still want me, you stay. If you aren't tired of it and I still want you, *and* I have someone to take over, I'll come with you. If you don't come back, well I guess I'll have my answer.'

He grinned like a schoolboy who just found out his crush likes him.

'Deal,' he said, thrusting out his hand.

Claire, also smiling, batted his hand away and pulled him in for another kiss.

Marly made Ragland a breakfast of bacon, eggs and toast and a steaming mug of black coffee.

'That really is the last of Simon's supply, so think yourself lucky.'

He raised his mug.

'You didn't need to do this but thank you.'

'It's nothing. Where did you race off to last night? And what time did you get in?' she asked, a glint in her eyes.

He shrugged, a coy smile on his face.

'Fair enough.'

Marly cleaned up the breakfast dishes as he went upstairs to collect his pack and weapons.

'I'll see you to the door, I won't come and see you off, too much to do,' she said quietly.

Ragland paused on the doorstep, then turned and drew Marly into a hug.

'Take care Marly.'

'You too old man,' she said gruffly, her eyes glistening. 'Drop in if you're ever in the neighborhood.'

'I might just do that,' he said. 'So long.'

She closed the door and he sighed gently.

He was halfway to the gate when a familiar figure emerged from a side street. It was David leading his horse. He turned when he saw Ragland and headed his way.

He hadn't seen much of his nemesis since the battle. He stopped and waited, every nerve in his body jangling, ready to meet any aggression with extreme prejudice.

David walked right up to him but instead of aggression, he offered the reins of his horse to him. Ragland, his hands still by his side, raised both eyebrows.

'I want you to have her,' the hunter said. 'As payment for… for all the trouble I caused you.'

'I don't need a horse.'

'Need? Probably not. But she'll make your life a hell of a lot easier.' He shook the reins. 'Please, no tricks. She's yours, saddle and all, my way of saying sorry.'

Ragland had a horse briefly in the second year of the After Days, and it had certainly made traveling a lot easier and faster. He'd been on the lookout for one ever since but had only come across wild ones, and he was no horse breaker.

He weighed up the man in front of him, and decided on this occasion at least, he was being genuine. Ragland was a man who might forgive eventually, but he certainly didn't forget. He took the reins and nodded.

'I'll take payment, but not the apology.' he said. 'Some things can't be made right with a sorry.' He began to lead the horse away, calling over his shoulder as he went. 'What's her name?'

'Reliable.'

'Well David, Reliable and I'll be back in a year. In the meantime, make things right with Marly... I don't want to have to kill you.'

He waited for a smart ass reply from David that didn't come. The Baker's Town local just stared after him, his face devoid of expression.

At the gate, Ragland was provided with one last surprise. Nearly the whole town was congregated and clapping as he led Reliable down the last stretch of avenue to the gates that had been freshly repaired by Rahul, Charlie and a few other willing hands.

Ragland shook his head, blushing at the fuss,

but waved anyway.

At the gate, he paused in front of the core group minus Marly and Claire but this time, including Viola. There were more heartfelt goodbyes and hugs, Ragland wincing at a few misplaced claps on his still smarting shoulder.

'Thanks again, Viola,' he said when he reached her. 'How are you feeling?'

'Oh, I'm fine,' she said, waving the question away and hugging him tightly. 'I'll miss you in the fields old timer, you have a job any time you want to come back, you hear?'

He chuckled.

'I'll keep it in mind.'

Odin ducked out from behind her and grabbed Ragland's hand before he could move on.

'Odin, I wondered where you were!' he said returning the vigorous handshake. 'You look after Viola, okay?'

'I will Mister Ragland.'

Alex and Kit were the last in the line and he hugged Alex before reaching out to hug Kit.

'Not yet Gramps,' she said, pointing a thumb over her shoulder. 'I have a going away gift that I want to give you in private.'

She avoided his gaze and headed towards the gate without looking back to make sure he was following. He shrugged and gave the crowd one more wave, his eyes seeking out the one person who had said their goodbye the night before.

He found Claire well back and standing apart

from the crowd, with her arms folded. With a knowing smile, he gave a wave. She returned it with one of her own and then turned and began walking back up the avenue.

Ragland gave one more wave to the rest and began leading Reliable after Kit.

'Safe travels Joshua Ragland!' boomed Simon, as he went through the gate.

'I'm going to walk you to the lodge,' said Kit, when he caught up to her.

'You don't have to-'

'I want to!'

'Okay… that would be nice, kid.'

There were no words between them the whole way, the kind of easy silence that only friends could share without feeling awkward, and certainly different to how it had been when they first met.

Finally, the old road leveled out into a sweeping curve revealing the Hunter's Lodge.

It looked like an old Christmas card, with snow packed on the cabin roof and smoke spiraling from the chimney. Kit led the way over the bridge and stopped on the other side, turning and waiting as Ragland and Reliable made their way across.

Kit approached Ragland, her eyes set and purposeful as he pulled the horse to a halt.

'Open your hand.'

Ragland did as she asked and held out his right hand, palm up. Kit pulled something from her pocket and dropped it into his hand.

It was the onyx necklace.

He opened his mouth to protest, but she held up her hand.

'I don't need this anymore,' she said. 'It's done its job but it's yours, and you'll need its protection now.'

Ragland stared down at the necklace, then back to Kit. She stood on tiptoes and kissed him on the cheek.

'When you look at it, it shouldn't remind you of loss. It should remind you of life and that there's more to this than just surviving.'

He nodded, not trusting himself to speak as his eyes welled up.

Kit smiled, wiping a tear away.

'This cold! Stings the eyes huh!'

He laughed and pulled her into a bear hug.

'Stay safe, Kid. I'll be seeing you.'

Ragland put his foot in the stirrup and heaved himself onto the saddle.

'You better,' she called as he shook the reins and began trotting away on his new steed.

He looked over his shoulder with a grin.

'Count on it.'

EPILOGUE

On a clear, sunny day six weeks later, Ragland halted Reliable beneath a peeling and weathered road sign.

WELCOME TO NEW HAMPSHIRE

LIVE FREE OR DIE

While he knew the motto of the granite state predated the Fall by many years, it was certainly prophetic. He didn't linger long; he wanted to find a suitable campsite and hunt while there was still light.

Two hours and nine miles later, he was spit roasting a chicken of all things. He hadn't had chicken in what seemed like a hundred years and the aroma of the cooking meat and skin made his mouth water.

He'd set his camp four hundred yards off the highway in a shallow glade and hadn't even bothered with his tent. Late in the afternoon the day had turned overcast, and the clouds bottled in the unseasonable warmth but didn't threaten rain. A light blanket would do for the night.

He'd finished the chicken and buried what was

left when he heard a sound on the wind. It was faint, but it sounded like a woman's laugh. It was as brief as it was unexpected and Ragland cocked his head, trying to work out if he'd heard it or imagined it.

A minute later, he was about to dismiss it as his imagination, when he heard another sound, what could only be conversation. He quickly stamped out his fire and picked up his bow, darting into the trees and heading towards the highway he'd traveled that day.

He didn't want trouble, but it always paid to know who one might be sharing the road with. He drew closer to the roadway and settled low in the shadows of the trees to observe. From the even tone of the quiet conversation, it appeared they hadn't spotted the smoke of his fire. Still, his heartbeat was fast as he waited for the group to appear.

They did after another minute. It was a group of seven. Two men, three women and two children, a boy and a girl. One of the men was wheeling a barrow, its inflated tire silent on the cracked tarmac.

What a strange group to see traveling at night, Ragland thought to himself. *But no threat.*

The thought had barely manifested when he felt a cold edge of steel pressed hard against his throat.

'I'm not going to hurt you, dude,' said a low voice behind him. 'But I need you to put your hands behind your head nice and slow and interlace your fingers. Got it?'

Angry at the ease with which he'd been snuck up on, Ragland swallowed. There was no way out... *yet*.

'Got it,' he rasped, before doing as he'd been ordered.

'Good. Now stand up slowly.'

Ragland obeyed and when he was on his feet his assailant pressed something hard into his back then took the blade away.

'That's a .44 Magnum right over your spine. I won't use it unless you make me, understood?'

Ragland nodded.

The man whistled loudly, and the conversation of the group stopped as they came to a halt and looked around expectantly.

'Okay, we're walking out onto the road. Nice and easy,' the man said and gave him a gentle shove between the shoulders.

The eyes of the group fell on Ragland as he emerged with his captor. In their faces, he saw only fear and mistrust, no aggression. That was a positive.

Ten feet from the group, his captor clamped something hard over his shoulder, bringing him to a stop.

'Are you armed?'

'Just my bow and a knife in my boot.'

'Good, slip the bow off and let it fall to the ground,' the unseen man said, plucking the three arrows in his quiver free.

This guy is careful, Ragland thought grudgingly, dropping his hand briefly to let the bow fall.

'Okay, with your left hand, pull out the knife holding the end of the handle with the tips of your finger and thumb. Nice and slow… and drop it too.'

Ragland bent over and pulled out the knife hand made by Rahul many months before. When he was done, he put his hands back on his head.

The muzzle against his back was removed, but the object on his shoulder was pressed down firmly as a big hand made quick work of patting him down.

Suddenly the pressure on his shoulder disappeared and he heard the man step away.

'Okay you can put your hands down now, but don't try anything.'

Ragland slowly lowered his hands as the man stepped around and came into view.

His captor was an impressive sight, at least two inches taller than Ragland, he was big and lanky without being skinny. He had red hair and a darker beard. Over his shoulder the drifter could see the well-worn handle of an axe, and against his chest, in slits through a leather strap over his other shoulder, were three throwing knives.

Moonlight glinted off the steel of the hook where the man's left hand should have been.

'You're an old one!' the big man said, his eyes widening. 'What's your name?'

Ragland locked eyes with him.

'What's it matter?'

His stare was met evenly.

'I'm just being polite. That's why I didn't ask your age.'

The answer drew a grunt of real amusement from Ragland.

'Fair enough. My name's Joshua Ragland

'Okay Joshua Ragland... my name's Luke Merritt. Pleased to meet you.'

The End

I hope you enjoyed *The Drifter.* While you're waiting for the next America Falls Adventure, why not check out my other post-apocalyptic series ***Rabid States***, available on Amazon.

You can listen to my audiobooks free here: **https://www.youtube.com/c/scottmedburyauthor**

The America Falls Series:

Hell Week
On the Run
Cold Comfort
Rude Shock
Luke's Trek
Civil War
Lone Wolf
Texas Fight
Messenger

The Rabid States Series:

Unleashed
Alpha Pack
Fox Hole

Standalone novels:

INGA

www.scottmedbury.com

Made in United States
North Haven, CT
02 July 2023